P9-CFY-693

# BENEATH
## *Wandering*
## STARS

★ Ashlee Cowles ★

Merit Press | fw

Published by
Merit Press
an imprint of F+W Media, Inc.
10151 Carver Road, Suite 200
Blue Ash, OH 45242. U.S.A.
*www.meritpressbooks.com*

ISBN 10: 1-4405-9582-8
ISBN 13: 978-1-4405-9582-0
eISBN 10: 1-4405-9583-6
eISBN 13: 978-1-4405-9583-7

Printed in the United States of America.

10   9   8   7   6   5   4   3   2   1

Cover design by Colleen Cunningham.
Cover and interior images © iStockphoto.com/kentarcajuan; Clipart.com.

*This book is available at quantity discounts for bulk purchases.*
*For information, please call 1-800-289-0963.*

# Dedication

For my parents, LTC Steven H. Chowen, USA, Ret., and Lea Anne
Chowen, who gave me the childhood that enabled me to write this story.
And for Danielle. None of this would have happened without you.

# Acknowledgments

Although this story and its characters are fictional, they were stirred awake by a lifetime of impressions and memories. I want to thank my parents and sisters for being the core of the adventure that is the life of a military brat. I am also grateful to my in-laws and the rest of my extended family for their love and support. Thanks especially to Tia Julie, for proofreading my Spanish and teaching me about Spain's cuisine.

Thanks to Marlys Sowell and Lucia Hrin, for walking the *Camino de Santiago* with me back in 2011—the journey that inspired many parts of this story. I'm glad we survived the snoring, the aching feet . . . and the *vino*. Finding time and energy to write is a challenge for any writer with a day job, but perhaps even more so for a writer who is also a teacher. I am indebted to several organizations for providing tangible resources that made this work possible. To start, many thanks to the people behind the Glen Workshop, a program put on by *Image* journal, and the place where I typed the first words of *Beneath Wandering Stars*. A generous scholarship made attending the workshop possible, and this book is proof that a week can truly change a life. Many, *many* thanks to the Russell Kirk Center, especially to Annette Y. Kirk and Andrea Kirk Assaf. Not many writers are fortunate enough to receive the kind of support and resources the RKC has provided me, and I am truly blessed to have spent an entire year writing among this life-changing community, where the "circles of destiny" are particularly pronounced. In Colorado, I am very grateful to the Anselm Society, which provides spaces where artists of all stripes can connect and realize, "Hey, I'm *not* the only one."

Writing may be done in solitude, but writing is never solitary. A sincere thank you to Katherine Khorey and Anna Vander Wall for reading an early draft of this story and for providing such heartening feedback. I am grateful for my wonderful critique partners, Anita Romero and Adrianne Hanson, who have given extensive comments on this and other works. Last but not least, I am forever indebted to Danielle Stinson, my very best friend, fellow Army brat, Ideal Reader, and the most talented writer I know. I'm so glad we share half a brain because without your brilliance and unwavering encouragement, this book would not exist. Whenever I had doubts, you always believed. Thank you from the bottom of my heart.

All my love goes to my husband, Jordan, who is always open to whatever crazy notions I come up with, whether that's moving to the other side of the world or becoming an author. Your steadfast support and willingness to endure the hours I spend glued to my laptop have made this dream possible. Thank you.

Many thanks to my editor, Jacquelyn Mitchard, and the rest of the team at Merit Press, for "getting" this story and for strongly believing it was one young people ought to read. I am so encouraged by Merit Press's vision for young adult literature, and I feel fortunate to be a part of it.

Finally, I would like to thank the millions of men and women who currently serve, or have served, in the United States Armed Forces, along with their spouses and children, who also sacrifice so much. I wanted to write a book for and about military "brats" because I wanted to tell *our* story. Please forgive any errors in my interpretation. I sincerely hope I did the wild ride that is our upbringing justice.

# CHAPTER 1

Mail service in the midst of a war. It's crazy when you stop and think about it. Some guy's job requires him to dodge bullets just so messages like the one that arrived in my mailbox today can make it from soldiers to their families.

The book in my hands is almost as tattered as the manila envelope it came in, postmarked in Kabul. There's no letter, no note of explanation, only this dog-eared paperback that's seen better days. An image of a golden galley—one of those ancient Greek ships that wandered the waves of the wine-dark sea—sits in the center of the cobalt cover, right below the boldfaced title.

**THE ODYSSEY**

"That from your soldier?"

*My* soldier? For the record, I will never have a soldier.

I look up from the book and meet the smiling eyes of a stocky lieutenant. I can tell he's a first lieutenant because of the silver bar on his camouflage uniform. His name badge reads Martinez. Idle chitchat doesn't fly in the Army, so it's best to have vital info up front and out in the open.

Soldiers are getting off duty, so the post office is crowded. I slam my mailbox shut. "It's from my brother."

The smile in the lieutenant's eyes travels to his lips. "Always fun to get a gift from the Sandbox."

"Lucas isn't in Iraq," I reply. "He's in Afghanistan."

"Even better," says the lieutenant, shuffling through his junk mail.

I can't tell if that's sarcasm in his voice or not, so I return to the equally cryptic communication from my brother, to the book that makes no sense. Lucas left one clue, scrawled on its title page:

*Do you remember that day, Gabi? How much we wanted to see the lights in the sky?*

I do. Only instead of lights, we saw the sky crash down 110 flights of stairs.

I was young, but I can conjure up every detail of that September morning. How excited Lucas was to glimpse the green swirls of Alaska's northern lights. The sweet smell in the car from the banana bread Mom packed for our breakfast. That Odysseus was about to outwit the Cyclops when Dad switched from my audiobook to the radio, and we heard the news about the towers, the Pentagon, the planes. How my father—who wasn't in uniform, but still wore the insignia of the military in the pinched corners of his mouth— looked more anxious than I'd ever seen him, which made me more afraid than I'd ever been.

Most of all, I remember the way Lucas held my hand. He kept holding it through all the moves, goodbyes, and deployments that followed. Lucas is only eleven months older, so we've always been close. But after that day, he never let go. Not until he followed in Dad's footsteps and joined a war that started when he was still playing with G.I. Joes.

"You okay, kid?" asks Martinez, who's watching me stare at this book like I'm famished and it's food. "You look like you're about to pass out."

"I'm okay," I lie.

Lucas and I never talk about 9/11. That means this book isn't a gift.

It's a message.

Sweat beads along the back of my neck as I flip through the paperback and notice specific verses highlighted in neon green. One reads, *Ares in his many fits knows no favorites.*

Weird. Ares is the Greek god of war, but what exactly is Lucas trying to tell me?

My brother deployed six months ago. He's pretty good at keeping in touch, thanks to e-mail and Facebook, but Lucas and I aren't exactly old-school pen pals. I'd expect him to send a souvenir from an Afghan market, or maybe a stash of flavored *shisha* tobacco for the hookah he had me hide in my closet. But a book?

Now, I love books. They're the most portable friends a military brat can have, but this isn't any book. Lucas and I used to listen to the audio version of the children's *Odyssey* during long drives and cross-country moves. I'd imagine our family's station wagon was our galley ship, the open road our Mediterranean Sea. The only thing missing was our Ithaca—the home we were trying to return to despite the detours.

I haven't read or listened to the *Odyssey* since that dark day over a decade ago, but I'm certain we have a copy buried in a moving box somewhere. Why would Lucas send another one?

Maybe it's a warning.

*Or* maybe I'm just paranoid.

Soldiers file into the post office like it's a Great Depression bread line, which means it's time to get out of here. I bury my nose in pages that smell of Lucas's aftershave and head towards the exit.

"Uh, miss, I think you forgot something."

I turn and see my mailbox door hanging wide open—even though I just shut it. "Oh. Thanks."

There's one more padded envelope shoved inside, the one with the San Antonio return address I've been waiting for. It's the reason I stopped by the post office after soccer practice in the first place. Thankfully, this package contains a note.

*Hey Gabi girl,*

*Thanks for offering to pass out these free samples for the band. It would be awesome to build a fan base over there in Germany. Maybe we'll be able to do a European tour and I'll get to come visit you! Miss you, babe.*
*Brent*

My heart takes a nosedive towards the floor.

*That's it???*

The last time we talked, Brent said he mailed me something "special." Sample CDs are cool and all, but I was hoping for something more personal and, oh I don't know, *romantic*. Saying you miss someone is not the same thing as showing it.

I study one of the CDs, which has me smiling in spite of the lump that has taken my throat hostage. Brent's rockabilly band is the Psychopathic Penguins. Kind of a ridiculous name, but the guys only wear black and white, so it's also kind of appropriate. As the lead singer, Brent takes center stage on the shiny new CD cover. He's wearing his signature pinstripe trilby hat, pulled down so low that his dark eyes are barely visible.

Okay, I'm getting dizzy again. This photo is one hundred percent swoon-worthy.

Man, do I ever miss this boy, especially right now when I'm confused about Lucas and need someone to talk me down off the crazy ledge. Thanks to his lip ring and Day of the Dead skull tattoos, Brent is *not* the kind of boyfriend my clean-cut soldier dad approves of, which is exactly why I like him. The military is all straight lines and sharp angles. "*Order*: the first step to fixing a broken world," Dad likes to say whenever it's time to clean my room. I've never dated anyone like Brent, a drifting spirit who prefers a realm of chaos where the road is always swerving, where every day is new. We're opposites in a lot of ways, but we work. So *why* did I move a million miles away from him in the middle of my senior year?

Because the Army is awesome like that.

*Two more months*, I remind myself as I step outside. The second I graduate, I'm headed back to Texas. Brent and I will go to the same college with our other friends, and everything will be just like it was before I left.

A giant cargo plane soars overhead, pulling my eyes to the overcast sky. The wall of gray clouds battles with the green backdrop of the German Rhineland, colliding like the camouflage pattern of the U.S. Army's uniforms. As the roar of the plane fades, an unfamiliar sound on this post of strangers puts a stop to my forward-march.

"*Gabi!* Wait up!"

Oh no. I recognize that overly enthusiastic voice. A quick glance back confirms my suspicions. It's Chloe Ross, my soccer team's goalie and a girl so nice she doesn't mind that I scored on her during our scrimmage in front of the boys' entire starting lineup.

I'm tempted to avoid small talk by hiding out in the mailroom, but a relentless bugle starts blaring on loudspeakers across the post, sabotaging that strategy. *Fan*tastic. It's 1700 hours. How do I know? It's called the retreat ceremony, and when the music plays and the flag is lowered, you *stop*. It wouldn't matter if you were giving an unconscious person CPR; for forty-five seconds no one moves a muscle.

A woman leaving the post office slows her stroller, the toddler inside already trained to stay silent. Cars pull off to the side of the road and any soldiers inside get out, raising hands to temples in a statuesque salute. I stand still, too, since this ritual is all about respect, though it also means I'll never escape chatty Chloe now. Normally I wouldn't blow her off like this, but I want to get home to see if Lucas called.

The bugle music stops, the frozen toy soldiers return to life, and Chloe rushes towards me, gasping for breath. "Gabi, I just had to tell you, that was an amazing goal today! I'm *so* glad Coach made you captain and moved you to center-mid before tomorrow's game."

"Thanks. Me too."

Another lie. Sure, my soccer-fanatic father will be thrilled at the news, but team captain isn't a responsibility I wanted, especially when I hardly know anyone at this school.

Still smiling like she has a pantheon of gods on her side, Chloe pulls a pack of Lucky Strikes out of her pocket and lights one up. The cigarette she waves around brazenly tells me that even though this warrant officer's daughter looks like she should be on a box of Swiss Miss, there's another story beneath her squeaky clean exterior.

"Geez, Chloe. Wait until we're off post, will you?" I glance around for personnel garbed in the ciphers of governmental authority, which on a military installation is pretty much everyone.

"Aye, aye, captain." Chloe drops her cigarette and stamps it out with her cleat. Grass and clumps of dirt cake her knees from diving for shots, most of them mine. "I know, I know, it's stupid. Not to mention the reason my asthmatic grandmother can outrun me, hence why you're team captain and I, the least coordinated person on the planet, got stuck in the goal. Hey, my apartment building is across from yours. Want to walk the rest of the way together?"

"Sure," I lie again, seeing how this girl's cherub face won't take no for an answer. Unlike me, Chloe has blond hair and blue eyes that enable her to blend in with the German population beyond our post's walls. Not to mention weasel her way into people's affections. For some reason, my corkscrew curls and tan skin do not have the same effect.

"You sure? You don't sound too enthusiastic about having company."

"Yeah, I'm sure," I say with a little more gusto. To be fair, Chloe is a nice person. It's not her fault I despise everything about this place. She isn't really someone I can picture myself being friends with, but at least she'll distract me from the questions crouched down in the back of my mind, waiting to launch their assault. No matter how hard I try, I can't shake the disturbing hunch that Lucas's book is a message.

But a message about *what?*

My phone vibrates in my pocket. I forgot to turn the ringer back on after school, so I've missed a lot of calls. Common sense assures me they're from Brent, though he rarely calls my cell phone since talking online is so much cheaper.

There it is again. That feeling. The gnawing sensation that things are about to get flipped upside down and turned inside out. My fingers chart the familiar territory of the touch screen as the pounding behind my temples smothers all sounds, including Chloe's inquiries into why I'm acting like an antisocial psycho. The calls are from my parents. There are texts, too. My father *never* sends texts. He's a total Luddite and doesn't believe in them.

"Gabi?" Chloe's shrill voice, like an echo racing down a subway tunnel, pulls me back to the solid earth. "You look like you're going to be sick."

That's because the worst tragedies are the ones you anticipate in advance. When Fate is out for blood, she'll cut you to the bone and you'll know she's coming—the same way you know you've nicked your finger while chopping vegetables, because you can feel the sharp sting long before red starts welling up in the clean white slice.

I open Dad's text.

CALL US ASAP. LUCAS IS WIA. ON OUR WAY TO LANDSTUHL.

Chloe rests her hand on my trembling arm and looks down over my shoulder. "What does WIA mean again? I can't keep all the Army acronyms straight."

"Wounded in Action." I stare at the screen until it becomes a bright blue blur.

My legs buckle and I meet the pavement. There's no surge of adrenaline, no merciful detachment, just stabbing pain and a crimson smear as my knees kiss the white cement.

# CHAPTER 2

Chloe walks with me to the front gate of the U.S. Army Garrison Kaiserslautern, known to us Americans as K-Town. A petite woman in blue Air Force fatigues waits for us.

*No, no, no.* A chaplaincy escort means Lucas is already dead, or he's dying.

"Gabriela Santiago? I'm Sergeant Doyle. I'll accompany you to the hospital. If you'll follow me?" The woman's red hair is secured in a bun so tight, it stretches the pale skin around her eyes. But with one sympathetic smile, her severity melts. Sergeant Doyle's freckled cheeks make her look like a little kid, yet the steely glint in her eyes assures me she's as tough as they come. She has to be. Her job is to tell people the worst possible news.

What's strange is that my dad is also a chaplain's assistant—the perfect job for him, since he's uber Catholic and probably thinks serving as the priest's bodyguard is a direct pass to skip through purgatory. Only this time, he isn't the one comforting the family members of a wounded soldier. He's the one being comforted.

I shake the woman's hand, unable to find words. All I can focus on is the raspberry burn above my right shin guard. The rest of my body is numb, but the raw, stinging flesh assures me this is real, no matter how fake my surroundings now seem.

"He's, he's going to make it, right?" I stutter as we climb into a black car with government plates. *Crap, Chloe.* In my daze, I forgot to thank her for waiting with me.

"Last I heard, Private Santiago is stable," Sergeant Doyle replies. "But I'll let the doctors explain his . . . condition. Your brother is a hell of a fighter. That's for sure."

Thank God. Lucas is still in the game. I want to press Doyle for details, but the woman's direct manner means she's told me everything she knows.

Time to get a grip.

Even if Lucas is badly injured, he's always lived by the "push through pain" philosophy our father instilled in us through extra soccer drills and summer hiking trips. If anyone can pull off a mind-over-matter maneuver, it's Lucas.

But if I'm so sure, then why won't my hands stop shaking?

"Food is probably the last thing on your mind, but help yourself if you're hungry." Sergeant Doyle nods towards a gooey *käse-brezel* in the car's cup holder, wrapped in an oily napkin.

Under any other circumstance, I would never turn down a German baked good, but my stomach can't handle a cheesy pretzel at a time like this. I focus on the airfield runway strip outside the window instead, where a C-17—the Pacific gray whale of military aircraft—takes off, likely on its way to pick up the next batch of wounded men. A train of Blue Bird buses marked with red crosses speeds across the tarmac, looking like toy Matchbox cars next to the enormous planes. It's crazy to think that Landstuhl Regional Medical Center—about twenty minutes from K-Town—is the first stop for injured soldiers coming back from the front lines. After all, it's not like Germany is in Iraq or Afghanistan's backyard.

How much agony did Lucas experience in the back of that dark, noisy cargo hold? Was it an IED or a bullet? Oh God, what if he lost a limb?

I roll down the window for some fresh air. Smells of hot asphalt, jet fuel, and damp canvas sail in with the cool breeze. I picture a much younger Lucas, running through the airplane hangar where soldiers and their families had gathered for a Thanksgiving feast. While the adults set up long tables among the metal beasts, Lucas and I played hide-and-seek in a maze of Huey helicopters.

This smells the same, minus the turkey. But the memory only makes things worse.

There's no time to cry. And as soon as we enter the hospital, I know I have no right to. Not when I'm walking around just fine.

Not after seeing all the soldiers covered in bandages, the amputees limping through the halls on crutches, the grief-stricken faces of the spouses and children filling the waiting rooms. *These* are my neighbors, my extended family. Over fifty thousand U.S. citizens live in this American corner of the Rhine river valley, but I've never visited this hospital before. I've never had a reason to, never had to *see* where so many of the men and women missing from our post wound up.

I follow Sergeant Doyle to the security checkpoint and hand over my military ID card. Over the guard's shoulder, I see Mom in a waiting area dominated by a gigantic television airing an old rerun of *General Hospital* (seriously, *in* a hospital?). Only this woman looks nothing like my mom. My mother is charming and perfectly put together—the model military wife—but the woman sitting in that orange plastic chair has her shoulders hunched forward like she's carrying the weight of the world. Which makes sense, since Mom's kids *are* her world.

My father stands erect by her side, rubbing Mom's neck beneath her strawberry-blond ponytail. She looks up at me with the hazel gaze we share—the one fair feature all her kids inherited despite the dominance of Dad's Latino coloring. The afterglow of weeping makes her irises pop bright green. When Dad's eyes find mine, I see that his are also wet with tears.

My breath catches in my chest. I have never—and I mean *never*—seen my father cry. Not a single solitary tear. The thin stream sliding down his cheek slices into my heart as deeply as the image of Lucas lying bloodied on some foreign battlefield, far from home. And by "home" I mean *us*, his family.

People are the only home the Army issues.

"Gabi," Dad croaks in a hoarse voice, hauling me into a hug more heartfelt than his signature back tap. "I'm glad you got here so quickly, *mija*."

Mom's body shudders as I embrace her next. She doesn't speak. This is a woman who is never short on words, which is how I know that what happened to Lucas is bad. Change-your-life-forever bad.

I turn back to my father as he gently pulls my five-year-old brother (another of life's unplanned surprises) off of his leg. The poor kid has wrapped his entire body around Dad's army boot like it's a lone tree in the midst of a tsunami flood. Matteo stares at me with eyes as round as bottle caps. He idolizes his big brother, and I hate seeing his innocence obliterated by life's dirty little secret: In the real world, no one is dipped in the River Styx and made practically invincible like Achilles. In the real world, heroes can be stripped down to nothing, just like everyone else.

I turn from Matteo's confused little face and cut to the chase. "How bad is it?"

My parents exchange tense glances, but neither responds. A switch flips inside me, igniting enough fuel to power ten fighter jets back across the Black Sea. "How *is* he, Dad?"

Normally I would never speak to my father in this tone, and normally he would never take it. Paternal respect is a big deal in Latino culture, and an even bigger deal when that *padre* is a soldier who lives and breathes hierarchy. Too bad "normal" no longer exists and hierarchies no longer matter.

Dad's sigh tells me he's too sad to be angry, which makes me feel a million times worse. He grabs my hand and pulls me towards a small window on the door of what must be Lucas's room. Except that when I peer inside, I do not see my athletic, almost nineteen-year-old brother. I see a little boy, shrunken by bandages that make him seem more like a mummy than a soldier. His right leg—the rocket launcher that earned him the soccer scholarship to UT-Austin I *really* wish he'd taken—hangs in a sling. Behind all the wires and tubes, a small portion of his face is visible. It's purple and bruised, like an overripe eggplant.

I press a hand to my mouth, but the sob still escapes my throat. "What happened?"

My body goes to jelly. I reach for a concrete wall, but it feels like it's made of foam. The entire waiting area turns to stare at me. I don't care. I need answers, and my parents are treating me like a crystal bowl they must handle with care. Matteo starts crying, so I resist the urge to rant and rave. But once Mom quiets him, the full-on body ache turns to rage.

I will *kill* the person who did this. And I don't mean the insurgent; I mean Seth, the moron who got Lucas to enlist and go infantry in the first place.

"Come on, *mija*." Dad takes my arm and pulls me away from the view of my brother's dim room, which already looks more like a tomb. "Let's go grab a *café con leche*."

Dad doesn't have to wink or give me a conspiratorial look—I understand his code. Whatever stale sludge this hospital cafeteria is serving, it won't be anything like the fresh coffee with frothed milk my grandmother made for me and Lucas when she lived with us during one of Dad's deployments. Mom wasn't aware of our *abuela*'s covert coffee ritual and wondered how Lucas and I had so much energy after school. Now Dad likes to use the term *café con leche* as shorthand for "not in front of your mother."

It's strange—the random memories that assault you in the midst of bone-crushing grief, the childhood secrets only you and your sibling shared. Too bad the aroma of *abuela*'s coffee dissipates as that distinct hospital smell—rubbing alcohol mixed with latex gloves—attacks my nostrils from the other end of the fluorescent-lit hallway.

Trailing Dad, who always walks like he's on a mission, I turn a corner and collide with a nurse heading towards the operating room, a stack of empty IV bags piled high in her arms. The woman locks her jaw like a pit bull and keeps moving, as though she's walking through a flimsy screen door. The synthetic fabric of her saltwater taffy–pink pants swishes between her thick thighs. Soon that *swish* is the only sound I can hear as everything else turns to white noise.

"He isn't in any pain," Dad says once we reach the cafeteria. His posture perfect, he sits utterly still, staring into his cup as doctors swirl around us in waves of seafoam-colored scrubs. He avoids my gaze, but that's nothing new. Ever since "the incident" back in San Antonio, Dad hasn't initiated a real conversation that doesn't involve soccer technique.

Apparently that's what happens when you almost ruin your soldier father's career.

But now is not the time for daddy issues. "What do you mean, Lucas isn't in any pain?"

"I mean he hasn't been responsive since they airlifted him from the battlefield twenty-four hours ago." My father takes a sip of coffee, his mouth twitching at the bitter aftertaste. "Gabi, your brother is in a coma."

I clench my empty cup until the Styrofoam crumples. "No."

That's all I can say. *No.* My brother—a guy who can't sit still for more than five minutes—is on his way to becoming a vegetable. Why does this news feel worse than the thought of him dead?

"The doctors are hopeful. They say these first few weeks are crucial. If he shows signs of response, anything at all, there's a chance he'll come out of it."

"A few weeks? That's how long Lucas could be lying there before we know if he's still *in there*?" My eyes burn as I picture Mom setting up camp in his hospital room, refusing to leave his bedside. And what happens if he doesn't wake up? Who gets to make the tortuous decision to play God and take him off life support? Not that God seems to be playing much of a role in this anyway.

Otherwise a decent human being like my brother wouldn't be here when there are rapists and terrorists running around free.

Dad ignores my question and finishes his drink. "*Vamonos.* It's visiting hour."

When we reach Lucas's room, someone else is already seated by my brother's bedside. The instant I see his combat boots and ice-blue eyes—eyes that always laugh at my expense—something snaps. Every emotion I've been straining to hold back washes over me in one massive torrent that no sandbag of self-control can stop. Seth Russo is the *last* person I want to see right now, so I march over to my brother's best friend, to the guy who convinced Lucas to turn down his soccer scholarship and suit up.

And I punch him in the face.

# CHAPTER 3

Well, I *try* to punch him in the face. But his hand—the one that's not in a sling—is larger and stronger and faster than mine. There isn't even a hint of surprise on Seth's face as he effortlessly catches my fist before it can slam into his cheek. After six months at war, I suppose his reflexes had better be top-notch.

"Gabriela Guadalupe Santiago!" my mother yells from the doorway. She only uses my full name when I've crossed the line. Most of the time, I can't help chuckling at the way she pronounces Spanish words with a Midwestern accent, but today I don't laugh.

"Nice to see you, too, kiddo," Seth mutters, clenching my fist like it's a live grenade.

I despise this guy. For multiple reasons, but mainly because Lucas never would have joined the Army if he hadn't filled his head with glory stories and told him about some "buddy program" that would allow them to stay together their first tour if they signed the dotted line at the same time.

"What are you doing here?" I haven't seen Seth since we left Texas. We didn't get along then, and I don't appreciate his condescending use of the word *kiddo* now.

Seth's face is humbled only by scrapes and a severe burn across his forehead. Your typical soldier with a buzz cut, he'd blend into any formation line if not for the dark eyebrows framing his big, doleful eyes, which are clueless and forever in mourning.

At least now they have a reason to grieve.

Seth doesn't respond to my question. His bloodshot gaze drifts across Lucas's bed, like he can't even believe I could ask it. Encountering an enemy who's already defeated diffuses the bomb waiting to go off inside me, and the heat of Seth's palm absorbs my wrath. He has no interest in fighting back, so I have no interest in him. I let my fist fall and take a seat across the room, where Matteo crawls into my lap.

"Private Russo, I apologize for my daughter's disrespect and lack of maturity."

Thanks for taking my side, Dad. Oh wait, I forgot. When it comes to supporting me or supporting a soldier—no matter how big of a Neanderthal he is—the Army will *always* win.

"We're glad you're here." Dad nods at Seth's arm, cradled by the sling. "Is it broken?"

"Just a sprain, sir. Nothing major." He sounds so guilty, like he can't accept that whatever happened to them downrange didn't even break his arm when it left my brother with a broken body and maybe a broken brain.

Good. I can't accept that either.

Mom's bloodshot eyes travel from the tan blanket draped across my brother's motionless body to the taupe walls behind Lucas's bandaged head. I know exactly what she's thinking.

*This drab room needs some color.*

It's the thought of a seasoned military wife who knows that even the most temporary landing pad should feel like a home. Only this time, she has her work cut out for her. Mom touches the plum swirls of Lucas's bruised hand, pulling back like she's grazed a hot stove.

*Hold his hand! Squeeze it! He can't feel a thing,* I want to scream. But I don't. I just clench Matteo in a death grip, breathing in graham crackers and Elmer's glue, which is what Lucas smelled like as a kid. Maybe it's what we all smell like as little kids.

"Lucas," Mom whispers, as though he can actually hear her. She looks up at the rest of us, a hint of crazy on her lips. "He's so dark. Why is he so dark? His name means *light*. Lucas means light!" As the panic in Mom's pitch increases, Matteo starts crying again.

"Come on, *cariño*. Let's go for a walk." Dad lifts Matteo from my arms, gently grabs Mom's shoulders, and guides them both from the room.

Alone with Seth, I approach the bed and see that my mother is right. Everything about Lucas was goodness and light. He was the perfect son, the perfect brother, and, I'm sure, the perfect soldier. Yet a shadow hovers over his face, suffocating his light with a darkness that goes much deeper than bruising. Wherever my brother resides in this state suspended between life and death, he is far, far away from all of us. I wipe a renegade tear from the corner of my eye, my cheeks burning beneath Seth's concentrated gaze.

"What happened?" I ask, my eyes never leaving Lucas. And by that I mean: *Where were you? How could you let them do this?*

"I don't know what happened. You'd have been proud of him though," Seth says softly as my dad re-enters the room with a doctor.

I was proud of Lucas *before* he got himself blown up, but I'm too drained to get into another confrontation with this meathead G.I.

Dad and the doc are in a tense conversation of their own. "Months? I thought you said a few weeks."

"Early signs of movement are the best reason to hope, but even if your son responds over the next few weeks, the coma could last for months." The doctor places his hand on Dad's shoulder. "I don't say this to discourage you, but so that your family can prepare for a potentially long haul."

The doctor leaves and Dad turns to me. "Your mother and brother are beat, *mija*. We all need to go home and rest. The nurses will call us if anything changes."

I can tell by his tone that he doesn't think anything will. At least, not so soon.

Eyes closed, Dad kneels before Lucas's bed for a moment, then kisses my brother's cheek—something he hasn't done since Lucas was about eight. He herds us out of the room.

"Wait, Sergeant Major." Seth follows us into the waiting area. "There's something Lucas wanted me to tell you. To tell both of you, I think." His eyes meet mine, searching for an ounce of openness.

This soldier may be on my bad side, but if he's here in this hospital, he's been to hell and back, too. I suppose the least I can do is make an effort to be a little less hostile.

I sigh. "What's that, Russo?"

"I wasn't going to share this so soon, but seeing how long the doctors think the coma could last, I don't see any point in waiting. Hell, maybe it will even help." Seth reaches into his pocket and pulls out a paperback. The instant I see the cover, my heart scrambles up my throat.

The *Iliad*. By Homer. Ancient Greek Homer.

"Where did you get that?" I demand.

Seth stares at me like I'm nuts to be getting so worked up over a book. "Lucas left it on my cot the night before he . . . ."

Trailing off, the private opens the book and pulls out a folded piece of notebook paper. Seth doesn't need to tell us what it is, because Dad and I already know. Lots of soldiers write a "last letter" before they head off to war and give it to a close buddy to bring home, in case they don't make it. The fact that Lucas *has* made it home, just not completely intact, causes a blend of rage and revulsion to bubble up inside me.

The letter has a similar effect on Dad, who crosses himself like Seth is about to read the words of an ancient curse. "Put that away. My son isn't dead yet."

"I know, sir, but I think Lucas would want me to read it. Especially given the circumstances." When my father's rigid eyes fail to soften, Seth continues, "At least let me explain what he wanted you two to do for him."

After a tense thirty seconds, Dad nods and I sigh. Then we both listen.

"Lucas told me that when you guys were stationed in Alaska, you started taking hiking trips every year," Seth begins. "Just the three of you."

This is true, and those trips were glue. Not only did they give us rare time with Dad, they were how I learned that Lucas would always walk my pace and have my back, even when our father was out of sight, leading the charge up ahead. Thanks to a string of back-to-back deployments, it's been years since we went on one of our trio treks.

"What does that have to do with anything?" I snap, wondering if I'll ever walk a trail or climb a mountain with Lucas again.

"Let me backtrack. In Afghanistan, most guys spent their R&R time playing video games or surfing the Internet, but not Lucas. Never Lucas." Seth actually has the nerve to grin. "The guy read so many books that the rest of our battalion called him the Philosopher."

A bittersweet smile starts to curl my lips, but I bite it down. "That's why Mom sent Lucas an e-reader for his birthday. Less cargo to lug around the mountains."

"He definitely made use of it." Seth swallows hard. "Anyway, after we experienced our first firefight over there, Lucas started withdrawing from the rest of us. A lot of the time he wouldn't even talk to me. He started making lists of all these places he wanted to see when he came to visit you guys in Europe. Places like Rome, northern England, some remote island in Scotland, the Holocaust memorial at Dachau. He called these sacred places. Holy ground."

I don't see how these random dots connect, but time has become a marked-down commodity on clearance. "Get to the point, Russo. What does this have to do with Lucas's letter?"

Sending a scowl in my direction, Seth holds up the crinkled document. "Lucas wants you to revive your old tradition by taking another trek. He wants you to do a pilgrimage. He claims people have made journeys like this on behalf of absent soldiers, the sick, and the recently deceased for thousands of years."

"That makes no sense. Lucas isn't exactly devout." I wince, realizing this admission must feel like a dagger in my dad's pious little heart. "I mean, why would he want us to do something so . . . strange?"

"I don't think his request has much to do with religion, though a lot of guys start asking questions when they're staring death in the face on a regular basis." Seth points to the only window in the dismal waiting room. "Most people walking around out there, they don't even realize they're mortal. That this could all be over in an instant."

Dad keeps his eyes glued to the sheen of the linoleum floor, bobbing his head like they're in on some sacred soldier truth. Seth falls silent, but keeps staring out the window, like he's waiting for someone to return. Right when the ticking wall clock is about to make me lose my mind, he releases a deep exhale. "Lucas wanted you to walk a very specific route, mainly because it's your namesake."

Dad's head snaps up. "You mean the *Camino de Santiago*?"

I recognize the name, too. The Spanish city of Santiago is at the top of Dad's European travel bucket list. Apparently it's where his ancestors came from before they set sail for Mexico a long, long time ago, and I guess he feels the need to touch the soil. Or something.

"That's the one." Seth's eyes bore into mine, the gleam of his gaze somewhere between mockery and anticipation. "There's one condition, though."

Doesn't matter. No matter what Lucas's stipulation is—even if it's something ridiculous like making the journey in the nude or on the back of an albino camel—I'll figure out a way to do it.

*I promise, Lucas.*

I may not understand this whole pilgrimage thing, but I'm banking on the hope that wherever my brother resides in his unconscious state, he'll see that we're honoring his request and maybe, just maybe, come back. Come home.

"And what condition is that?" I ask, my eyes locked on Dad.

I don't need to see Seth's face because the hint of triumph is evident in his voice. And I honestly, unabashedly, hate him for it. I hate him for once again making me feel like the tagalong afterthought of an all-boy soldier club I can never fully be a part of, even if I followed family tradition and enlisted in the Army myself.

"In his letter, Lucas wrote that if he wasn't able to walk to Santiago with you two for any reason, then he wanted me to go in his place."

# CHAPTER 4

Why are there so many stupid magazines in the ICU waiting area? Does anyone actually think celebrity gossip and "Ten Tips for Losing Winter Weight" is going to provide a drop of comfort?

I study the latest cover of *Outdoor Life* magazine, featuring a glossy photo of an isolated tent in a desert lit up by stars. There was nothing Lucas loved more than the sky. Starry skies, stormy skies, sunset skies—he was always looking out and staring up.

Speaking of staring, Seth is daring me to speak first. He's on the other side of the waiting room, slouched down in the orange chair with his legs splayed open like he's watching the big game on TV. Just gawking. He hasn't said a word since he told us about my brother's request. He's waiting to see how I react, so the best way to stick it to him is to not react at all.

"Is your copy of the *Iliad* highlighted?" I ask, sending a jagged crack down our icy wall of silence.

"'Without a sign, his sword the brave man draws, and asks no omen, but his country's cause,'" Seth recites. "Makes for easy rereading. He chose all my favorite lines."

What a showoff.

"So you think Lucas is the one who highlighted it?"

"Who else?" Seth gives me that look again. The one that makes me feel like I'm either the most naive person he's ever met, or I'm nuts. "Lucas said every soldier should keep the *Iliad* beneath his pillow at all times. I figured he was passing along his own copy."

I doubt that was all Lucas was up to, but I'm not about to tell Seth I received a similar gift in the mail a few short hours ago. Not yet. There's something about Seth's cool, casual attitude towards everything that I don't entirely trust.

My dad, who's retrieved my mother and little brother, pokes his head into waiting room. "Ready to go? I'll pull the car around. Matteo is exhausted."

I fix my gaze on Seth. "Me too. Some people suck all the energy out of the room."

He's not the only one who can play "let's see what gets a reaction."

Seth almost smiles. Almost. "Sleep well, kiddo."

How is it possible that even his goodnight sounds like a dare?

"And then get yourself some decent hiking boots. We've got a long way to walk."

• • •

Just to prove to Seth that I can, I do sleep well. And long. The smell of Mom's blueberry pancakes, served with the Michigan maple syrup her uncle taps and ships to us overseas, is what finally wakes me. My heavy eyes focus on the crumpled soccer uniform at the foot of my bed. It goes without saying that I will not be making my game this morning. So much for being team captain.

"Good morning, sweetheart," Mom says as I enter the kitchen. Her cheerful voice is fake, but well-meaning. She turns from the stove where her round cakes are sizzling and hands me a wooden spoon, covered in what looks like purple plaster. "Pancake batter?"

"Thanks." I stick the entire spoon in my mouth. Mom's looking much better after a good night's sleep, so I dare to ask, "Heard anything from the hospital?"

"Not yet." She flips a slightly overdone cake. "*Scheize*. Pardon my French. Or German, rather." Mom sighs and shakes her head. "I was going for a perfectly golden dozen."

Despite this minor setback, Mom's optimism does not falter. She pours another round of batter onto the skillet before looking at me, a fierce fire in her eyes. "He's going to wake up, Gabriela. Believe me. Mothers can sense these things."

I nod and take another lick of blueberry paste. I wish I had Mom's confidence—or knack for denial—but military life has left me a cynic as of late. Or maybe I'm just a realist. I don't want to burst her bubble, so I carry the plate of hot pancakes into the dining room.

Dad stands there in his PT running shorts with both hands on his hips, looking down on a table covered in paper instead of placemats. He's either planning a very detailed battle strategy for a ten-hour game of Axis & Allies, or he decided to get up early and print out every map he could find of the *Camino de Santiago*.

Seriously, am I the only person in this house holding it together without resorting to some sort of delusion or manic behavior? I peer into the living room where Matteo watches SpongeBob dubbed in German—which is as horrifying as it sounds, but part of his normal morning routine at least.

"You really intend to go through with this?" I clear a spot among the paper and set down the pancakes. When Seth first revealed Lucas's request, Dad had been hard to read, but he's never one to make whimsical, spur-of-the-moment decisions. "How long does the walk take?"

Dad points to a detailed map of the pilgrimage route, his finger trailing a thin red line that hugs the top of Spain before breaking into a dozen tributaries into the heart of Europe after the French border. "The most traditional route, the *Camino Francés*, starts here in the Pyrenees mountains. It takes five or six weeks to reach Santiago, depending on your pace."

"Five or six *weeks*?" I was all for fulfilling Lucas's request at first, but now that I've slept, I'm thinking like a sane person. What if something life-altering happens while we're gone? "There's no way we can leave Lucas for that long."

"I know, *mija*. I didn't plan on leaving your brother's bedside for a day, let alone a month." Dad looks out the window, focusing his gaze on the red glass hummingbird feeder that hangs from our balcony. "But then last night I had a dream."

Oh God, here we go.

"Lucas was a little boy, fast asleep inside a giant scallop shell—the symbol of the *Camino de Santiago*." Dad's eyes glisten with liquid crazy, which is how my father tends to look whenever he's feeling enthusiastic about something. "It's a sign, *mija*."

I don't want to hear another word about signs, omens, or secret messages hidden in Homeric epics. "How is walking across Spain supposed to help Lucas? Don't tell me you're actually hoping for a miracle."

If he is, my father is way more superstitious than I ever imagined, and I have years of therapy to look forward to when his mission fails. "Lucas wants us to visit Santiago, but why do we need to walk all the way there? Can't we just take a plane or train like normal people? Then we'd be back at his bedside in no time."

Dad shakes his head like my mere suggestion is sacrilege. "It's supposed to be a pilgrimage. In the Middle Ages, penitents walked this route barefoot. *Escucha mija,* let me tell you a little story about the *real* world . . . ."

Ladies and gentlemen, enter one of my father's "you narcissistic American youth with your constant selfies have no idea what it's like to suffer" diatribes.

"Do you know *why* I had to quit Mexico's national team after only one season?"

"Because when *abuelo* died, you had to support your mother and five siblings all by yourself," I recite, knowing by heart the story of how Dad gave up soccer and enlisted in the U.S. Army as a path to American citizenship.

"That's right. And because I caught a rare infection that put me in the hospital and could have left me lame. Your *abuela* traveled all the way from our village in Oaxaca to the Basilica of Our Lady of Guadalupe in Mexico City to pray for my healing. So yes, I believe in the power of pilgrimages."

Time to try another tactic. I want to do what Lucas asked, I really do. But I also want to make sure my father realizes what we would be giving up, even if I can't say the words *but Lucas might die while we're gone* out loud because that might make them real.

So I choose an easy scapegoat instead: the public education system. "Have you forgotten that I'm graduating in two months? How can I miss that much school? How can we leave Mom to deal with this alone?"

"Your mother is tougher than you think, and I'll talk to your teachers. Besides, spring break is next week, so that takes care of the first nine days." Dad folds up his research material. A vulnerable expression I've never witnessed consumes his face. It's the face of a helpless man. A man with no backup strategy and no other options.

"I hate to leave him, and when I really think about it, I'm not sure I'll be able to. But I hate sitting here doing nothing even more. This is the *one* thing we can do for him, *mija*. Don't you see? A miracle is all we have left to hope for."

Maybe so, but I'll hedge my bets and put my faith in modern medicine. Still, if Dad wants to get me excused from school, he can go for it. The teachers are the only ones who will notice I'm gone anyway. That reminds me—I need to call Brent. Based on his last text, he's wondering why I went MIA.

Tried calling yesterday, but it kept going straight to voice-mail. Haven't seen you online either. Everything okay? Call me soon. I miss you, Gabi girl.

In spite of everything, the hint of desperation pleases me, I'm not gonna lie.

Dad pulls his credit card out of his wallet. "Your mom and I have a meeting with Lucas's doctors this afternoon. Why don't you take Matteo and go look for a backpack and boots at the Base Exchange."

"The selection will be limited, but I'll check." Taking Dad's credit card almost feels like taking an olive branch—a small sign he's starting to trust me again.

That or he has no other choice.

Mom brings out the rest of the pancakes and calls my little brother to the table. We eat beneath an oppressive silence. Each of us, even Matteo, glances at the one empty chair. Lucas's absence is as thick as maple syrup. It sticks to everything.

A golden glob falls from my fork, landing on the oak table. Most of the furniture we bought for this apartment is that cheap Scandinavian stuff that looks like it was designed for a space station, but the one exception is our dining room table, which we shipped from the States. It's nothing special, but it's been with us everywhere. I could tell a story about every dent, every scratch, every finger-painting episode gone wrong. When we were little, Lucas and I staked permanent claims to our seats by carving our initials into the wood. Mom was upset, but even she had to admit that it cut down on our dinner time squabbling over who sat where.

I run my fingers across the *L.S.* gash, tracing serrated lines etched by a much younger hand. Lucas hasn't sat at our table for all the months he's been deployed, but this feels different.

This absence doesn't feel so temporary.

"I should have known this was a bad idea." Mom throws her fork down and scoots her chair across the hard floor, slicing the room in half. Into *before* and *after*. "It will never be the same. Never."

A moment later we hear her muffled sobs in the kitchen as she throws Lucas-sized portions into the garbage disposal and starts washing the dishes.

Matteo drowns his last bite in syrup and gives me a look that's way too perceptive for a kid who just turned five. Then again, Matteo has already seen more of this world than most kids three times his age.

"Mommy forgot," he whispers, eyes wary. "Blueberry pancakes are Lucas's favorite."

• • •

"We'll pick you up in a few hours," Dad says from the rolled-down window of his beat-up bimmer. I help Matteo out of the old BMW and onto the sidewalk that leads to the main gate of Ramstein Air Force base. Army kids like to joke—okay, *whine*—that Air Force kids get all the best facilities on their bases, but at least we live close enough to benefit, too. No other installation abroad can boast the largest shopping facility in Europe, complete with a Macaroni Grill and a movie theater with stadium-style seats. God bless America.

"Why don't you grab dinner on your way out," Mom adds. "Your pick."

"Robin Hood! Robin Hood!" Matteo shrieks at the mere mention of the Exchange food court. He's not cheering for an outlawed archer in green tights, but for a sandwich shop that serves subs with names like Maid Marian and Little John—a chain I'm pretty sure only exists on military installations.

I take Matteo's hand and approach a gate guard wearing navy blue camouflage, a bulletproof vest, and a blue beret. His partner is busy searching beneath a car with foreign plates, using a mirror on the end of a long pole to look for bombs. Just another day in the life.

I dig through my purse while the gate guard stands in front of me like a statue. Finally, I locate my ID at the bottom of my bag. "That's a relief. My dad would kill me if I lost this thing for the third time in six months," I say sheepishly, hoping for a human reaction . . . like a smile.

Nope.

After wiping the smudges of lip gloss off on my jeans, I hand the guard my ID, which he scans with a device that looks like it's straight out of an original Star Wars film. The soldier's flint face fails to reveal a single emotion as he studies my birthday and eye color to make sure the person in the photograph is really me. You know, just in case terrorists are trying to sneak on to military bases disguised as teenage girls.

"My turn!" Matteo holds up the laminated library card Mom gave him; that way he can pretend to have this shackle around his ankle, too. We get actual ID cards on our tenth birthdays, which is sort of a rite of passage for military brats. The day we receive our very own government-issued identity.

The gate guard chuckles at Matteo's eagerness and gives him a miniature salute. "All set, buddy. Go on through."

What a little charmer. Why can't I have people skills like that?

Inside the Exchange food court, half of the tables are filled with kids from my school, and the opposite side is occupied by kids from the Air Force school. Seriously, it's like *West Side Story* Department of Defense style, only without the singing and pirouettes. Racially speaking, the military has to be the most diverse, integrated institution there is, but we often segregate ourselves by service branches. Don't even get me started on the Army vs. Navy football game.

The food court is the popular hangout place, but I've never taken part in this excessive loitering. That's partly because I've spent enough time working afterschool jobs in the majority of these eating establishments, from Baskin Robbins to Anthony's Pizza. The other part?

Oh yeah. I have no friends.

My goal is to make it through the food court without running into soccer teammates who will ask me questions about Lucas. No one here really knows him, but news travels faster in the military than it does in the smallest town. Too bad Matteo sabotages my attempt at stealth by making a break for a nearby craft stand selling Polish pottery and these cutesy wooden signs with burned engravings of corny German phrases. Naturally, this kiosk is also where Chloe Ross orders a Mother's Day plaque with an idyllic image of Neuschwanstein Castle and the verbose declaration *Ich Liebe Meine Mutter!*

I grab my little brother's arm as he reaches for a Hummel figurine that costs more than my annual allowance. "Matteo, no! You can't just run off without telling me."

"Oh my gosh, Gabi," Chloe squeals, enveloping me in a vanilla body spray–scented embrace. "We missed you this morning, but the team totally understands. How's your brother?"

"The doctors say he's stable," I reply, my voice shaking. No way. I can't do this right now. I can't break down in front of all these people. Chloe is only trying to show sympathy, but Lucas is my family's concern. No one here knows him, and no one here knows me.

Chloe grabs my hand, forcing my eyes up to where hers shine with the optimism of a cloudless blue sky. "Your brother is a hero and you can bet we all know it. A lot of people are praying for him and for your family, too. We're all here for you, Gabi."

The fact that Chloe received the Nicest Person superlative three years in a row must have something to do with the ease with which she speaks on behalf of others, whoever this collective "we" happens to be.

"Thanks for your support. I appreciate it." And then I move on before the unstable, nameless thing inside me splatters across the floor like a tray of spilled nachos.

Unfortunately, I make the rookie mistake of walking past the toy section first.

"Legos! Legos!" Matteo jumps up and down like a frog on crack.

"Sorry, buddy. Dad didn't give us security clearance to purchase any Lego toys." I press on towards the shoe department. Then I freeze. "You have got to be kidding me."

Yep, this outing was a huge mistake. Seth Russo sits in the shoe section, attempting to try on a pair of boots with only one arm. So far he's managed to get the left boot on despite his sling, but tying up those laces is going to be a problem.

Good. Now he knows what it's like to be left hanging. I'll never forget the birthday party we both attended back in Texas almost three years ago. The group we were hanging with wanted to play "seven minutes in heaven," and of course I got sent into the closet with Seth. For seven full minutes he ignored my existence. He never said a word, just stood there in the dark, playing on his phone. I didn't want to kiss him, either, but I swore I'd never forgive him for the slight.

Only now my childish grudge feels kind of stupid.

I release a groan. The guy is injured and I can't ignore him no matter how I'd like to, so I drag Matteo over to his chair. Seth bends forward, awkwardly shoving his foot into the Gore-Tex shoe. His dog tags dangle out in front of him, smacking against his chest as he sits back up.

"They already let you out?" I ask.

"You talk like I was in prison." Seth's lips turn up slightly, but his eyes stay sad. "I thought about breaking out in nothing but my hospital gown, but the doc ruined my commando escape plan by telling me I was free to go."

My lack of laughter solidifies into a thick silence. Seth clears his throat. "I see that you've come to grace me with your fashion sense. What do you think about this pair? I'm going for the 'I'm a baller too cool to tie my laces' look."

"Or you *can't* tie them." I pick up a pair of yellow and black cross-trainers. "Fashion sense, huh? Last I recall, you used to make fun of me for dressing like a tomboy."

Seth's eyes flicker across my moderately short cargo skirt—which is khaki green and has enough pockets to store a decent supply of weaponry, but still qualifies as a skirt. His smirk widens. "Last *I* recall, you never used to show that much leg, kiddo."

"Cut the 'kiddo' crap, all right? You're not even two years older than me. Besides, I'm not the one who needs help tying my shoes. Come on, Matteo, let's show him how it's done. Remember how to make the bunny ears?"

Of course he does—the kid's smart as a whip. Matteo follows my lead as we kneel in front of this big, tough soldier and tie his shoes right there in the middle of the store, my brother reciting, "One bunny ear, two bunny ears" as he goes. I glance up, expecting Seth to either be pissed or embarrassed, but instead he's staring at my brother like he's the most precious thing he's ever seen, not to mention the most painful.

"Thanks, kiddo," he says in a husky voice, patting Matteo on the head. "You too, *Gabi.*"

"It's the least we can do," I reply. And I mean it. It doesn't matter that I've always thought of Seth as the flippant jerk who scorned me. It doesn't even matter that Lucas wouldn't be in the hospital right now if Seth hadn't convinced him to enlist. I may not like the guy, but his scars tell me he's been through more than I can imagine. "You're serious, aren't you? You're really going to walk to Santiago?"

Seth's eyes turn hard. Dry. "For your brother, I'd walk anywhere."

# CHAPTER 5

One lightweight sleeping bag.

One pair of waterproof hiking boots.

One thirty-two-liter backpack.

That's all it takes to blow through the remainder of Dad's paycheck, but at least the Exchange has a flexible return policy, which we'll need when my father returns to planet earth. That moment of truth ends up occurring sooner than expected.

"What do you mean the trek is off?" I demand over the Robin Hood sandwiches no one but Matteo is enjoying. My parents seemed tense in the car ride home, and now I know why. "What about Lucas's request? What about your dream?"

"Believe me, *mija*. This pains me more than it does you."

I don't want to leave my brother's bedside, but I also wanted the decision to be *mine*, not the Army's. The fact that they're intruding on this of all things changes everything.

Besides, I made a promise.

"Screw your commanding officer, Dad. We have to go."

"Um, are you going to eat those?" Matteo asks over our elevated voices, pointing to the untouched pickles on our plates. Dad and I shake our heads no—a flicker of unity that extends to nothing else. My little brother gathers up the spears and moves into the living room to play with the unauthorized Lego blocks I bought him. Because this situation sucks, and he deserves the small joy that is multicolored, stackable plastic.

Mom sits across from me, hands folded on the table in front of her, lips pursed in an unyielding silence. My parents are good at presenting a united front, like they agree on absolutely everything, even though the hushed fighting I sometimes hear behind their bedroom door suggests otherwise. I don't expect Mom to choose sides, but I wish she'd call my father out once in a while.

"It isn't that simple," Dad replies once Matteo is out of range.

"So that's it? We give up?" I persist. "The Army says you can't go and we just ignore what could very well be Lucas's final—"

"Don't," Mom snaps. "Gabi, don't you dare."

Dad studies my mom like she's a ticking bomb. "Two nights ago there was another suicide attack, not far from Ghazni. Six soldiers from the same unit were killed and all of their families are stationed here in Germany. The chaplaincy in Vilseck is short-staffed as it is, so I've been asked to fill in. I'll be able to come home on weekends to visit Lucas in the hospital, but I certainly won't be approved for several weeks of leave. Paid or unpaid."

"But why can't the Army get someone else? *Your* family is grieving, too." It's a selfish thing to say in light of what these poor people are going through, but the thought of Dad counseling another soldier's kid instead of fulfilling his own son's dying wish makes me furious. I let the bittersweet indignation wrap itself around me like a warm hug.

"The Vilseck chaplain was one of the six," Dad says softly. "So there *is* no one else."

I know he's right, but I don't care. Budget cuts. Back-to-back deployments. Missed birthdays. There's *never* anyone else. It will always be *him* because to us, he is everything.

"Then let me go on my own." The words pour out without my consent. Ten minutes ago this pilgrimage felt like a bad joke, but now it feels like our lives depend on it. I don't scheme, I don't think, I just speak. "Let me walk to Santiago for Lucas."

Dad laughs. I'm one hundred percent serious, and the man suddenly finds me hilarious. "I don't think so, Gabriela. Not after what you pulled back at Fort Sam. You're not walking anywhere you can't be supervised. Not until you walk across that graduation stage first."

"That's less than two months away! What difference will a few weeks make?"

"In two months, you'll be your own liability. Not mine." Dad shrugs and Mom, well, Mom doesn't say anything. I can tell something is bothering her, but she refuses to back me up, just like she refused to tell my father that a month-long house arrest right before the Army moved us to a foreign country was an excessive response to my so-called crime. "I've made my decision, *torito*. You may be stubborn as a bull, but you also know that my word is final."

Yes, I'm familiar with *El Jefe*. An army of one.

Only this time, my father's control-freak tendencies have crossed the line. "Dad, I can do this. I already have the gear. *Please*. Someone has to walk to Santiago for Lucas."

There's a knock at our front door, almost as if he planned it.

"And someone will," Dad says. "*Hablando del diablo.*"

"Mom, listen," I whisper while Dad gets up to answer the door, my final shot at an underdog alliance. "You know he's being ridiculous. It's not like I'm asking to spend my senior spring break partying at Daytona Beach. This is for Lucas."

Mom stares at me hard, but it's impossible to tell what she's thinking behind the spiderweb of her bloodshot eyes. Before she can respond, Dad returns with the visitor of the hour. I'm starting to think of the guy as an irksome horse fly that won't go away.

"Hey, Gabi." Seth's T-shirt is drenched and his face glistens with sweat. I can feel the heat radiating off of him from where he stands.

"Did you seriously run all the way here?"

"Gotta start training for the *camino* somehow."

"It's a walk, not an eight-hundred-meter sprint." I point to his sling. "What about your injury?"

Seth pulls an orange bottle of large white pills from his pocket and gives them a shake. "Thanks to the good doctor, I am feeling *no* pain."

"You want to tell us what this meeting is about?" Dad interrupts.

The young soldier hesitates, his eyes flitting from Mom to me, then back to Dad. "Sergeant Major Santiago, do you think we could, er, talk alone in the other room?"

Dad nods and Seth follows him into his office. Mom avoids my guilt-tripping gaze by telling Matteo it's time for his bath. Once they're gone, I tiptoe down the hall and press my ear against the office door. Most of what I hear is muffled and unintelligible, but one of Seth's statements rings out loud and clear:

"Because of what I experienced over there, I've been given extended leave time."

My Dad's response is too low to make out.

Seth speaks again: "You can trust me, sir. I won't let you down."

• • •

"*What*? He was wounded? Wow, babe. I am so sorry." Brent looks pensively torn up, which is kind of his standard expression, but it's as poignant on a pixilated screen as it is in the flesh. "Man, I wish I could be there for you right now."

I wish that, too, but that would require jumping through my desktop, and unfortunately technology hasn't advanced that far yet. Brent is a sensitive soul—one of those super comforting people to have around when things get rough because it's obvious he *feels* everything you're going through. That kind of empathy reminds me why I'm lucky to be with a guy like Brent. An additional reminder is seeing his face, since we haven't video-chatted in over a week. His chestnut hair is extra curly around his ears—a sign Texas is already hotter than Hades. People always say he looks like the lead singer of fill-in-the-name-of-whatever-band, but to me he's just Brent. *My* Brent.

"I miss you, Gabi. I know I've been busy with the band, but I really do." Brent tugs anxiously on one of the gauge holes in his ears—an accessory my father deplores ("Tell me, *mija*. Just what Amazonian tribe is your boyfriend a part of?"). "Is it bad?"

"Well, he's in a coma. So yeah. It's bad."

I don't elaborate because I can't do so without losing it, but I'm surprised when Brent's face does a free fall. He and Lucas never hit it off, in part because Brent isn't a military brat. His dad is the regional manager of all the AAFES retail stores in Texas, so Lucas always thought of Brent as a rich kid just pretending to be one of us.

It doesn't help that my brother is annoyed by fashion-driven subcultures of any kind. Hipster, goth, skater—he detests them all. Whenever I teased Lucas about his boring wardrobe of faded T-shirts and worn jeans, he'd smirk and say, "Classic old-school is the most radical thing a person can be these days, Gabs. Want to be original? Then stand for something time has proven to be solid."

Sure, Brent pays extra attention to trends because he's a musician, but I don't mind, seeing how I'm the one who gets to enjoy the view. Besides, even if he and my brother are never best friends, Brent is there for me when it counts. Like right now.

"You said Lucas left a letter with instructions. What does he want you to do?"

"Go on a pilgrimage. Apparently." I explain my brother's strange request, which Brent doesn't get *at all*.

"Seriously? Lucas wants you to walk all the way to Spain just to visit some dead guy's tomb? Why not fly? It'd be a lot faster. Oh wait, is this supposed to be some weird way to save your brother's soul?"

Based on how my brother's mind works, Lucas orchestrated this little adventure to save *us*, not himself. He's always been a natural mediator, and I have no doubt that Lucas saw this trek as a way to repair the broken bond between me and my dad. Too bad there's no chance of a truce now. Dad has made it perfectly clear that he's counting down the days until I am no longer a military dependent and a potential threat to his upwardly mobile career.

"The three of us used to do hikes all the time," I explain. "I'm guessing Lucas's plan has to do with how messed up things have been lately. You know, ever since—"

"Believe me, I know." Brent's flushed cheeks are even visible digitally. "The man hasn't looked me in the eye, shook my hand, *nothing*."

"Yeah, well, that's what happens when you break the circle of trust." I roll my eyes and change the subject from my father's resentment issues to something hopefully less futile. "Have you received anything from UT-Austin yet?"

Brent shakes his head and stares into his lap, like he's embarrassed that he hasn't heard back. From the moment I arrived in Germany, my plan has been fixed and my goal singular: to return to Texas as soon as possible. Our entire group of friends applied for admission to UT-Austin as a way to reunite the old crew after graduation. I got my acceptance letter in the mail a few weeks ago, but we're still waiting to hear back on Brent's application. He's a decent student with a lot of extracurriculars like me, so I don't get the holdup.

"Don't worry," I tell him. "You'll get in and we'll be together. Just like before."

Brent nods, but he still won't look at me. There's something buried beneath the surface that he doesn't know how to unearth, but now is not the day for me to dig.

"So when are you leaving for Spain?" he asks.

I sigh. "As of thirty minutes ago, it looks like I'm not. Dad's boss won't let him go, which means I can't go."

"And so you're giving up? That's not like you, Gabi girl."

"What else am I supposed to do?"

"Go anyway." Brent shrugs, as if this is the most obvious solution to my problem. To his credit, Brent's parents are fairly hands-off, so it's hard to blame him for failing to grasp life under an oppressive, dictatorial regime. "You're about to graduate, Gabi. They can't call the shots forever, and letting Lucas down is something you'll regret for the rest of your life. Buy the plane ticket and go do this thing."

"Uh, with what money?" Brent makes it sound so easy. And for him, it would be. "As of today I've made $264.78 bagging groceries at the commissary, which will hardly be enough for last-minute airfare, let alone train tickets, hostels, food . . . ."

"Relax. I can spot you," Brent interjects. "Let me buy your plane ticket as an early birthday present. E-mail me the dates and I'll book it right away."

Why is he pushing this? His offer is super generous and that's one thing Brent has always been, but five minutes ago he could barely grasp the concept of a pilgrimage. Now he's volunteering his patronage.

"That's sweet of you, but I can't let you do that." My family has lived paycheck to paycheck for most of my life, and it seems I've inherited my father's self-made-man vanity.

"Yes, you can. You never let me pay for movies or concerts, which means I've got, hmmm, let's see . . . ." Brent counts his fingers, his blithe smile an assurance he intends to win this one. "Yep, according to my calculations, I owe you fifty-four dates. Come on Gabi, it's the least I can do. I doubt I'd be graduating, let alone getting into college, if you hadn't kicked my butt into gear. Let me help *you* out for once."

"This isn't about me," I realize out loud. And that's the very thought that makes this act of treason plausible. My brief stint as a rebel in San Antonio didn't last long, but I *do* think I could play a martyr. Lucas's cause is worth imprisonment or exile—the two most likely sentences *El Jefe* will inflict once he discovers I've disobeyed a direct order.

So be it. When I picture my brother lying in his current prison, neither punishment sounds all that bad.

"Okay, Brent. Buy the ticket. I'm in."

• • •

Nylon is noisy. There's no escaping it. My backpack is huge and awkward and I feel like a drunken Santa Claus stumbling down a dark hallway with an overstuffed gift sack.

Dad left for Vilseck and Mom has spent most of her waking hours at the hospital, so making travel preparations wasn't difficult. Seth had already decided to do the walk with or without me. I told him my dad changed his mind, and I'd meet him at the airport in time for our 7 A.M. flight.

Now the trick will be getting out of this house in the dark without my ginormous backpack taking out Mom's favorite lamp in the process.

Why did I pack so much? I doubt Bilbo Baggins ever had to deal with this nonsense.

As I creep through the living room, a floorboard creaks beneath my extra weight. I freeze. The lamp I was worried about breaking switches on, the colors of its Tiffany shade blinding me like a watchtower spotlight. Mom is on our new Ikea Söderhamn sofa, her hand clutching the cord of the Victorian lamp. I'm struck by how these two styles don't go together *at all*, but right now shaky interior design is the least of my worries.

"Were you going to leave a note at least?" Mom sits up like she's been expecting me. Her face is hard. Gangster hard.

Yep, I am so busted.

I lower my eyes to the pristine hiking boots I'll never get to use. "How did you find out?"

Mom yawns and wraps a crochet blanket around her shoulders. "You never do your laundry without me pestering you about it a dozen times first. Last night you did three loads."

*Laundry?* Are you kidding me? After all my scheming, that stupid Snuggles bear was the one who sold me out?

"So that's it. You tell Dad and none of us accomplish the *one thing* Lucas asked us to do." I unclick the shoulder straps of my bag and let my Matteo-sized backpack fall to the floor. "All because Sergeant Paranoid doesn't believe I can travel with a member of the opposite sex without getting pregnant in the process. Can't you see how ridiculous this is? In seventeen years, I screwed up *one* time."

Now my mom is wide awake. "Your father has a lot on his plate, Gabi. Lucas is plenty, but he's also got six devastated families to serve, and the last thing he needs to worry about is his only daughter wandering around a foreign country."

"Which is why he should just—"

"Let me finish, Gabriela." Mom runs her hands through her hair, like she's about to make an important announcement to important people and wants to look the part. This is a demeanor I've seen before, most often when Dad was deployed. It means my mother is about to ditch the passenger seat and take the steering wheel.

"As I was saying, your father has a lot on his mind, so I'm not sure he's thinking clearly about this, about how important this journey must be to Lucas." Mom takes a deep breath. "The last thing I want is to undermine your father. We make our decisions together as a team, despite how one-sided it may look on the outside. *But* I've also been married to the man for twenty years, and sometimes I suspect I know what he truly wants even more than he does."

"And what does he want?" I demand. "For me to live with the guilt of having failed Lucas for the rest of my life?"

"Cut the melodrama, Gabi. What your father wants is simple— for his children to reach adulthood safely, without having to experience the kind of struggles he had to. What he sometimes forgets is that this world will never be safe, and two of his children are practically adults already." Mom gets up from the sofa, picks up my pack, and helps reposition it on my back. "I'll talk to your father. Now you'd better get going, otherwise you'll miss your flight."

Salty tears line the back of my throat as I give my mom an unexpected hug goodbye. "Thank you. For being on my team."

"I'm always on your team, Gabriela. You just have to give me the chance to play."

I break Mom's embrace and turn towards the door.

"Gabi, wait."

My shoulders sink. She's about to change her mind. Mom disappears down the hallway towards Dad's office.

"Take this," she says when she returns, holding out a plastic bag.

Now I'm really confused. "What is it?"

"Something your father wanted to do for Lucas while he walked the *camino*. Something your Grandma Guadalupe did for him when he got sick." Mom hands me one hundred extra euros and the clear plastic bag filled with tiny tealight candles. "Now it's up to you."

I accept this parting gift, aware that I'm walking this route for Dad as much as I am for Lucas. Maybe if I do this one thing right, he'll trust me again.

Maybe I'll start trusting myself.

# CHAPTER 6

Seven hundred and eighty kilometers. Five hundred miles. The distance between Cleveland and New York. That's how far we're walking. Well, almost that far. Mom will talk to my teachers, but two weeks of class plus spring break is probably the most I can miss and still manage to graduate, so we'll have to take a short bus ride in the middle of the route to speed things up. Still, walking for this long is *insanity*. And I willingly agreed to take part in it.

Not to mention that I most certainly overpacked. This is the first detail I discern as I study the other tourists—oops, I mean *pilgrims*—on the train ride from Paris to the Spanish border. Let's start with the young woman across the aisle, the one who hasn't looked up from her magazine in almost two hours. Her stylish sporting gear makes me wonder if she's a model for Eddie Bauer or The North Face. She's got to be either Dutch or Norwegian. Tall and very Heidi-looking with white-blond hair worn in two long braids. Like the rest of these passengers, her equipment tells me Europeans take hiking *very* seriously. Their fancy trekking poles, super lightweight packs, and layers of waterproof material make it look like they're about to tackle Everest.

*My* contribution to the world of *camino* fashion? A ratty pair of Adidas warm-up pants that should have been thrown out two seasons ago. Seth brought his camo-green rucksack, which holds a lot of junk, but stinks like canvas and makes us stick out like silly Americans who have no idea what the heck they're doing.

Seth has uttered maybe three words the entire overnight train ride. He rests his head against the window, looking like he's in desperate need of an energy drink. I decide it's time for another round of "let's see what gets a reaction," so I dig through my daypack, hoping that what I'm about to reveal will remind Seth we're doing this pilgrimage for Lucas, not as a ridiculously long penance that requires him to glower 24/7.

I pull out the Barbie-sized G.I. Joe action figure—*action figure*, not doll, Lucas always insisted—that sat on my brother's nightstand most of his childhood. Only I've made a few alterations. To start, I taped a small photograph of Lucas's face over the G.I. Joe's face. Then I stripped the soldier of his gun and wrapped his arm in a mini-rosary, just to give him a more pilgrim vibe.

"Get it?" I say. "It's like that traveling gnome. You know, the one from the commercials?"

Seth just stares at the toy. Okay, so maybe it isn't genius in the sense of being highly original, but I still think Lucas would find it hilarious.

"I figure we take pictures of G.I. Joe at all the major stops along the pilgrimage route, and then show Lucas the photos once he wakes up."

For a second Seth seems upset, like this is some sort of sacrilege, but then he holds up his phone and grins. "I can post the pics online, if you want. Make our little soldier his own Facebook profile and everything."

Hmmm, I never actually thought about *sharing* the photos. While I'm on the *camino* I'm using Mom's international prepaid phone, which is so old and bare-bones it doesn't even have a camera. "I don't know about that. Maybe. I'm just praying Lucas won't be pissed that I took Army Ken out of his mint-condition collector's box."

Seth studies his phone's screen, searching for a signal now that we're pulling into the final train station. He lifts the device to his ear.

"Miss your battalion buddies already?"

"Uh, no. I highly doubt Sergeant Major Santiago considers himself part of my posse."

"Wait, *what*?" Like a cat swatting at a bird, I strike the phone from Seth's hand. It soars across the aisle, stopping to rest between Heidi's perfectly petite feet.

Seth glares at me, then gets up to retrieve his phone. The North Face model gives him her best Claudia Schiffer smile and hands it over. They exchange a few words and a flirtatious laugh before Seth returns.

"What was that about, Gabi? This phone cost most of my tax return."

"Sorry. I overreacted. But you *cannot* call my dad."

"Uh, yeah, I can. He'll want to know we arrived safely."

"It's not a good idea," I insist. "He's got a lot going on right now. We shouldn't bother him unless we absolutely have to."

Seth's frigid eyes lock onto mine. He's waiting for me to blink, willing me to crack. "You're lying." He sighs, like he knows he's going to regret his next question. "Okay, Gabi. Why don't you want me to call your dad?"

I cross my arms and lean back into my seat. "Correct me if I'm wrong, but I didn't think the Army trained lowly privates in interrogation tactics."

"It's a simple question, though I suspect you've already answered it." A sneer lurks on Seth's lips. "Your dad doesn't know you're here, does he?"

I don't respond. Instead, I stare out the window at the walled town of Saint-Jean-Pied-de-Port, at the base of the Pyrenees mountains. The place is all cobblestone streets, red-tile roofs, and overflowing window boxes, but Seth's swelling anger manages to suffocate the quaintness.

After muttering a series of colorful words that could only be strung together by a soldier, he gets up from his seat, ready to disembark the train. "I can't believe this. Your dad is going to murder me. That's what I get for trusting the word of a high-school kid."

The train stops and Seth hurries down the aisle with the rest of the eager crowd, but I still need to get my backpack down from the overhead storage compartment. It's so awkward and heavy that I nearly fall over trying to get the stupid thing back on.

"Thanks for the help," I mutter at the back of Seth's head.

And who says chivalry is dead?

At least figuring out where to go next is easy. All I have to do is follow the mob of pilgrims getting off of the train. Most wear these large white scallop shells (the one from Dad's dream) around their necks or on their packs. Apparently it was worn in the Middle Ages and tells everyone you're a pilgrim. Talk about *the* original statement piece.

I weave through the crowd and catch up to Seth. "Why are you freaking out? My mom knows I'm here and she'll tell my dad soon enough. It's not like the military is going to issue a Missing Person notice for me."

"Not for you. But they'll need one for *me* after your father buries me six feet under." Seth's pace doesn't slow one bit. "I'm supposed to be looking out for you, not kidnapping you."

"Looking out for me? What, like I need your protection?"

The fact that Seth sees himself as my chaperone is infuriating, but I'm momentarily distracted by the man crossing the street in front of us. He leans on a long shepherd's crook and is trailed by a border collie who herds three brown cows right down the middle of the main street. It's like we've walked onto the set of *The Sound of Music*, but Seth doesn't even notice.

"You have no idea the position you've put me in," he seethes. "Then again, why would you? This is all a big game to you."

"No. It's not. Chill out. My dad will come around." At least I hope he will, though that can't happen unless Mom breaks the news in her own diplomatic way. But if *Seth* turns me in, my father will be on the next plane to Barcelona, intent on dragging my sorry butt home.

I hold up the G.I. Joe and wave it in Seth's face. "Don't worry, the Sarge will be fine once he sees our photos and realizes what we're doing for Lucas. *Lucas*, Seth. Forget about my dad. Think about Lucas."

Seth does think. In total silence. For the next quarter of a mile.

We reach a bridge crossing a river lined with stone houses that must be hundreds of years old. Other than church bells, chirping birds, and lots of pilgrim footsteps, the town is quiet. Whenever I exhale (which, given the altitude, is often), my breath turns to mist as it mixes with the steam rising from the river.

Seth's expression isn't one of contemplative awe. He doesn't look angry anymore, just uncomfortable, like he knows he doesn't belong here. Like he has no idea *why* he's walking through a medieval village in southern France with a bunch of strangers on holiday when his best friend is in a hospital bed and the rest of his buddies are being shot at. Seth's short haircut, solid build, and busted arm draw a few curious glances from the other walkers, but his stay-away body language makes it clear he isn't taking questions.

Where are we going? Why is he torturing me like this? *Are you going to call my dad or not?* I want to shout. Instead, I try summoning patience, which is so not my virtue.

"I'm sorry I didn't tell you, okay?" We close in on the official headquarters of the *Camino de Santiago*, the place where we're supposed to pick up these pilgrim passports that enable us to stay in the cheap municipal hostels.

*Please stop, please stop, please stop.*

"Did you hear me?" I repeat. "I said *I'm sorry.*"

If only Seth knew the rare and precious value of these words, coming from me.

"Whatever," he mutters. "Let's just get our credential."

*Hallelujah.* My heart pumps liquid relief. I speed-walk towards the pilgrim office door before Seth can change his mind.

"Hold up," he says from behind me. "I have one condition."

Of course he does. I turn. Slowly. "And that is?"

"You have to be honest with me from here on out. You have to give me no-bullshit answers to all my questions, no matter what I ask."

But that makes no sense. What could Seth possibly want to know about *me*?

"Fine."

"I'm serious, Gabi. No more BS," he repeats, arms crossed like he's a bouncer standing in front of an exclusive nightclub.

"Got it."

Seth nods. "Then let's get going."

"First, let's make it official." I set G.I. Lucas down on a stone ledge for his inaugural photo in front of the *camino* logo—a golden scallop shell against a bright blue background.

Then we enter the credentialing office. Now, if the Middle Ages had its own version of the living hell that is the DMV, I'm pretty sure this was it. A lengthy procession of pilgrims wait to see *one* little old Frenchman armed with a rubber stamp. As we stand in line, multiple languages assault my ears from every direction.

Seth gives me a look that pretty much sums it up: *What are we doing here?*

Finally, I'm next. With a gnarled, shaking hand, the elderly man slams his stamp down on my pilgrim's passport like he's squashing a ridiculously large bug. He smiles and lifts his crinkly blue eyes to mine. "*Buen camino, mon chéri.*"

I take hold of the document and suddenly this is *real*. I don't know why I'm here, or why Seth decided not to call my dad, or what my brother even wants us to accomplish, but I am now an official pilgrim on the Way of St. James.

• • •

Nobody—not even Rick Steves—told me we'd be scaling cliffs on Day One. Most photos of the *camino* that I found online were of these long, winding roads that stretched through wheat fields and rolling vineyards, the occasional steeple of an old church reaching up to kiss a clear blue sky. Nope, none of that here. For the first few kilometers the incline is gradual, but then the road turns steep and doesn't quit. The scenery becomes breathtaking, literally, as we approach a series of switchbacks.

To make matters worse, Seth is still pissed. His brutal pacing proves it.

As we march single-file up the mountain, I suddenly understand why so many pilgrims regard this journey as a profound spiritual experience. After all, I'm already praying, "Hail Mary, full of grace, slow this guy's pace before he kills me." Yet there's no way I can ask Seth for a break so soon. That would mean showing weakness, and that's the worst thing I can do.

We reach the next summit, where a blue and white statue of the Madonna and Child overlooks the valley behind us. The shrine is draped with wilting flowers, empty wine bottles stuffed with handwritten notes, even a few pairs of worn-out hiking boots. I approach the statue and see a hiker in a neon yellow windbreaker drop to his knees. He lights a small candle, moving his lips in a silent prayer as he sets it on the altar. Seth waits in the shade nearby, watching this display of unabashed piety like he's observing an endangered species in the wild.

"I don't get people who pray," he whispers. "Doesn't this guy realize his trail of tealights could start a forest fire?"

The mockery in Seth's voice makes it clear he regards this behavior as an evolutionary step backwards. I'm still trying to catch my breath, so I don't respond, but I feel the bag of candles from Mom pressing into my lower back. My father would be lighting them up like a pyromaniac if he were here, but I leave them buried at the bottom of my pack. Dad may have viewed this trek as a spiritual mission, but that doesn't mean I need to see it that way. So the candles stay put, taking up space and adding extra weight I could do without.

"Better keep moving." Seth turns to leave the praying pilgrim in peace.

"After you," I mutter, prepared for another thirty minutes of gasping for air.

Before long we cross the border into Spain and ascend Lepoeder Pass, the highest point of the day. A grove of twisted beech trees coated in florescent moss provides shade for a while, until we reach a hillside covered in the kind of grass found on a golf course. A few sheep dart across the trail in front of me, which explains the exceptional lawn-care service. My feet slow when I approach an overlook showcasing emerald peaks from every angle. The road descends into a valley filled with golden mist as the sun begins to set. Seth, far ahead of me by now, all but disappears into the sea of orange sherbet clouds.

"This isn't a race, Russo!" I shout across the valley. Seth climbed this mountain like it was nothing, and now he's descending it even faster. He's punishing me, and he's enjoying every sociopathic second. "Whatever, dude. I'm stopping."

My feet throb like someone went to town on them with meat tenderizer. The familiar burn promises fat, oozy blisters on the back of my heels, so I sit on a boulder and take off my boots. Sure enough, two spots of raw, pink flesh peek out from my woolen socks.

Awesome. What a great first day!

It doesn't help that Seth makes it look so easy with his firm soldier calves and his stiff soldier stature. Even with his immobilized arm, Seth's movements drip with arrogance and his gaze remains fixed ahead on his goal. I spend the rest of our descent into Roncesvalles boring my eyes into the soldier's rigid, too-good-to-stop-and-smell-the-roses back, hoping he can feel every shard I throw at him.

"Did you know this place is famous for Charlemagne's conquest in the year 778? We're right near the spot where his prized general,

Roland, was killed," Seth announces casually when I catch up to him at the village entrance. He sits on the side of the road with his nose buried in his guidebook, like he just finished up a nice evening stroll.

Seriously. I want to kill him.

"Thanks for the random trivia," I mutter, sucking down oxygen.

Maybe Roncesvalles was a hopping town back in the eighth century, but there isn't much happening here now. From what I can tell, pilgrims make up most of the population. They're all walking towards the same building, which looks like an old monastery. Or a morgue. My aching body, longing for an eternal rest, almost hopes for the latter.

"My trivia is more relevant than you think. You know how Roland died? Charlemagne's army was ambushed by a band of Saracens who had invaded this part of the Pyrenees." Seth shuts his book and stands. "Which proves that some things never change."

"Uh, better fact-check your guidebook. See that plaque back there? You know, the one you were in too much of a hurry to stop and read? It said most historians now believe the ambush was by a guerilla army of Basques, the native people from this part of Spain. So your stereotyping can take that."

Seth bites the inside of his cheek. "Funny you should think so highly of the people responsible for your brother's injuries. If you'd been there, Gabi, you would have—"

"Funny you should think so highly of people at all," I interrupt. "We've been killing each other since the dawn of time. Over race, religion, whatever. Humans have never needed much of an excuse. *That's* what never changes."

I survey the small mountain town, wishing the Basques had the entrepreneurial foresight to open a drive-through KFC. "Take me, for instance. I'm starving and if someone waved a juicy drumstick in front of my nose, I might just attempt murder to get it. That's how the world works. When it comes to survival, the ruthless will always win. Or have you never seen a single zombie apocalypse movie?"

Seth's glare turns to pity as he shakes his head. "For the record, kiddo, you have no idea what you're talking about."

His retort is real and it stings, but I'm too worn out to give it much thought. We enter the *albergue*. A bored attendant waits to stamp our pilgrim passports before showing us to a large room with a vaulted ceiling and stone walls, lined with approximately fifty bunk beds, half of them already taken. Looks like we will not only be sleeping in a dank and drafty monastery, but there will be *no* privacy.

Not to mention the place smells like feet. Hundreds of pairs of filthy, stinking feet.

"Wow, this is one step below the Ritz." I unbuckle my backpack and toss it onto a bare mattress with more stains on it than I care to count. "I call top bunk."

The bunk beds are pushed together in pairs, so there are two twin beds on top and two on the bottom. Talk about awkward. Thankfully, no one has claimed the bed next to mine yet. I hope to whatever saint is responsible for such matters that it stays that way.

While we're getting settled in, two Spanish women in the next bunk cluster mention a special pilgrim's Mass about to take place in a nearby chapel. I don't think Seth can understand what they're saying, but he starts following them out the door.

"Don't tell me you're headed to confession?" I call after him. The thought that Seth may be more willing to pray for my brother's healing than I am is not only a shocker, it makes me feel a tad guilty.

Seth tenses up at the word *confession* like I've hit him upside the head with it.

"I'm the product of a lapsed Baptist and a secular Jew," he replies, adding a silent *so what do you think?* "I'm off to find a drink."

Good riddance. If the prickly tension between us is an indication of how this trek is going to be, I doubt we make it to the next town before our fragile alliance is severed permanently.

Okay, shower time. I dig through my backpack for flip-flops and clean clothes, but everything I packed is tainted by that damp travel smell that never goes away once it settles in. Still, a hot, steamy shower is the one thing that can salvage this letdown of a first day. I grab my toiletry bag and make my way to the bathroom, but the line is already a mile long. Naturally. So far this *camino* has been nothing but a rush through beautiful scenery and a lot of wasted time standing in queues. As the British would say.

"All yours." A woman emerges from stall number three. She saunters out buck naked—I kid you not—strutting around like she owns the place. I try to keep my eyes to myself, but a quick scan of the locker room assures me Europeans have no issues hanging out in the buff with strangers in super confined spaces. Overweight and eighty years old? Not a problem.

Finally, it's my turn. Fully clothed, I hurry into the stall before the suspicious woman behind me—the one with the crafty look of a professional line cutter—makes a break for it.

"*Scheize!*" The lukewarm water that erupts from the showerhead stings my bleeding feet, turning the water around the drain a rusty brown. Gross. The stall already has a collection of hair from twenty different people, along with used razors and a disgusting Band-Aid some courteous individual left stuck to the wall. But the harsh spray feels good on my sore back, so I stand there, selfishly using up the remaining warm water. A new thought washes over me.

*If you had been there, Gabi.*

That's what Seth said when he mentioned the insurgents responsible for Lucas's injuries. It's a statement that suggests Seth *was* there, which means he lied to me at the hospital when he said he didn't know how Lucas got hurt. I *knew* it. The guilty puppy look in Seth's eyes proves he knows every detail and isn't willing to share. Fine. If he wants to turn this trek into a power struggle, he has no idea what he's up against. Seth may break my body, but I won't relent until he gives me answers. Until he tells me the truth about Lucas.

"*Hola, chica.* Time's up!" booms a voice beyond my shower stall.

"Oh, come on," I groan. A *minimum* of ten minutes is required for a proper shower. I still have conditioner in my hair, but when I step out of the stall—wrapped in a towel like a normal person—I'm greeted by a wall of irritated faces.

There's another line for the mirrors in front of the sink, which is where I make a futile attempt to defrizz my hair with a tiny travel tube of gel designed for a hobbit, not a Latina. Yeah, this whole communal shower routine needs to be seriously streamlined.

Back outside, I find Seth sitting on top of a stone wall next to the *albergue*, drinking from a full-sized wine bottle in a brown paper bag. Classy. I reach into his open jar of anchovy-stuffed olives and pop one into my mouth. "You like to get the party started early."

"You like to spend forever in the shower." He takes another swig, a deep purple stain lingering on his lips. "Red wine is crazy cheap here. This bottle cost me a whole euro."

Seth offers me a drink, but I decline. "No thanks. I'm so hungry that I'll get the spins from a single sip."

"Then let's go find something to eat."

Now he's talking. Once I've trapped him inside a restaurant, Seth won't be able to speed-walk away from my questions.

"Uh, what's wrong with you?" he asks after a few steps.

"What do you mean?"

"You're walking like a duck."

"No. I'm not."

"Yes. You are. You're waddling."

"It's my stupid feet," I groan. "They're covered in blisters. Those crappy boots I bought at the BX are worthless."

Seth pats the wall. "Have a seat."

I climb onto the stone ledge and let my flip-flops fall to the ground. My green polish is chipped, which makes it look like I have some sort of fungus, but the red blisters and cuts along my toes overshadow this cosmetic neglect. Seth kneels in front of me and opens up his daypack, removing a small first-aid kit.

"Boy Scouts always come prepared," I tease, temporarily forgetting that just a few minutes ago, I declared war on this mortal enemy.

Seth smirks as he removes a needle, some alcohol swabs, and a few moleskin bandages, all with one hand. "Yeah, well, I hope the U.S. Army has provided me with survival skills a little more advanced than tying cool knots."

Seth drains and cleans each blister, covering the wounds with moleskin. I hate my feet, aesthetically speaking, so it's strange having someone else touch them in their extra gross state. Fortunately, Seth's movements are as fast and methodical as any medical professional. He never looks up, but I swear I see a rosy flush spreading across his cheeks. His hands are a lot gentler than I'd thought they'd be. Only a few calluses. An itchy warmth travels up my legs, even though Seth's fingers never move past my ankles. The tingling is unexpected. And weird.

"All set. Hopefully the blisters heal soon, otherwise you'll be miserable for the rest of the journey." Seth stands up and puts his supplies away. "Make sure you take your boots and socks off to air out any time we stop to rest."

"Which, based on your pace today, will be never." I jump down from the wall. "But thanks. My feet feel a million times better already."

Seth smiles. Like *really* smiles. "My Scout leader would be proud."

We head up the gravel path leading to the only restaurant in town. Seth's grin, a minor fissure in his defensive wall, makes me think this is an opportunity to gain the higher ground. "Why do you think Lucas asked us to do this pilgrimage? His letter made it sound like he wanted to revive an old family tradition, but there must be more to it than that."

"There is," Seth replies. "But I wasn't sure how your parents would handle it."

I grab his arm. The injured one. Not too hard, but hard enough for him to know I mean business. "I can handle it, Seth. Whatever it is. Lucas always told me everything."

"He didn't tell anyone about this. Not even me." Seth breaks off a piece of tall grass growing alongside the footpath, where a chorus of crickets emerges. "Remember how I told you that Lucas became more withdrawn once our missions started? How he started isolating himself?"

"I remember."

"Well, I was worried about him, so I went through his e-reader to see what he was so absorbed in during R&R. Lucas had almost finished this history book about medieval knights during the Crusades who weren't allowed to reenter their villages until they confessed their sins to a priest and were absolved of the violence they'd taken part in. I guess these warriors felt a strong desire to purge themselves of war before returning to their communities." Seth hesitates, like he's trying to connect the dots.

"So what you're telling me is these knights were sent to fight in a war sanctioned by the government and the church, but the people in power had the audacity to make them apologize for it when they got back? Wow. That's a whole new level of messed up."

"See, that's what I thought at first too, but then I read what Lucas typed in the eBook's margin: *It's the only way home. There's no other way home.*"

Now I get why Seth didn't tell my parents any of this. It's hard enough when your kid is wounded in action, but hailed as a hero. It's even worse when your kid considers *himself* a coward, or worse, a criminal who has no right to return to the people who love him most. "What do you think Lucas meant by that?"

"PTSD is the big buzzword, but the symptoms are pretty specific. Flashbacks, nightmares, extreme anxiety. All that. A lot of people throw the label around as if every returning soldier has it, but there are other types of trauma."

"That makes sense." My dad has mentioned this before too, though I'm ashamed to admit I didn't pay much attention to his meditations on life as a chaplain's assistant until they applied to my own brother. "What kinds of trauma?"

"Moral wounds. Regarding yourself as one type of person—G.I. Joe, the good guy—but feeling like you're forced to become someone else." Seth lets out his breath in a slow, even exhale before stringing together more words than I've ever heard him speak in one sitting.

"Taking human life is heavy shit. There's no easy way to process it, regardless of our justifications or claims that it was necessary. Then afterwards we're supposed to return to the regularly scheduled program, as if nothing happened. Strangers at the airport buy you drinks and everyone treats you like a hero, but you don't feel like one, even if you love your country and believe in the mission. You feel like there's this giant stone hanging around your neck, but you don't know what to do with it because no one who cares about you would dare suggest you've done anything wrong. They all say you did what you had to do, what a soldier is *supposed* to do. There's no middle ground. Either antiwar protesters on the street call you a baby killer, or people turn you into some kind of idol. They don't acknowledge that the only reason you're back home at all is because other people are dead. And not all of them terrorists."

Seth's tone has gone from frustrated to morose in a matter of seconds. I wonder who we're talking about here: my brother or him? Does Seth have something to feel guilty about, too?

"Do you think Lucas believed walking this pilgrimage route would alleviate his conscience somehow?" I ask. "Do you think that would even work?"

"That's the only way I can make sense of his sudden obsession with pilgrimages. A lot of people think 'right' and 'wrong' are just a matter of opinion, but if that's the case, I don't think soldiers—you know, like Lucas—would experience inner anguish over simply doing their jobs. We have a conscience and you can kill it eventually, but your brother isn't the type to numb himself."

But is Seth?

He falls silent as we approach the café. I can feel him rebuilding his walls, layer by unspoken layer. Our conversation has hit a nerve. Something *is* eating away at Seth's scruples. Something that has to do with Lucas.

This is my chance. He's already opened up this much, so I might as well push in further. "Seth, how did my brother get hurt in the first place? I *know* you know."

Nothing but a stony silence.

"For real. What happened to you guys over there?"

Seth opens the gate leading to a covered patio, his lips pressed into a thin line. The distance settling into his eyes is one I recognize, given that I saw it on my father's face every time he returned from a deployment. I can be relentless when I want to be, but I also know that if you press in on a door that's bolted shut, all you end up with is a bloody fist and a busted frame.

Seth sighs. "That, kiddo, I can't tell you. Not yet anyway."

Then I can wait. Maybe I'm more patient than I thought.

# CHAPTER 7

"Try the *queso con miel*. Trust me, you'll never be the same."

And that's how we made our first pilgrim friend: Bob from Australia.

Bob is a sixty-seven-year-old ex-hippie, and he's forever changed my life. When he overheard us arguing about an appetizer, Bob suggested we try homemade bread served with fresh goat cheese and Spanish honey so dark, it looks more like molasses.

Seriously. Life-changing. The perfect blend of savory and sweet. Forget KFC, I'll never crave those butter-drenched biscuits again after this nectar of the gods on toast.

Bob pulls his chair over to our table, unbuttons his Hawaiian shirt, and props his Birkenstock-clad feet onto the empty seat. "So where are you newlyweds from?"

"Uh, she's seventeen," Seth says in a way that makes it sound like I have Ebola.

"Yeah, we are so *not* married," I reiterate.

"Could have fooled me with that proficient bickering." Bob chuckles and removes a bag of sunflower seeds from his shirt pocket. "Don't worry, there's plenty of time for you two."

Time for what? To kill each other in new and creative ways?

"Hell, I've been on the *camino* so long, I can't tell how old anyone is anymore. Younger than me, that's for sure." Bob cracks a few sunflower seeds with his teeth, spitting the shells into his empty beer bottle. It's gross and endearing at the same time.

"How long have you been walking?" I ask.

"Oh, I've come back every spring for the past seven years."

"You just keep walking the same route?" Seth asks before swooping in on the last chunk of goat cheese. "Aren't there any good hikes back in Australia?"

Bob laughs. "It's hard to explain, but there's something special about this road and the people who walk it. It isn't even the most beautiful hike out there, though there are parts that will take your breath away. But of all the treks I've done, the *camino* is the most surreal. It's like everything is orchestrated—every stop, every person you meet. Just wait, she'll steal your heart. You'll see." Bob lowers his feet from the chair and slaps both thighs. "Well, kids, it's been fun, but I've got old friends to visit and you two have a lovers' squabble to resolve. See you around."

Before either of us can correct him on our relationship status, Bob saunters off to find his drinking buddies from pilgrimages past.

Once he's gone, I'm attacked by a killer yawn. "Ready to turn in?"

"What are we, eighty?" Seth snickers. "It's nine o'clock. That old guy puts us to shame."

"Give me a break, okay? I don't usually walk fifteen miles in one day. Besides, I'm sure Bob did enough shrooms in the sixties to kill the parts of his brain most perceptive to physical pain." I get up from my chair and rub my full belly. "I, on the other hand, am sore, sleepy, and stuffed with more honey than Winnie the Pooh. It's bedtime."

Smiling, Seth tosses a stack of euros onto the table. "Okay, grandma. Let's go."

• • •

*Una oveja, dos ovejas . . . .*

Nope, still can't sleep. I've tried counting sheep in English *and* in Spanish, but neither method is effective. Studying the cracks in the ceiling doesn't work either. I'm exhausted, but there are snores coming at me from every direction. The most annoying octave, by far, is the bellowing baritone in the next row. It doesn't help that my bed keeps shaking every two minutes, thanks to Seth tossing and turning below. I hear him click on his LED flashlight. Its blue glow appears along the wall by my head.

Rolling onto my stomach, I press my face to the crack between the mattress and the wall. Seth is reading the *Iliad*. He's got this pensive look on his face—like he isn't reading the book for fun, but because he's searching for something.

*That, kiddo, I can't tell you.*

What's Seth hiding? Why won't he tell me what he knows about Lucas? And why does he keep calling me "kiddo" when I've told him how much I hate it? All I can figure is Seth thinks he's protecting my feminine virtue by not disclosing the harsh realities of war. That thought makes me furious, which in turn makes me thrash around on my poor excuse for a mattress like a baby seal stuck in a fishing net.

"Easy there, squeaky," Seth whispers from below.

"Can't get comfortable." I bury my face in my lumpy pillow, but it doesn't matter. I can still smell the potpourri of human sweat and hear Darth Vader breathing next door.

To make matters worse, a rude latecomer decides *now* is the perfect time to check in to the already packed joint. Naturally, this latecomer chooses the empty bunk next to mine.

The empty bed *pressed right up against* mine.

I should have seen this coming. Do I even need to say it?

The straggler is Bob. Pissed drunk, senior citizen, Aussie Bob. He shakes the entire structure as he climbs onto the top bunk and barely has his sleeping bag unrolled before he does a face plant into it. The old guy is literally inches away from me. He releases a hearty belch before adding his tenor to the chorus of snores.

Move over, Darth. This old guy produces the most guttural, "oh my God what is that poor animal dying?" noise I have ever heard.

"Enough!" Seth shoots out from his lower bunk, even more distressed by Bob's imitation of a water buffalo than I am. "Come on, Gabi. Get your things. We're going."

"Are you crazy?" I hiss, which receives several annoyed *shhhs* in response. "Where will we go? We can't just leave in the middle of the night!"

"Want to bet?" Seth almost has his sleeping bag rolled up, so there's no use arguing with him. Besides, it's not like I *want* to lie here wide awake while Bob serenades me until sunup.

I gather my things and chase Seth into the dark night. The sky is an inkspill sea filled with a million starships. There's no more sweat. No more feet. The altitude strips the air of all smells. I'd forgotten what mountain skies are like—how they make you feel insignificant and infinite at the same time. But now is not the moment to get caught up in their spell. Seth is far down the road in front of me, like usual, walking towards the edge of town.

I break into a jog. "Seth, wait! What is *up* with you?"

"Too many people," he says in a hushed voice. "I'll never be able to sleep in that open warehouse. It's too . . . vulnerable."

"You do realize we aren't at war, right? I thought pilgrimages were supposed to be about seeing the best in humanity." I'm annoyed at being dragged out of a warm bed, but I also see Seth's point. Deployments don't exactly turn a guy into a free spirit. War is not how carefree, friend-of-the-world Bobs are born.

Seth heads to the entrance of the only hotel in town, though if you ask me, the place looks more like a barn. I wait outside while he checks to see if there's any room at the inn.

He returns with a single key. "Don't worry, it's on me. They only had one room left, so we'll have to share. After twenty-four hours of nonstop travel, I really need to sleep tonight. Trust me, you don't want to be around if I don't."

Oh, goodie. Sharing a hotel room with Seth is one more thing I can add to the list of reasons my father is going to kill me when I get home. Not that I'm concerned Seth will try something sleazy. He's made it clear he views our arrangement the same way I do: as a functional part of fulfilling Lucas's plan.

We enter a room that smells like mold and cigarettes. It has an orange shag carpet, tacky floral wallpaper, and a cube television from the 1980s. None of these outdated amenities concern me. What concerns me is the *one* double bed.

"Relax, Santiago. You think I don't know that your dad *and* brother would have me hung, drawn, and quartered if they ever found out we shared a sleeping surface?" Seth drops his bag, grabs the thin outer comforter off of the bed, and slumps to the floor below the only window. "Besides, I'm an old-fashioned gentleman. If you couldn't tell."

"Riiight. I'm sure your string of one-night stands can all attest to that."

To be honest, I know nothing about Seth's romance record, though my instincts tell me he isn't steady boyfriend material. I climb into the bed fully clothed and turn out the light. "Are you sure a stained carpet that's been around since Nixon is worth the extra money? I thought you said you needed a good night's rest."

"After sleeping in sand for six months, the floor will be fine, so long as you aren't one of those deceptively pretty girls who snores like an ogre."

I laugh. Extra loud, to cover up the fact that Seth just called me pretty and I have no idea what to do with that. "As far as I know, I'm a silent sleeper."

"Good. Can you pass me a pillow?"

I toss one in Seth's direction and he goes quiet, but his breathing doesn't get any heavier. The charged silence keeps his casual compliment ringing in my ears.

"For your information, I've never had a one-night anything," Seth says after a few minutes. "Though I'm flattered you think there are ladies who'd be willing."

"Uh, it wasn't meant as a compliment."

"Well then, neither was my ogre comparison."

I snort out another laugh. "I can't believe Lucas told you that."

"Told me what?"

"Don't play dumb. Lucas always teases me about having giant feet for a girl my size. It's his favorite insult, so I'm practically immune to it by now."

"Ah, so *that's* why you wear green toenail polish. In honor of your people."

I shoot up in bed and hurl another pillow at Seth's head. He releases an exaggerated grunt, but I can feel him smiling in the darkness.

"I really miss him," I say after an eternal minute.

"I know. So do I."

And with that, I'm ready for lights out. I don't want to think and I don't want to feel. The room's many shades of orange blend to black as I pass into that hazy realm of half-dreams, somewhere between consciousness and sleep. Childhood snapshots pass through my mind like images on a projector screen. One moment in particular stands out. That's because most Americans remember exactly where they were on September 11, just like most Americans a generation prior remember where they were when JFK was assassinated, or when Pearl Harbor was bombed a generation before that.

I remember, too.

• • •

"C-H-E-N-A. Chena?"

"That's right, *mija*. Chena Hot Springs. The best place in Alaska to see the northern lights," Dad said as he drove our station wagon through a dark forest that never seemed to end.

I tried showing Lucas the spot on the map, but he was too busy looking out the window, watching for colored lights and wandering stars in the predawn sky. In the rearview mirror, I watched Dad's eyes shift from the road to the clock on the dash.

"Wait," I said as he reached for the dial. "Odysseus is about to blind the Cyclops."

"Just for a minute, *mija*. I'll go back to your story, but I need to check the news."

With a sigh, I returned to my map. Army dads always needed to check the news. That's because sometimes, the news sent them halfway around the world.

Today was one of those times.

"It'll be okay, Gabi," Lucas said when the woman on the radio told us about the towers.

Dad pulled over and got out of the car to make a phone call to his superior. While he was gone, Lucas climbed into the backseat with me—one hand clutching his G.I. Joe while the other gripped my clammy fingers.

"We've got to go home!" I cried. "We've got to get home right now."

"Don't be scared, Gabs. Odysseus made it home. We will, too."

I stared at my brother through my tears. Lucas spoke with so much certainty that I could hardly glimpse the fear hiding behind the mossy color of his eyes.

The crumbling buildings weren't what frightened us most. The men who flew the planes into them didn't scare us either. What we were afraid of was war, because a war would change our family, change our world. Change everything.

I stared out the rain-sprinkled window at my father. "Daddy's going away, isn't he?"

Lucas nodded. A lonely silence stretched between us like the vast Alaskan wilderness, and somehow I knew my brother had made a decision.

"Heroes always have to leave the ones they love," he said, eyes glued to the chunk of camouflaged plastic in his hand. "That's what a hero is."

Then Lucas pressed the play button to continue our story.

# CHAPTER 8

Seriously, you're hiking through Spain with some G.I. you hardly know?! What the hell, Gabi??? You failed to mention that little detail.

My fingertips hesitate over the keyboard. We're in Pamplona, the largest city on the *camino* so far. I entered the first Internet café I could find to chat with Brent. This "café" consists of a cramped room stuffed with a few PCs that are five years too old, plus a vending machine. Thankfully, the Europop music on the radio is almost drowned out by the hum of a large fan pointed at the front desk, occupied by an even larger woman with an impressive uni-brow. Wi-Fi costs two euros for ten *minutos* and the clock in the corner of my screen is counting down, which makes explaining my situation to Brent feel even more urgent.

*He's not a stranger*, I type back, which is only partly true, since Seth is so distant most days he practically feels like one.

*He's my brother's best friend. My parents think he's a saint.*

*Whatever. You should have told me. I don't like the idea of you backpacking through Europe with some shell-shocked soldier. How'd you like it if I went on a three-week camping trip with another girl?*

He has a point, but I didn't even think about Seth when Brent offered to buy my plane ticket. Besides, this isn't a normal situation. This is about my brother, who's fighting for his life. Brent's tone makes my blood boil, and my heavy typing proves it.

*It's not like I'm on vacation. This walk is for Lucas. That's it! We've been apart for half a year, Brent. If I wanted to cheat on you, I could have done it a long time ago.*

Brent doesn't reply for almost a minute.

*Maybe you have*, he finally writes. *How would I know?*

The growl rising up inside me must become audible, because a chat box from Seth pops up in the corner of my screen.

*Trouble in paradise?*

Seth sits at a desktop across the café, giving me his signature holier-than-thou smirk.

"You have no idea," I say out loud before telling Brent where he can shove his self-centered attitude. For months I've been the perfect girlfriend, to the point of making *no* new friends so Brent wouldn't worry about what I was doing on weekends or who I was with. *He's* the one who still goes to parties and has flocks of half-naked groupies following his shows.

*Ditch the boyfriend, Santiago,* Seth types. *It's time to move forward.*

I assume he's talking about the *camino,* so I tell Brent I'll e-mail him later before sending my response to Seth.

*Yes, sir, drill sergeant, sir.*

• • •

"Why are you reading the *Iliad* again? It's not like you're in school."

My question is kind of random. We should be sitting here in silence, mouths gaping at the amazing scenery. The outdoor restaurant is sheltered from the setting sun by a trellis of flowering grape leaves. As the orange globe disappears behind Pamplona's walls, the sky glows like it's smeared with crushed chalk the color of a pink rose. Something about the coolness that settles in with the dusk makes me bold enough to take another stab at getting Seth to come clean. This time, I have enough sense to start out slow.

"I'm reading it because it's the greatest war epic ever written," Seth replies, confused that I have to ask. "Ever heard of the Trojan War?"

"You mean it was an actual war? Huh, and all this time I thought it was a campaign to combat the STDs sweeping college campuses across America."

Humor tends to be the best attack against an impenetrable fortress, but Seth is immune. He stares at me like I'm an imbecile, so I release an exaggerated sigh. "Yes, Seth, I've heard of the Trojan War. Though I have to say, I liked the *Odyssey* a lot more."

"That's because you're a wanderer, not a warrior."

Interesting. Could that be the logic behind Lucas's gifts?

"Okay, *warrior*. Tell me how you sustained your wounds." Though I'm pretty sure I know how he sustained his wounds, since I've seen facial scars like his before. "An IED?"

Seth downs the rest of his beer, his third in under an hour. "You never quit, do you? What part of 'I don't want to talk about it' is getting lost in translation?"

"The part that involves my brother, which I have a right to know about."

"A right? You have *a right*?"

Yeah, I shouldn't have said that.

"What's with people these days thinking they have a right to everything simply because they exist?" Seth's brow furrows into an even deeper scowl as he waves over our server to order another adult beverage. This time it's hard liquor. Not an evening has passed on the *camino* without Seth having a drink or two, but tonight he's really on a roll.

"Fine, maybe I don't have a right to anything, but you should talk to *someone* about what happened over there. My dad says one of the most challenging things about soldiers suffering from PTSD is they don't feel like they can talk about it."

"First of all, I don't have PTSD," Seth snaps. "Why do people automatically assume that every pissed off soldier has a disorder? Maybe war just makes people pissed off."

"Okay, fair enough—"

"But even if I was struggling with something," Seth continues, "it's no wonder soldiers don't want to spill their guts when people like you either treat us like wounded puppies, or like some anonymous *nobody*. We're all the same, right? Just your standard issue G.I. Joe. Trained killers who come back damaged and need to be drugged ASAP."

"I never said any of those things."

"You didn't have to. Just know that there are a lot of different reasons guys come home from war changed, and not all of them have a convenient acronym. Sometimes it's because of what we did. Sometimes it's because of what we didn't do." Seth throws back his shot and wipes his mouth on his sling. "All right, kiddo, I'll make a deal with you."

Our meals arrive before he has the chance. The waiter sets down a hearty stew of tender meat chunks soaked in a red, oily sauce that smells amazing. Because we're in Pamplona, I ordered *rabo de toro*—tail of the bull.

"*Muchas gracias.*" The food smells glorious and I'm starving, but I return my attention to Seth. "If we keep eating like this, I'm going to burn through my money quick. But back to this deal. What do you propose?"

Also a meat and potatoes person, Seth digs into his *tortilla Española* and the largest steak I've ever seen outside of Texas. "Pilgrimage, the *camino*, it's supposed to be this big metaphor, right? One of those 'life is about the journey, not the destination' kind of things."

"Yeah, I guess. What's your point?"

"Well, seeing how you're so damn inquisitive, at each place we stop along the *camino*, I'll give you an answer to a different question. You can ask me anything, just not about what happened downrange. That has to wait for Santiago. *Maybe* by the time we get there, I'll have thought through things more. *Maybe* I'll know how to explain what happened."

"Somehow I doubt that."

Seth's fist tightens around his fork. He's on the verge of rage, an emotion I have a knack for inciting. "What don't you get, Gabi? I can't talk about something I haven't even processed myself. Lying on a couch sharing feelings all day doesn't work for everybody."

What I *get* is that Seth is on his way to getting seriously drunk. "Fine. What do I have to do in return?"

"The same. Give me honest answers to anything I ask."

I take a bite of stew and burn my tongue. If I were to be honest right now, I'd say I'm flattered that Seth cares to know anything about me at all. I assumed he saw me as his buddy's little sister. Someone he got stuck babysitting. A *kid*, as he so frequently likes to remind me despite my repeated objections. "Okay, what do you want to know first?"

"Why are you with that whiny emo boyfriend of yours?" Seth asks without missing a beat. He smirks and shoves more fried potatoes into his mouth.

"Brent isn't emo. Which isn't even *a thing* anymore, by the way. Wait—is that how Lucas described him?"

Seth wipes his face with a napkin and leans back in his chair, still smirking up a storm. "Is that your final question for the evening?"

"Heck no. When I ask my question, you'll know. I want dirt."

"Sorry, babe. I'm Mr. Clean."

Again, I seriously doubt that. The hard glint of steel that never leaves Seth's gaze assures me he's more complicated than he is clean, no matter how hard he tries to hide it.

"Lucas never talked about Brent much, but he didn't seem to like the guy either. The truth is, I perused your Facebook page before we left Germany, and I swear I saw a photo where the dude was wearing eyeliner." Seth winks. "Not to mention skintight jeans that revealed parts of a man no self-respecting young lady should ever see."

"So he likes his jeans tight. I'll give you that, but Brent does *not* wear eyeliner." With my fork, I launch one of my potatoes at Seth's chest, which results in snooty glares from an older couple seated nearby. "Why were you stalking my profile to begin with? Creeper."

Seth flicks the smashed potato off his shirt and shrugs. "Surrogate big brother duties."

At the mention of Lucas being out of commission, the banter between us falls flat. I'm almost touched that Seth cares enough about Lucas—and maybe even about me—to keep an eye on the guy I'm dating, but it's annoying how they've both misjudged Brent big time. That's how soldiers tend to be with nonmilitary types. When it comes to red-blooded manliness, no one outside their tribe can ever measure up.

Seth's face breaks into a slightly sloshed smile. "Ah, you're a sneaky one. I asked *you* the question, and you turned it around and interrogated me. Perhaps we'll make a secret agent out of you yet, my young Padawan."

"Have no fear, the U.S. government can't afford me. Once my eighteen years of involuntary service are up, I'm out. As for your initial question: I'm with Brent because he makes me laugh, because he's artistic, because he has talents that don't involve disassembling semiautomatic weapons in under a minute. We've been together for almost two years."

"And that's enough of a reason to go to college with him? To give up on the once-in-a-lifetime experience of being an independent young woman striking out on her own, armed with nothing but a portable shower caddy and bunny-rabbit dorm slippers?"

I can't help but laugh. "What, like you did when you joined the Army all by yourself? *Oh wait.* You couldn't cut the cord, so you asked my brother to sign up *with* you."

It can get intense when Seth and I go back and forth like this, but the lightning bolt of self-loathing that flashes through his eyes tells me I've gone too far. Seth gets up from his seat, even though I'm not finished eating yet. This time he doesn't offer to pay.

"It's getting late. I'll see you back at the *albergue*. We'll start out at sunup."

It's only when Seth disappears into the dusky shadows that I realize I never got to ask him *my* question. Maybe that's what he had in mind all along.

# CHAPTER 9

Seth wasn't kidding about the early start.

"Ugh, it's still dark outside," I moan when he shines his LED flashlight in my face. The stupid thing is so bright it feels like I'm having a close encounter with a UFO.

"We've got to walk thirty K today. Look at all the other people leaving."

I peer over the bars of my top bunk. Right now there's a lot of shuffling going on. Pilgrims roll up sleeping bags and stuff laundry into their packs, but there's a common trait that unites these early risers. "Seth, they're German! Germans are *always* the first ones out the door. It's like this pilgrimage is a new way to conquer the world."

"Funny. Now get up."

"Seriously. Look at the flag patches on their packs." I point out examples to support my case. "Swede. German. Finnish. These are Northern peoples. I come from the Southern Hemisphere, where we honor the concept of *siesta* and the health benefits of sleep in general."

"You're only half Mexican."

"And you're only half Jewish, but we both like to claim our more exotic sides."

Seth is smiling now, but that doesn't stop him from whacking me on the head with a pillow. "For real. Up and at 'em, soldier."

We're out the door in fifteen minutes flat. Before I have a chance to down my first *café* of the morning, I'm accosted by a trio of lady pilgrims who materialize out of the predawn mist.

Their leader pulls up alongside me like a police car. Flashing a toothy grin, she points to the action figure attached to my pack. "Oh, I *must* hear the story behind this."

The woman's silver hair hangs down her back in a thick braid. Add to that a smattering of amber jewelry plus a billowing skirt, and I'm guessing she's a recovering flower child who recently slipped out of remission. This seems to be a common theme among North American pilgrims over the age of forty-five.

"It's a tribute to my brother," I reply. Yep, this could be bad. I hadn't considered that G.I. Lucas might serve as an inconvenient conversation starter. "He's a soldier."

The woman gasps as though I've discovered the cure for some rare disease. "What a wonderful idea! I'm a pacifist, but those boys need us to focus all our positive energy on finding a peaceful solution to this conflict."

Yeah, I'm sure al-Qaeda members practice the Law of Attraction and tap into the power of positive thinking on a regular basis. It's probably part of the terrorist training manual.

Hippie lady holds out her hand. "I'm Harmony Jones from Vancouver, BC. And these are my traveling companions for as long as the *camino* wills it: Mary Kim Nguyen from Vietnam and Julia Ribeiro from Brazil."

The older Vietnamese woman wears a wide-brimmed floppy hat and white knee socks beneath her sandals. A dozen rosaries hang from her pack, so I'm going to go out on a limb and assume she's walking the *camino* for religious reasons. Next to her is the smiley girl from Brazil. Minus her nose ring—which my father would rip from my nostril without hesitation—Julia and I could be sisters with our dark, curly hair, light eyes, and *café con leche* complexion. Based on the bottle of Campari stuffed into the side pocket of her pack, she must be walking the *camino* for "cultural" reasons, if by culture we mean a nonstop party.

"Nice to meet you all." I look down the road and see that Seth has sped up, leaving a considerable gap between us. Thanks a lot, comrade.

"Julia and Mary Kim only speak bits of English, but we communicate in other ways. Through the language of common humanity," Harmony explains, beaming like a common light bulb. "Having such quiet companions works out well when the only sound you want to hear is the crunch of the *camino* beneath your feet."

"What made you want to walk to Santiago?" It's a dangerous can of worms and I already suspect this lady's answer will have something to do with shifting energy fields, but I ask in an attempt to avoid more probing questions about Lucas.

Harmony snorts out a laugh. "Oh, I'm afraid my story is one massive cliché. Recently divorced woman seeks adventures abroad in a foreign land as a way of dealing with midlife crisis, and hopefully meets younger men while she's at it." Harmony studies Seth with animated eyebrows. "Men such as that fine specimen up ahead, though he looks a little *too* young. And probably a little too gladiatorial for my liking."

"Trust me, he's too gladiatorial for most people's liking."

"The *camino* may change that. It tends to give us what we *need*, not necessarily what we want. Though that's the way of the Universe in general, isn't it?"

Yeah, I'm sure a nice blow to the skull was *exactly* what Lucas was missing.

"Sure," I reply, hoping that will be the end of her New Age nonsense. But no.

"I see the *camino* as an opportunity to ask the Universe one big question that takes many miles to answer. My question is, where do I go from here?" Harmony twists her torso so she's looking right at me as we walk, which is kind of creepy, I don't care how much yoga you do. "And you, Gabi? What will your question be?"

"I don't have a question. I'm walking the *camino* for my brother. He's hurt and—"

"No!" Little Mary Kim pumps her fist into the air, her docile demeanor Viet Cong–intense all of a sudden. "Walk for other people okay, but also have own reason. Must have own reason!"

"*Por qué estas hacienda el camino?*" Julia repeats in Spanish.

Wow, talk about a cohesive team strike. I look out over the ridge to our right, where a row of giant wind turbines whip through the air, generating electricity for all of Pamplona. Beyond their white blades, the indigo peaks of the Pyrenees fade into the distance, a reminder of how far Seth and I have already come. Watching the prongs slice through the clear blue sky makes me wonder what's moving me. Where's my motivation coming from? Why am I on the *camino*? Not my brother's reason, or Seth's reason, but *my* reason?

All I get as an answer is a surge of anger. Why do I need a reason at all? Frodo didn't leave the Shire to "find himself." Odysseus wasn't wandering the Mediterranean because his desk job sucked and he needed an adventure. None of the heroes in the stories I love left home because they *wanted* to, but because they *had* to. Maybe everyone else on the *camino* is here on some profound personal quest, but a spiritual search is a luxury I can't afford. I'm walking for my brother, and to make my dad proud. That's it.

And that's enough.

•••

"All right, Seth, my turn. Why did you join the military?"

My strategy is to start out slow. We've stopped to rest on a sea of fallen almond blossoms. It's the perfect place to pin Seth with my query of the day, since neither of us is in a hurry to leave this magical spot anytime soon. I strip off my shoes and socks and stretch out beneath the almond trees, eager to soak up the warm sun on what looks like a bed of snow.

"And your answer can't be that it's a family tradition. You've got to have your *own* reason." Even if I don't believe it, Harmony's appeal to narcissism seems to work when you want to get people talking.

"Serving in the military because it's a family tradition *is* my own reason." Seth slices a fresh baguette with his pocket knife. We've agreed to more picnics because eating in restaurants is rapidly burning through my funds. Today's *menú del dia* is tomato and manchego cheese sandwiches, anchovy-stuffed olives (a Spanish staple), and a bar of Swiss chocolate for dessert.

"My grandfather lived on an American post in Germany right after WWII because his father was stationed there during the Nuremberg trials. He even witnessed a few."

"Really? That must have been so bizarre."

Seth nods and passes me a sandwich. "My great-grandfather was in one of the first units to liberate the concentration camps. Even he didn't realize how horrible they were until he saw Buchenwald with his own eyes. After that, he requested to stay in Germany for as long as possible."

"But why would he *want* to stay? He was Jewish, right? You'd think Germany would be the last place he'd request to be stationed."

Seth shrugs. "I guess he felt a duty to all the survivors he encountered in the camps, and he wanted to witness the trials to see that justice was done. So he stayed."

"And all the men in your family have served in the Army ever since?"

"Every generation." Seth slowly picks the white petals off an almond flower, one by one. "I don't do it because I have to. I do it because I want to."

I set my baguette down in the grass and a brigade of ants scurry towards it like a wall that must be sieged. Suddenly, I'm not so hungry anymore. This whole time I thought Seth convinced my brother to enlist because he wanted to drag a friend along while he fulfilled some silly tradition, but his reasons go much deeper than that.

"Don't be fooled into thinking it's *all* about honor. I have other motives, too." Seth hesitates, like he isn't sure he should tell me. "I don't think I could ever live a civilian life after growing up a brat. Some people see needing the military structure as a sign of weakness, but what's the alternative? Working in a cubicle like a dog so you can own a big house in the 'burbs full of crap you don't have time to enjoy? It seems so pointless. Like a merry-go-round of empty promises you get stuck on your entire life."

Seth is afraid. This tough, tightlipped guy is terrified of one specific thing and he fears it more than pain, more than death, more than anything else—and that's a life without purpose, without meaning.

"Maybe," I reply, "but the military can't be the only option. Couldn't you find some kind of do-gooder job out there in the real world?"

Seth shrugs again and passes the chocolate. "The military is as real as it gets. In the Army, we're all on the same page. Sure, it's the most hierarchical institution there is, but everyone is working towards the same goal, supporting the same mission. You'll see when you get to college. There are a lot of entitled little punks out there. No one knows how to commit to anything greater than King Ego, and pretty soon the whole thing is going to implode."

Now there's a glass half-full picture for you. I've met my fair share of jerks in the military too, not to mention every other walk of life, but I don't want Seth to launch into a doomsday lecture about how America's finest hour is behind her thanks to texting and Instagram. It's too peaceful here, eating chocolate beneath almond trees, listening to the breeze playing with the dog tags attached to Seth's pack.

As I twist blades of grass into little knots, I study Seth out of the corner of my eye. He's lying on his back, head resting on his pack, eyes turned towards the cotton-ball clouds. Each day he seems a little more tranquil and less weary, even though our bodies are taking a beating. Most of the time Seth's muteness feels like a bandage keeping his rage from spilling out, but sometimes his silence emanates strength. A strength that's almost electric.

This is one of those times.

"What about all these people walking the *camino*?" I ask when the tingling sensation traveling up my skin becomes too much. "It's not like they're doing this trek to get ahead in life. Most of the pilgrims I've met seem like decent people. Eccentric, but decent."

"That's because they're trying to live awake, trying to see what's out there, what's real." Seth pauses and sits up. "It's weird . . . ."

"What's weird?"

"How the *camino* is beautiful the way war can be beautiful."

"War beautiful? Yeah, that is weird."

"I know, but how often do we live in the *immediate* present? Not via social media? Not tied down to a to-do list?" Seth asks.

"Not often, I guess."

"And it only gets worse as you get older," Seth says, like he's got twenty years on me instead of two. "But in war, every second is *now*. Visceral. The buddy beside you could be gone in an instant. The past and future don't matter. That's what makes war beautiful—even addictive. Walking the *camino* is kind of like that, too. I never minded our PT ruck marches because that's what walking *does*. It slows down time and makes you see everything, including all that's broken."

Seth's tone makes me think he includes himself on that list of broken things. I just wish I knew why. But by now I also know that pushing him will shut down our conversation faster than screaming "Bomb!" in the middle of a crowded military base.

"Maybe that's why Lucas thought this walk would be a good way to get me and my dad talking again." A small part of me is frustrated that Lucas's plan didn't work out, though most of me is relieved that Dad isn't here. Dealing with my brother's situation *and* my father's perpetual disappointment doesn't sound like a good time. Then again, maybe the difference between a pilgrimage and a vacation is that a "good time" isn't the goal.

Seth looks intrigued. "What happened with your dad?"

I'm surprised Lucas never told him about the Fort Sam incident that left a black mark on my permanent record (if such a thing even exists). My brother's discretion makes me miss him even more, but I'm not about to share an embarrassing story that would only give Seth one more thing to tease me about. If he's going to keep his secrets, then I can keep mine.

"Let's just say I'm currently at the top of Sergeant Major Santiago's *scheize* list."

I can tell Seth wants to press me for details, but he doesn't. "Yeah, I know that game. My dad thinks I'm a failure, too. You're right about Lucas, though. He's good at building bridges between people." Seth passes me the last piece of chocolate, his smile fading. "Sorry you got stuck with me instead."

Our fingers touch as I take the chocolate, and the warmth that accompanies it makes me realize I'm not sorry. Of course I wish Lucas was here, but this trek is fast revealing there's more to Seth Russo than I ever thought possible. When he offers up more than sarcastic one-liners, I actually like talking to him. He gets the life I've lived because it's his life, too.

Sometimes, he almost seems to get me.

• • •

"How is he?" I practically shout, that way Mom can hear me over crunching footsteps on dry ground. It's weird using a cell phone while walking a stretch of the *camino* paved with ancient stones from the Roman road. "Has anything changed?"

"The doctors don't think so, but I swear I saw Lucas's eyelashes flutter. Hasn't he always had the most beautiful eyelashes? So thick and dark, they can't help but make a girl jealous," Mom replies with a sad chuckle. "Where are you now? Getting close to Santiago yet?"

"Only seven hundred and thirty-five kilometers to go," I grumble, watching Seth study our guidebook like it contains a map to the Holy Grail. "We're near a town called Puente la Reina. It's beautiful here with everything in bloom."

Neither of us mention my dad, so I hope things didn't go south between my parents once Mom told him she let me go. They don't have the option of a civil war, not when Lucas's condition demands that our household establish a more perfect union to "establish justice, insure domestic tranquility, provide for the common defense, promote the general welfare, and secure the blessings of liberty to ourselves and our posterity."

That's right, my father—the proudest immigrant you'll ever meet—made me memorize the Preamble to the United States Constitution. At age five.

"Take your allergy medicine, Gabriela. And don't forget to say prayers for your brother. You've been lighting the candles I gave you, right?"

I'm not quick to supply an affirmative. So far I've lit *one* candle, which I placed in the almond grove where we had our picnic when Seth wasn't looking. Even so, it felt ridiculous to be doing something that has no basis in scientific fact.

Candles don't cure people, doctors cure people.

"Gabi." Mom's tone is surprisingly stern. "Unless you walk this road with your heart's intention in the right place, it won't matter. You have to believe with every step that Lucas will get better. With *every step*."

Great. Not her, too. My mother has never been quite as religious as my dad, but for years we all went to church because that's what

*El Jefe* demanded. After Dad got back from his last deployment, I started putting up a fight about going, which resulted in my father not speaking to me most Sundays. Mom seemed to support my freedom of choice in this matter, which is why it's so strange that she's buying into Dad's ritualistic nonsense all of a sudden.

"I'll try, Mom. I promise I'll try."

For the rest of our walk into Puente la Reina, I keep my eyes alert for a good place to light a candle. We pass a small church made of bricks the color of sand. A stork guards the bell tower from its giant nest, and beneath the sanctuary's arched doorway rests an old woman dressed in rags. I nod a greeting in her direction, and she responds with a placid grin that reveals her few remaining teeth. I look down. The poor woman has no legs beneath her kneecaps. She's holding a dirty cardboard sign that reads: *Rezo por limosna*. Prayers in exchange for alms.

If there's any justice in the cosmos, then this woman's pleas have a far better chance at getting through than mine do. I can feel Seth watching me from a safe distance as I remove one of the tealights from my pack, approach the woman, and drop a few euro coins into her basket.

"*Por mi hermano.*" I hand her the candle, along with the one and only prayer I have in me. "Wake up, Lucas. *Please*. Wake up."

# CHAPTER 10

G.I. Lucas is about to get tipsy.

We wait in a long line of pilgrims in front of a monastery winery called Bodegas Irache, positioned along the *camino* near the town of Estella. At the end of the line there's a stone wall and a statue of a medieval pilgrim, but this isn't some touristy photo op. Right below the sculpture sits a fountain with one spout labeled *agua* and the other labeled *vino*. Now tell me, where else but Spain can you find *free* wine being pumped out of a wall on the side of the road?

It's almost our turn. The man in front of us leans over to sip the red wine flowing freely from the fountain. I can tell from his long brown cassock that he's some kind of monk. A Franciscan, I think, if the Name That Saint flashcards from my catechism days actually did their job. The monk wears simple Jesus sandals and travels with nothing but a walking stick and a small leather satchel, just like the *peregrinos* of old.

"*Con pan y vino se hace el camino. El camino de la vida!*" he exclaims, raising his hands to the sky, as if miraculously revived by this fountain of youth.

"Uh, what did that Jedi master say?" Seth whispers in my ear.

All the hairs on the back of my neck stand up. "With bread and wine you can walk the way. The way of life," I quickly translate before approaching the fountain.

First, I position G.I. Lucas so it looks like he's taking a nice big gulp, and Seth snaps the photograph. Then we take another picture of him below the fountain's sign, which states:

Pilgrim, if you wish to arrive at Santiago full of strength and vitality, have a drink of this great wine and make a toast to happiness.

"This bodega must give away a ton of wine each day. That's super generous."

"Or it's a super smart way to take advantage of a unique marketing campaign," Seth replies.

"Says the guy who filled his entire water bottle with wine when the sign *clearly* states that pilgrims may help themselves to a glass, but should drink in moderation." I shake my head. "And I thought I was cynical."

"Hey, I never said I wasn't an opportunist myself." Seth takes a swig from his water/wine bottle. "Besides, they don't call it the *vino camino* for nothing."

"I've never heard it called that before," I reply with a chuckle.

"Okay, *I* call it that." Seth's grin showcases a row of purple teeth. "Maybe I even made the phrase up. It's possible I am just that clever."

"And humble." I tuck G.I. Lucas back into my pack. "You're on your way to becoming the *vino camino*'s poster child, that's for sure. Do you usually drink this much?"

"What do you mean, *this much*?" Seth's posture stiffens. "You've never seen me falling down drunk, have you? I'm up before *you* every morning, aren't I?"

I hold up both hands in surrender. "Okay, okay. It was just a question."

"Yeah, well, ease up on the offensive. I didn't have a single sip of alcohol the entire time I was in Afghanistan, so yes, I like to have a drink every now and then. Especially while I'm in Europe, given that our great nation has determined I'm not yet responsible enough to order a beer, but I'm sure as hell old enough to die for its sake."

My, my, somebody needs a *siesta*. You never know what you're going to get with Seth. Most of the time he's fine, but say one wrong thing and the rest of the day is shot. True, he's never been passed out drunk, but Seth likes to have more than "a drink every now and then." And I'm starting to worry. I'm worried about the wounds all that alcohol is meant to sterilize.

"Can I see the guidebook for a minute?" Seth asks. "We should be getting close to the turnoff for this detour I want to take."

"Go for it." I hand him the book and he flips through it while we walk. Suddenly, his feet stop shuffling.

"Oh. Crap."

"What's wrong?"

"We already passed it." Seth runs a hand over his shaved head, his face twisted in distress. "The place Lucas wanted to visit more than any other stop on the *camino*, and we walked right past the turnoff. I am such an idiot! I must have mixed up Eunate with Estella. The detour was all the way back near Puente la Reina."

I grab the guidebook, opened to a page that features a glossy photograph of Iglesia de Santa Maria de Eunate, this small, octagon-shaped building. "It says this church was built in 1170 by the Knights Templar."

"Exactly. That's why Lucas wanted to see it. The Knights Templar were mentioned in those books Lucas was reading about warriors in ages past. He'd gotten way interested in the military orders of the Middle Ages, especially knights who swore to protect pilgrims from thieves and bandits on the open road."

Tears blur my vision, so I pretend I'm reading the historical description beneath the photo to blink them away. My poor, idealistic brother. Lucas was searching for a code of chivalry in a world that hardly knows what words like "gallantry" even mean anymore.

"We have to go back," Seth says, point-blank.

"And backtrack over twenty kilometers? That's insane. We'll never make it to Santiago in two weeks if we do that!"

"Then we'll have to take a longer bus ride to make up the lost time. Pilgrims only need to walk the last hundred kilometers to get the *Compostela* certificate, and Eunate was the one place your brother specifically mentioned in his letter. We have to take a photo of G.I. Lucas there, and *you* need to light a candle."

There was never anything rational about Lucas's request to begin with, but I'm amazed by the way the ceremonial has taken over; how there are suddenly things we *must do* in order to make this journey "count." Seth has never taken an interest in my candle collection, so he must really mean it. Besides, he's right. It's what Lucas would want. "Fine, let's go back."

"For real?" Seth stutters when I make an abrupt about-face. "You're not going to put up a fight or tell me how impractical I'm being?"

I shrug. "This journey is about Lucas, not us."

"Cheers to that." Seth lifts his bottle and gives me a sly grin. "At least going back the way we came means we can stop for a free refill."

• • •

By the time we make it to Lorca—an additional ten kilometers on top of the twenty we already walked today—my feet feel like they're going to disintegrate into a pile of dust. Vineyard views surround us in every direction, and the evening breeze smells like thyme and wild oregano (which *really* makes me want to order a pizza). Too bad Seth and I are both hating life, and consequently hating each other.

"I told you to air out your socks or you'd open your blisters again," Seth accuses as we hobble towards a roadside bar for a much-needed break.

"Hey, this little detour was *your* idea."

"Yeah, well, if you hadn't flipped out and decided you needed to control the map, I would have known to make the detour," he snaps back.

"Seriously? *I'm* the control freak? You're the one who's too good to talk to any of the pilgrims we meet, seeing how that might cut into our ridiculous walking pace."

"You're really childish, you know that?"

I point to the bar's low doorway. "Careful, your gigantic head might not fit inside."

"Screw you."

"You wish."

"Hardly."

Yep, there's nothing like a little loss of control to bring out the best in *two* control freaks. We sit down at a plastic table covered in red Coca-Cola logos, order said sodas, and proceed to engage in a "I hope you die a slow and painful death" glaring showdown. Correction, *I'm* drinking a Coke. Seth claims he doesn't touch the stuff, so he orders—you guessed it—a beer.

"Since when are you a health freak?" I ask between sips of effervescent, teeth-rotting goodness.

"I'm not. That sugar water is just particularly lethal."

I take another swig and look around. The little hole-in-the-wall is packed. Strangers often share tables in Europe, so I'm not surprised when a man dressed in work boots and dirty overalls sits down with us. Based on his clothing, he must be a farmer who lives nearby.

"*Buenas tardes,*" the man grunts before digging into his meal—an aromatic stew made of pork and large white beans. The farmer turns to me after a few minutes of tense silence. "Why the long faces, *peregrinos*? Saint James hasn't been good to you?"

"We misread our map," I explain in Spanish. "Now we're falling behind schedule."

"You Americans are so funny. Always in a rush to get to the finish line, but the *camino* is not a race." The farmer's tan face breaks into a smile beneath his thick mustache, creating cracks in skin as parched as the dirt along this section of road. The wrinkled tributaries streaming out from his eyes are deep enough to carry tears through the dusty terrain of his cheeks, but I doubt this man ever cries. He has the hardened face of one who's worked outdoors his entire life—a face similar to the photographs I've seen of my *abuelo*, who toiled from dawn to dusk to feed his family, never leaving his region of Mexico once. "So you want to see *la Iglesia de Santa Maria de Eunate*, eh? *Si*, it is a special place. My farm isn't far from there. *Venga*, I'll give you a ride."

I translate the stranger's offer. As first Seth is resistant—you know, since he's such a trusting bleeding heart and all—but then he realizes our other options are few and my busted feet won't carry me much further. We decide to adopt the *camino* spirit by having faith that this man is, in fact, a farmer and not a leader of a terrorist cell hiding out in the Spanish countryside.

We pay for our drinks and follow the stranger outside to his old, rusty pickup truck. He gestures towards the flatbed in the back, already occupied by several cages of chickens, along with an obese goat.

"Well, Russo, I think it's safe to say our driver's story pans out." I toss my backpack into the flatbed and climb aboard. "He's definitely a farmer."

"Ugh. I hate chickens," Seth grumbles. "My mom has a ton of them on her property in New Hampshire. They're disgusting, evil animals."

"Sounds like someone was attacked by a rooster as a child and never got over it."

A tickling sensation travels along the top of my head. I glance back and see that *Señor* Goat has decided my braid makes for a tasty afternoon snack. The joke's on him—I haven't washed my hair in four days, though I suppose goats will chew on anything.

Our new farmer friend roars with laughter as he closes up the flatbed. "*Mira! Sancho Panza te gustas!*"

"*Sí*, we're best buds." I pull my braid out of the slobbering beast's mouth and turn to Seth—unflinching, immovable Seth, sitting across from me, scowling. What's got his panties in such a bunch?

"At least *one* of my traveling companions appreciates my company," I say, squirting my water bottle in Seth's direction. The chickens in the cage behind him detonate an explosion of squawks and flapping wings. Seth shoots across the truck so fast you'd have thought the flightless birds were a band of insurgents.

"What the hell, Gabi? I just told you I hate chickens!"

"Yes." I smile as Seth cowers against me in the corner of the truck. "You did."

• • •

We reach Eunate at sunset. I had no idea "slight detour" meant a venture into the middle of freaking nowhere, but that's exactly where we are, surrounded by fields fading to a thousand shades of blue beneath the blitz of twilight. The cloudless sky goes from bright cobalt to dusky lavender. It's going to be a Van Gogh kind of starry night.

The truck slows as we approach an octagonal structure. It sits alone in a golden field, the stout bell tower rising from its center like a lone stargazer waiting for the curtain to rise on tonight's performance. An unfinished cloister walk surrounds the small church, its tan stones blending in with the neighboring sea of wheat.

We jump down from the truck. A gust of wind laced with burning charcoal blows back my hair, which is already a tangled mess from the open air ride. Silence wraps around us like warm sheets fresh from the dryer. I look at Seth; Seth looks at me. We're struck dumb by the magic of this place. As the truck's taillights disappear down the road, I rip my eyes from the Templar chapel and take in the rest of our surroundings.

"Where, exactly, are we supposed to spend the night?" I ask, attempting to mask the rising panic in my voice. Other than the chapel itself, there are very few signs of civilization.

"The guidebook says there's an *albergue* not far from the church." Seth turns in a circle, taking in every angle of this place. "Look, there it is over there, beneath those trees. It's getting late, so we should check in right away if we want to snag beds."

The pile of dirty boots on the *albergue's* front porch makes me think a modern version of Chaucer's pilgrim brigade had the same idea. I have a sinking feeling, and it goes beyond having to wait in line for the shower.

A young woman finally responds to our persistent knocking. She greets us in Spanish, but she doesn't look Spanish. "*Buenas tardes.*"

"Hi. We're interested in two beds for the night," I reply in English.

"I'm so sorry, but we run a very small *albergue* and it's already full," the woman explains. "A few people over capacity, in fact. Several pilgrims will be sleeping on the floor as it is."

A man—the innkeeper's husband, I'm guessing—steps up behind her and points to the periwinkle sky. They both speak flawless English, but their accents sound like a song. "Looks like it's going to be a mild night. You're welcome to camp in the churchyard, that way you can use the hostel showers and take your meals with us. Dinner will be served in half an hour."

"Thank you," I say. "That sounds great."

This is a lie—sleeping on the cold ground is never great. But a warm shower and dinner after walking all day sounds fantastic, and we'll still have time to take our coveted G.I. Lucas photos before it gets too dark.

"Well, it's official. Tonight is going to suck," Seth mutters as we walk back to the church to set up camp. "Hope your sleeping bag is warm."

Seth may be pessimistic (big surprise), but I find the stillness that confronts us in the shade of Iglesia de Santa Maria de Eunate intoxicating. It's like a protective force field radiates from each and every stone. As the sun dips behind the church's dome, a golden glow chases gargoyle shadows down its walls and into the fennel fields beyond. My eyes meet Seth's as we unroll our sleeping bags in the cloister walk. The curious expression on his face tells me he feels it too. An "it" that can't be explained in words.

That farmer was right. This *is* a special place.

We explore the enchanted grounds without speaking. I stop in front of the arched entryway to stage a photo from an angle that makes it seem like G.I. Lucas is proportional to the chapel, but I need Seth to hold him in place. "Seth! Can you come here for a sec?"

No answer. I lower the camera and glance around, but Seth is nowhere in sight. Cold sweat drips down my back. This place is magical, but it isn't somewhere I want to hang around by myself at dusk. The air seems thinner and I don't feel entirely safe.

Maybe sacred things are never entirely safe.

"Seth?"

Nothing. The silence turns stifling as it presses in on my ribcage.

"*Seth?*" I call out again.

"Over here."

Thank God. My heart thuds in my chest like a bass drum, but I manage to jog to the other side of the sanctuary without passing out. Seth stands in front of a grassy plot along the churchyard's outer wall, staring at a row of unadorned headstones.

"These are graves of medieval pilgrims who didn't make it to Santiago. They died along the way," Seth explains in a reflective tone.

"It's weird to think there was a time that could actually happen." A gust of charcoal caresses my face, and I zip up my windbreaker as the coolness of nightfall descends. "I can't imagine going on a journey without any guarantee you'd live to see the next day, let alone reach your final destination."

"It isn't that hard to imagine."

Seth's solemn voice stabs me in the chest. I'd forgotten that the whisper of mortality, the uncertainty of ever seeing home again, is something soldiers experience on a daily basis. Yet sooner or later, the journey ends and we're all buried in the ground, just like these pilgrims. Sooner or later, we all find ourselves in a state of helpless surrender, just like Lucas.

"Not yet, Gabi." Seth, reading my mind, rests a hand on my shoulder. The extra weight makes my sore muscles relax beneath his fingertips. This is the first time Seth has ever touched me on purpose—except for that one time he bandaged my feet—but it feels normal, like he does it all the time. "Lucas isn't there yet. And he isn't going to be."

My arms twist around my waist as I bite down on my lower lip. I can't cry for Lucas because once I start, I won't be able to stop. I pour my grief into my pain instead—into my tired feet and throbbing joints. That kind of suffering I can manage, but as soon as my heart breaks open for Lucas, all self-control will be lost. The only way to keep walking is to make my heart as callused as my heels. Seth squeezes my shoulder, which tells me this is something he knows all too well.

"We should go," I say once the initial heat of his touch cools. "We don't want to be late for dinner."

Seth's gaze drifts from the neat rows of corn to the untamed hills in the distance. "I get the feeling that in a place like this, being late isn't really a possibility."

# CHAPTER 11

Seth is right. You can't be late to your own party, and that's exactly what this feels like. We enter the dining room and every pilgrim at the table raises his or her glass, cheering like they've been waiting for us the entire evening.

The place looks like a madrigal banquet or the wedding feast at a Renaissance festival. Arched ceilings float above thick stone walls, creating an open space illuminated by candlelight. Fat pillar candles, thin taper candles, and every size in between line the perimeter of the room. Something smells incredible, but it isn't food. That's when I notice the sprigs of dried herbs and wildflowers bundled with twine decorating the long table, which is set with wine glasses and terra cotta jugs filled with Spain's fruit of the vine.

"Um, I'm pretty sure we just time traveled. To the year 1492," I whisper as we stand there smiling awkwardly, taking in the pilgrim faces seated among the flickering shadows.

"Seriously," Seth replies. "Maybe the mystique surrounding the Knights Templar is justified. This definitely feels like the gathering of a secret society."

After mumbling a few shy hellos, we take our seats next to an Irish woman in her thirties and a young Sudanese man with skin so dark and smooth it's impossible to tell his age.

The husband and wife innkeeper team enters the hall carrying gigantic platters covered in grilled asparagus, blood-red tomatoes, and eggplant doused in olive oil. Then come the bowls of figs, olives, and grapes, along with fresh-baked bread and a spectrum of cheeses, starting with mild goat all the way to blue and super stinky. It isn't that much food given the number of people, but everything is garden-fresh and no matter how many times we pass the trays, nothing runs out.

"*Escargot?*" Molly, the Irish woman, hands me a plate of charcoaled grass stalks covered in small snails—shells and all. "I'm told the locals pick these stalks from the side of the road and throw the entire thing on the barbecue. Feeling brave?"

"Sure. Why not?"

Across the table, Seth cocks his head. He wears an amused smile, like he didn't expect a girl raised on Hamburger Helper to have the guts to try a glorified slug. Time to show him I'm more adventurous than he thinks. I lift the shriveled snail to my mouth. "When in Rome, right?"

"That's the spirit." Molly's accent is as warm and lyrical as her laughter.

All I can say about *escargot* is thank God for garlic. And bread. Pretty soon it's passed, the wine is poured, and we dig in.

"*Con pan y vino.*" Seth lifts his glass and winks. At me.

This small gesture warms my insides more than wine ever could. Flustered, I break Seth's gaze and study our diverse group of dining companions. In addition to the Danish caretakers, Greta and Karl, there's Molly from Ireland and Sudanese Jean Paul, a middle-aged Czech couple, an Argentinian mother and her ten-year-old son, an elderly South Korean man, and an Italian priest so baby-faced he must have finished seminary yesterday. Two more Americans sit to my right, a guy and a girl. I assume they're a couple, until the guy gets a little too friendly.

"Hey there. I'm Dennis from the San Francisco Bay Area."

"Uh, hi, Dennis from the Bay Area. I'm Gabi."

"So Gabi, where are you from?"

Seth's smile shifts into a smirk. He knows without me having to tell him that I hate this question with the intensity of a thousand suns.

"Texas," I reply.

"No, I mean where are you *from*? Like, originally."

Seth rolls his eyes, as if to say *here we go*.

"Well, *like*, I was born in Louisiana."

"But before that," Dennis presses.

"Uh, before my birth?"

Dennis laughs. "You have an exotic look. You don't look American."

Oh really? Then by "American" he means someone who looks like him, despite that I've sacrificed more for good old 'Merica in seventeen years than he will his entire lifetime. "Uh, my mom is Scottish, maybe a little French, and my dad is originally from Mexico."

"Mexico! That's it. I knew you had to be from south of the border. Texas, duh." Dennis slaps his forehead, totally oblivious that his lame attempt at flirtation might be offensive if I had thinner skin. "God, I miss Mexican food. You can't find anything like it over here, which wasn't what I expected, seeing how folks in both countries speak Spanish. Man, your people sure know how to make a tortilla."

"Yeah, well, I've never *been* to Mexico, *sooo* . . . ."

"What about Mr. Strong and Silent? Where's he from?" interrupts the young woman sitting across from Dennis. I think she said her name was Natalie, but I can't remember because I was too busy staring at her face. The girl is a total knockout, but in that very specific way where you're not quite sure if what you're looking at is an optical illusion. Most *peregrinas* on the *camino* don't wear much makeup, if any, and this girl has shiny, flat-ironed hair and perfectly manicured nails. "She's SoCal all the way, baby," as Brent would say.

Now, I'm not trying to be catty; it's just impossible to ignore the sight of a runway model after weeks of smelling like a sock. I should be impressed by what she's managed to accomplish in a hostel bathroom, but I get the feeling this couple doesn't stay in *albergues* often. They seem more like tourists who added a short stint on the *camino* to their all-inclusive vacation along the Costa del Sol. Maybe they're nice people and I'm just a judgmental jerk, but something about their posh vibe doesn't quite fit.

Natalie tosses Seth a suggestive smile, so she's either with Dennis solely for his money, or these people are total swingers. "You, my friend, look like you're starving. And not for more *manchego*." She leans over the table and brushes her fingers across the tattoo stamped on the inside of Seth's wrist.

ϖ

I've never paid much attention to it, but Natalie is intrigued by the foreign script. Her eyes light up like a cat staring at a shiny object. "What do all those funny letters say?"

"It's Greek," Seth replies, like that should be the end of it. But Natalie keeps staring at him with wide, expectant eyes, so he clears his throat. "It means 'either with your shield, or on it.' As in, return from battle with honor, or don't return at all. Mothers in ancient Sparta supposedly said these words to their sons before they went off to fight."

"How sweet." Natalie frowns and pulls back her hand. "What, did you just return from a war or something?"

*A* war? Please tell me that in between her salon visits, this girl at least learned the names of the countries we've been fighting in for the past decade. No wonder soldiers feel exiled from people so disconnected from reality. A warrior caste is right.

Seth stares at his food. "Yeah. Something like that."

I push my plate away. The sight of snails coupled with this conversation makes me want to puke. Is this really what it will be like for Seth and Lucas any time they get asked about where they've been for the past year? These two Americans should feel like familiar friends, but instead they're the most foreign of all the pilgrims we've encountered so far.

Dennis revisits an earlier subject in an attempt to fill the uncomfortable lull. "So Gabi, you said your mom's part Scottish?"

Okay, I am losing patience quick. "Sure, as in her ancestors came over from Scotland before the United States existed as an official country."

Jean Paul and Molly are deep in a conversation that has *got* to be more interesting than this one, so I shift my body in their direction. Seth shoves a finger in his mouth and pretends to pull the trigger. Believe me, buddy, I would if I could, but that means missing out on dessert and I've heard a rumor it's *flan*, my favorite. Luckily for Seth, Natalie has a short attention span, and soon she traps the young priest in a discussion of deep spiritual significance. The state of the Italian leather shoe industry, I believe.

"I'm Scottish, too," Dennis smacks, his mouth full.

I resist the urge to stab him, and then myself, with my fork.

"Really? Man, do *your people* know how to make a Scotch egg! Let me guess, you play rugby and the bagpipes, right? I bet you love the movie *Rob Roy*, huh? Why isn't your hair red? Why don't you have an accent, *laddie*?"

Okay, so I snapped. Lost my mind for a moment. I'm not proud of it, but it happened.

Dennis's mouth falls open, proving *escargot* can look even more disgusting than it does on the plate. He stares at me like I'm the biggest moron he's ever met in all his urbane travels, then turns his back to me, joining Natalie's one-sided conversation with the poor Italian priest on da Vinci and his secret code.

I almost feel bad for blowing up on the guy, but he's the sort of tourist who gives Americans abroad a bad name. Then again, he and Natalie are out here on the *camino* when they could be lying on a beach sipping cocktails, so maybe they're making *some* effort to expand their narrow little world.

Seth is cracking up behind his wineglass, his squinty eyes signaling an enthusiastic *bravo!* I can't help smiling back, but now I'm flustered and feeling unfit for a cross-cultural exchange. Fortunately, Jean Paul does most of the talking, and before long the entire table falls under his spell. He shares what it was like growing up in Sudan during the civil war. As he speaks, Jean Paul's hands move in graceful gestures that denote an inner calm I can't comprehend, given the horrors he's witnessed.

"Of all the long walks I've done, this pilgrimage is the most peaceful. When I was a boy, I fled the violence in my country by escaping across the border to Kenya, and we had to keep on the lookout for wild animals the entire way." Jean Paul's face breaks into a huge smile. "So far I have yet to see a lion or a crocodile on the *camino*. Although it often sounds like I'm sleeping next to one in the hostels."

Everyone laughs, but the fact that Jean Paul is the sole surviving member of his family makes my head spin. Hearing his story stirs up guilt for all the times I complained about having to pack up my room again, or because I was missing a school dance due to a move. Things my dad likes to call "first world problems," compared to the challenges most of the world faces on a daily basis. You know, things like hunger and disease and violence lying in wait around every corner.

Seth's subdued voice breaks into the dim space. "Do you mind if I ask why you're walking the *camino*, Jean Paul?"

I snap my head in Seth's direction. This is the first time he's actively engaged another pilgrim on purpose. *Ever.* Pay attention, people!

"Not at all." Jean Paul's glowing face brightens the room. "I'm here because I'm grateful. Grateful to be walking with all of you, grateful to be starting medical school in the United States this fall, grateful that I will be able to return to Sudan one day to help my people. Yes, that is my reason. My pilgrimage is one of gratitude."

"I'll toast to that," someone shouts from the other end of the table. "*Salud*."

"*Salud!*" we respond in unison, even the nonconformist Seth.

Seth chats with Jean Paul right through dessert, which blows my mind since he hates small talk with strangers. But this Sudanese kid has lived and breathed armed conflict for most of his life, so maybe Seth can relate to the rawness of that more than anything else.

"Attention, pilgrims!" Greta clinks the side of her water glass with a spoon. "After dinner, we'd like to invite you to a time of reflection in the sanctuary—a nightly tradition here at our *albergue*. Entirely optional, of course, but you are all welcome to experience the serenity of Eunate."

Seth and I make eye contact. Normally we'd "peace out" at the mere mention of a touchy-feely group *anything*, but ditching our hosts after this amazing meal feels rude. Besides, we're sleeping on the sanctuary's front stoop anyway.

After clearing the table, everyone heads outside and walks over to the churchyard. Karl opens the door to the chapel, and we step through a portal to someplace ancient. A thick darkness I can practically feel awaits inside, until Greta hands out white taper candles and the small space fills with a gilded glow. I breathe deeply and taste a thousand years. Beside me in the pew, Seth fidgets with his jacket. I'm a little uncomfortable too, though I don't know why.

For a while we just sit there with our flickering lights, surrounded by a silence that echoes across the centuries. I stare up at the octagonal roof, supported by eight arches divided like eight slices of pie. It's a design more Middle Eastern than European, and stars peek through the skylight holes in each of the eight segments. The ceiling reminds me of the bathhouse postcard Lucas sent us after he experienced his first *hammam* in Afghanistan.

*Lucas*. I remove a tealight from my pocket. As I touch it with my taper candle, Karl's voice shatters the hushed atmosphere. "Let's take a moment of silent intention for pilgrims who are sick or suffering, and for those walking on behalf of loved ones who are sick or suffering."

Musty earth assaults my nostrils as my gaze falls to the orange dust on the floor, tracked in by the thousands of pilgrims who have passed through this space in search of a silent moment. A still point in an otherwise spinning universe.

Is that what my fellow wanderers are seeking out here on the *camino*? A minute with no phone, no Internet, no television? A chance to think about someone they love? Or are they searching for something even deeper? For an ethereal instant that makes skin tingle, for a fleeting whisper that promises there's something more? Some part of us that goes beyond cell clusters and synapses?

The space is beautiful. Like all beautiful things, it makes me ache. Maybe because it reminds me of something else. Something I know in my bones, but can't quite name. The domed altar, the hand-carved pillars, the golden stones—all this beauty stirs up a longing for a place I *know*, even if I've never been there.

I'm not sure if this hunger for something sacred is real, but I'm certain the feeling will be over in a flash, gone as soon as I step outside and smell the manure sprinkled across these fields—a stark reminder that everything growing this spring will decay in the fall, no matter how delicious it tasted tonight.

But right now I can't help thinking this universe is a mystery that *wants* to be solved; a mystery trapped inside each and every one of us. The clues are all there—layered in the part of us that loves starry skies and sunsets, whispered by the muse who inspires painters and poets, hidden in the fractured piece of us that somehow feels more whole in a room full of strangers from around the globe. I don't know much, but I know this *thing*, this mystery, must be behind the desire that stirred millions of pilgrims across the centuries. Why else would people walk hundreds of miles to a place they've never seen? What is it that our restless hearts are searching for?

*Home.*

That's what we all left behind to find. And if this longing for Home is *real*, then maybe Lucas still exists somewhere, even if his brain and his body are no longer talking. Maybe there's more to him than both of those things combined.

My eyes fall to the individual shadows scattered across the floor, all blending into one massive blur of tears. Before I feel the warm wetness on my cheek, I feel Seth's thumb wiping the tear away. He's been watching me this entire time, staring at the tealight resting between my fingertips. The look on his face is as close as he's ever come to a prayer, but it's enough. It assures me Seth loves Lucas as much as I do.

"Would anyone be willing to sing a song from his or her native land?" Greta asks, rescuing us from the weight of this overbearing stillness.

Molly volunteers. She intones a haunting, Gaelic tune, her mournful voice rising above all of us. Then she launches into an achingly slow rendition of "Danny Boy," which almost makes me lose it entirely. Lucas's middle name is Daniel and my mom used to sing us this song whenever our dad was away.

"The summer's gone, and all the flow'rs are dying
'Tis you, 'tis you must go and I must bide.
But come ye back when summer's in the meadow . . . ."

*Yes, come back*, I hope. Or pray. Is there really a difference? *Please, Lucas, come back.*

• • •

"That was nice. I guess." Seth stretches out beside me in his sleeping bag, his face turned up to the night sky. "Nothing too weird or over the top."

I know what he means, but I wouldn't call anything about this evening *nice*. Eunate is spectacular, incredible, amazing. But there's something unsettling about it, too. Something transcendent and almost sublime. I suppose we *are* sleeping right next to a medieval graveyard.

"Are you all right?" Seth asks when I don't respond. He's lying a decent distance away from me, his good arm resting behind his head, his eyes fixed on a net of stars.

"I'm fine. Just tired." I roll over, struggling to get comfortable. A brigade of chirping insects fills the fields surrounding us, and their lullaby brings me back to that murky place where memories blur into dreams.

*Cicadas. Big Red soda. Chlorine.*

I'm in sixth grade and Lucas is in seventh—our ages the first time Dad was stationed in Texas. We lived off-post and had to go to a nonmilitary school for the first time. We hated it. All the other kids had known each other since kindergarten, so they ignored us. There was also this weird division between the white kids and the Latino kids, which we'd never experienced before. Military brats are used to hanging out with everyone, no matter if you're black, brown, or blue.

*September. Asphalt hot enough to fry an egg. All the grass in our subdivision is brown. Lucas is wearing his favorite San Antonio Spurs hat.*

On our walk home from school, Lucas got into a fight with another Latino boy who teased me for "acting too white." I had no idea what that even meant. All I knew was that I didn't fit in anywhere or have a single friend, which meant I spent most of the lunch period hiding out in a bathroom stall. Not my finest hour, in addition to being totally disgusting.

"Don't worry, Gabs. You'll always fit with me," Lucas said while Mom iced his black eye with the frozen pork loin she planned to cook for dinner.

*You'll always fit with me.*

The sound of Lucas's voice forces my eyes open. I can't tell if the sob pressing down on my chest actually escaped my throat. The sky is silky black, the color of Lucas's hair before the Army chopped it off. I rub my eyes and make out a murky mass above me. The Milky Way. Seth rests in the same position, like a sentinel on an all-night UFO watch.

"How come you're still awake?" I mumble. "Can't sleep?"

Seth doesn't move his head or break his focus. "Look at all that empty space. An entirely empty universe."

I can't tell if that's meant to be reassuring, or just depressing. Either way, the thought of black holes that consume all light makes me want to disappear into my sleeping bag.

"Have you heard the St. James legend yet? About how they found his body way back in the day?" Seth asks a few moments later.

"Nope," I mutter sleepily.

"Supposedly there was this old hermit, a holy man, who lived in the woods alone about a thousand years ago. One night he heard strange music and when he looked outside, he saw a bright star shining above an empty field. But it wasn't a normal star. This star wandered back and forth across the sky, then stopped. The hermit reported what he'd seen to the local bishop, which led to an official investigation. The Church discovered the bones of three men in the spot where the hermit saw the star come to rest. James the Apostle had been a missionary to Spain, so the Church determined that the bones belonged to him and his two disciples. That's why they built the cathedral we're walking to."

Santiago de Compostela. I never really thought about it, but it makes sense. *Santiago* is James in Spanish, and *campus stellae* means "the field of the star."

I turn on my side to get a good look at Seth. "Is that what you've been watching for? Wandering stars?"

Seth nods, but his eyes don't leave the sky. "So far I've counted three."

His response sends a shiver from my head to my toes, as if one of those stars falls right through me. After today's long hike, Seth must be exhausted. He doesn't seem like the stargazing type, so I don't even have to ask. I already know he's watching the heavens on behalf of my brother, wishing on all those shooting stars for Lucas. Knowing that Seth would stay awake for something so simple and silly floods me with feelings I don't know how to name. All I know is they make me want to kiss him with an intensity normally reserved for love or hate.

I burrow down in my sleeping bag, but there's nowhere I can hide from this holy fear, this startling wonder, this unnerving loss of control. Like a conviction that carries all kinds of unwelcome obligations, the last thing I want is to *believe* the emotions running through me.

Too bad the truth keeps existing whether we acknowledge it or not.

*I love Brent, I love Brent, I love Brent.*

The thing is, I *do* love Brent. At least, I think I do. And I would never betray him for the spell of a starry night, though that doesn't make the power radiating from the sleeping bag across the way any less frightening. This isn't just physical attraction. Hostel life is intimate, so I've seen Seth without a shirt on a million times, without a single spark.

This is something much, much worse.

*Get up. Act.* Don't wait for things to happen *to* you. *Make* things happen.

I unzip my sleeping bag and crawl over to Seth, but instead of pressing my mouth to his, I extend my hand. "Come on."

"What are you doing?" Seth looks up at me, a puzzled smirk on his lips.

"I want to try something. Something one of the other pilgrims mentioned."

With an exaggerated groan, Seth takes my hand and climbs out of his sleeping bag. I lead him to the cobblestone path that follows the churchyard wall. The moon is so bright we can see the glistening stones without a flashlight.

"The Argentinian woman at dinner shared another *camino* legend. Some pilgrims claim a healing miracle will occur if you walk around this church barefoot—three times on the inside of the wall, and then three more times on the outside. Afterwards, we're supposed to enter the sanctuary and light a candle on the altar."

Seth raises a dubious eyebrow. "Seriously, Gabi?"

"Hey, Jiminy Cricket, if you're going to stay up all night wishing on shooting stars, we might as well give this a try, too."

Seth's smile turns sheepish when he realizes I've discovered his little secret.

"Besides," I continue, "I forget if you're supposed to walk around the church clockwise or counter-clockwise, so we can each take a direction and cover all our bases."

Seth sighs. "Fine. Maybe I'll finally fall sleep afterwards. Oh hey, while we're on the subject of weird esoteric rituals, there's something I've been meaning to show you."

Seth extends his hand and drops a small object into mine, still warm from being pressed inside his palm. It's a stone. The most beautiful stone I've ever seen. Its edges are jagged and it looks like hardened lava. The sparkly black rock is marbled with streaks of intense blue and flecks of gold.

"Where did you find this? The moon?"

"It's called lapis lazuli and it's mined in Afghanistan," Seth explains. "It was with Lucas's letter. He said we should leave the stone somewhere along the way. He said we'd know the place when we saw it. Whenever that time comes, I think you should be the one to do the honors."

The stone is heavier than it looks, but it's nothing compared to the burden pressing down on me. Lucas is in a coma. How can all these laughable little customs change that?

"Let's just start the circling process," I suggest, "otherwise we'll both feel too ridiculous to go through with it."

We start walking, which gives me six opportunities to study the sandstone faces of the mythical creatures etched into the church's high walls. Each time I pass Seth heading in the opposite direction, his gaze burns into mine, his eyes like two blue orbs of lapis lazuli glowing in the moonlight. Neither of us says a word, but when we've circled the church the prescribed number of times, we meet in its darkened doorway.

I light a candle and Seth grabs my other hand. His palm is still warm, even without the stone. Together, we step inside.

# CHAPTER 12

After Eunate, something changes. Seth and I are a team. Maybe we're even friends. We find our stride. The long days of walking get easier, and we talk a lot more than we used to.

Talking is good. Talking means I don't have to think, which means I don't have to deal with the knot at the bottom of my stomach, a knot that increases in size and degree of entanglement each day.

*You wanted to kiss him.*

The accusation scampers through my mind any time I stop running my mouth. Whatever happened in Eunate, blaming it on enchantment, or on a spell cast by the alignment of stars, doesn't satisfy. Maybe it was the food. Yeah, that's it. I hear *escargot* causes horrible indigestion. And according to this article I read on the Internet once, serious indigestion can cause hallucinations and other erratic behavior.

Or something.

"You're looking mighty pensive this afternoon," Seth says as we approach the town of Santo Domingo. "What's up?"

"Nothing." I chug what's left in my water bottle. I'm pretty sure "I've been thinking about how I no longer hate you and might even like you a little" isn't the answer Seth wants.

He smirks. "*Nothing* doesn't make a girl blush. Let me guess. Brent texted you lyrics to a lame and gushy song he wrote just for you?"

"No. And I'm not blushing. I'm hot and out of water."

This is true. The further west on the *camino* we go, the warmer the weather gets. For the past two days, the landscape has been as dry as the layer of cracked mud on my boots. Everything around here is the color of sand. Tan road, tan tiles on all the roofs, tan fields. Seth's farmer's tan. A world of beige, except for the sky, which shines sapphire blue. The same color as Seth's eyes.

Beneath Wandering Stars

*Dammit, Gabi. STOP!*

Yeah, this introspection thing isn't working for me. "Hey, we haven't played your game of Twenty Questions in a while," I suggest.

"Okay, you start." Seth flips his baseball hat around so it's on backwards. Why this small, insignificant gesture makes my heart skip a beat, I'll never understand.

Me: "What was your worst move? The place you hated most?"

Seth: "Fort Rucker, Alabama. No Jews and lots of water moccasins."

Seth: "Where's the best place you ever lived?"

Me: "San Antonio because of the people, Hawaii because . . . well, because it's Hawaii."

Another mile and our questions turn a little more philosophical.

Me: "What do you think these wars will end up changing?"

Seth: "The people who fight in them."

Me: "Why are we walking?"

Seth: "Uh, because Lucas asked us—"

Me: "No, I mean why are *any* of us walking? Ultimately speaking?"

Seth: "Because once you stop moving, stop chasing something, you die."

One more mile and things get really serious.

Seth: "Why are you in such a hurry to go to college?"

Me: "One of us has to go or Dad will think he became a U.S. citizen for nothing."

Seth: "But what do you really want to do? Ultimately speaking?"

Me (after a lengthy pause): "I have no idea."

Me: "When were you most afraid over there?"

Seth (after a longer pause): "When I held Lucas in my arms until the medics arrived."

And there we have it. Seth *was there*. I should press him for details, but the image of Seth down in the dirt, cradling my brother,

120

is too painful to envision for long. My heart cracks in two and our conversation ends. Or at least I want it to, but Seth is on a roll.

"What do you hate most about being a military brat?" he continues.

Good. An easy way to change the subject. "You want the long list or the CliffsNotes?"

"You have *a list*?" Seth chuckles. "Remind me not to get on your bad side."

"It's called, 'Things I Hate Most about Life As a Military Brat.'"

"Catchy. Let's hear it."

I take a deep breath. "Number 1: Being called a military brat. The nickname isn't the problem, since I know it's one of endearment. What bothers me is being thrown into a club I never asked to join. My dad was the one who signed up for the Army, but the moment the doctor at some hospital with walls the color of lima beans smacked me on the butt and said, 'Welcome to Fort Wherever,' I was *in*, like it or not."

Seth laughs. "Yeah, I'm surprised we don't see more recruitment posters that say, 'U.S. Army. Enlisting infants since 1776.'"

"Number 2: That annoying question, 'So, where are you from?' I used to get tongue-tied trying to explain that I was technically born in Fort Polk, Louisiana, but we moved to Fort Drum, New York, when I was two months old. I couldn't tell you a thing about my birthplace, other than the cockroaches are allegedly the same size as the rats. So now I opt for the simplest response: 'Pick a place.'"

"See, that's the only good thing about my parents' divorce. My mom will never leave her hometown again, so at least I have that as a fallback answer. Continue."

"Number 3: Surprises. The constant changes that come with moving so much make it easy to latch on to anything remotely consistent, so even the silliest traditions start to matter when everything else descends into chaos. I like to know what to expect."

"Note to self: never throw Gabi a surprise party." Seth grins. "Not unless I want to get kicked in the *cojones*."

I smile back. "I'm glad we understand each other."

Santo Domingo de la Calzada
"Where the hen sang after being roasted"

I stop in front of the huge sign. "Wow. And I thought Maryland's state motto—'Manly deeds, womanly words,' whatever *that* means—was bad."

Twenty Questions comes to an end when we reach the town of Santo Domingo de la Calzada, in part because we're greeted by the most bizarre welcome sign I've ever seen. And I've seen plenty.

"I know, right." Seth scans the quiet town. "Why anyone would choose a chicken as their mascot is beyond me."

"Can I see the guidebook?"

Seth hesitates. "Do you remember what happened the last time I gave you the guidebook?"

"Yes. We met some amazing people and slept out under the stars. Now give it here."

Seth hands over the book. I flip to the page on Santo Domingo, read the short description, and slam the cover shut. "Follow me, *por favor*."

• • •

"You have *got* to be kidding me."

I can't help beaming at the look of horror on Seth's face. "Surprise!"

"Gabi." Seth swallows hard, straining to keep his voice calm in the quiet sanctuary. "Why are there chickens inside a church?"

I peer into the wrought-iron cage decorated with filigree designs, the opulent home of two white hens who stare back at us with shifty eyes. "They're here so that pilgrims will remember one of the most famous miracle stories of the *camino*."

"Let me guess. A man who loved chickens built them a cathedral and was cured of his raving lunacy?"

"Nope. Once upon a time, long before *albergues* had subpar showers, a young pilgrim walked to Santiago with his parents and they stopped in Santo Domingo for the night. The daughter of the innkeeper propositioned the young man, but being the good Catholic boy that he was, he refused her advances. In retaliation, the scorned girl hid a silver chalice in his bag and called the authorities. Since it was the Middle Ages and theft wasn't tolerated, the poor kid was promptly executed. His parents continued walking to Santiago to pray for his soul, and on their way home they stopped at this church to say their final goodbyes. That's when they discovered that their son was still alive."

"Dun, dun, *dun!*" Seth exclaims with fake enthusiasm.

"Hey, this is my narrative and that was *not* the decisive turning point." I pick up a feather from the floor and tickle Seth's cheek. He squeals like a little girl, I swear.

"That's disgusting! Okay, okay. Just finish your stupid story already."

I clear my throat. "As I was saying, the parents informed a city official of this miracle right as he was sitting down to lunch. 'Your son is as alive as this roast chicken on my plate,' the official scoffed. And because God can't stand haters, the moment the man said these words, his roasted chicken stood up, sprouted feathers, and flew away."

I take an exaggerated bow. "*Fin.*"

Seth glares at the two hens like they're solely responsible for the world's troubles. "And the moral of the story is: don't turn down promiscuous tavern wenches, otherwise your food will return to life and start attacking people?"

I struggle to contain my laughter as a few more pilgrims enter the church. "I don't think the roast chicken ever attacked anyone. According to the legend, these lovely ladies are her descendants."

"Do people in your religion actually believe this stuff?" Seth asks.

I shrug. "I highly doubt revived chickens are a doctrine one must accept, but this part of the *camino* is pretty boring, so why not add a little whimsy with some local folklore?"

"But why chickens? These two ladies would peck out your eyeballs if they had the chance. Trust me on that."

"Wow, Seth. You're a regular St. Francis of Assisi. If blessed hens who live inside a church can't defeat your irrational phobia, there's nothing more I can do for you."

"You're right," Seth mutters. "I'm a lost cause."

• • •

For some reason, I've lit a lot of candles lately. Sometimes I light them in the little churches at the center of every village. Sometimes I put them on these pagan-ish monuments pilgrims create by stacking stones. And sometimes I leave the candles in places that have no special significance, but just seem like a spot Lucas would appreciate.

"Can I light one?" Seth asks as we're passing through a grove of olive trees outside the town of San Juan de Ortega.

"Sure." I almost fall over in astonishment as I hand Seth half a dozen tealights so he can start his own trail for Lucas. Between the two of us, we might just set the *camino* on fire.

Speaking of getting burned, there's something I've wanted to ask Seth for a while now. The misty sunrise that started our morning walk was a taste of heaven, so now is as good a time as any to bring up the seven minutes we were supposed to spend in that eternal realm.

"Seth, remember that birthday party we both went to a few years back? The one Lucas missed because he was away at soccer camp?"

"Yeah," Seth replies, his face deadpan.

"Why were you so repelled? Was it because I had braces then? I mean, I didn't want to kiss you either, but it wasn't as if the thought made me physically ill."

The embarrassing words tumble out as though I am physically ill *right now* and can't control my verbal retching. I've never been one of those girls with horrible self-esteem issues, but I'm basically offering myself up on a silver platter, giving Seth the opportunity to spell out everything that's wrong with me. Every reason he refused to kiss me that day and decided Angry Birds was far more interesting.

Seth stops walking. "It wasn't like that, Gabi."

"Then what was it like?"

"It was, like, you were fourteen."

"And you were sixteen. As far as I know, that's not illegal."

"It is when it comes to your best friend's little sister."

Ah yes, the unbreakable bro code.

"Then why didn't you just say that? Why'd you ignore me?"

After everything we've talked about and been through these past few weeks, my questions feel so incredibly *tween*, but I have to know. Brent hasn't been great at keeping in touch lately, so I'm wondering if there's a reason boys find it easy to pretend I do not exist.

Seth starts saying something, then stops. He studies the layer of copper dirt dusting his boots. "I'm sorry, okay? I just didn't know what to do. Put a guy in a dark closet with a cute girl and there are things he *wants* to do, no matter how off-limits that girl is. So I checked out instead. It seemed like the easiest solution."

Forget setting the *camino* on fire. I'm more worried about my blazing face.

"I see."

That's all I can say. I'm mortified, and worst of all, I asked for it. Fortunately, the momentary awkwardness fades and we rediscover our stride. We don't talk for the next few kilometers, but the silence isn't uncomfortable. It's more familiar than most things.

How weird. The more at ease I feel around Seth, the more I miss Brent. I always miss him, but I've also gotten used to his absence. My mixed-up feelings from Eunate are a distant memory by now, but getting close to Seth after going solo for so long feels like chinks in my armor. I need to contact Brent as soon as we reach a city large enough to have an Internet café.

There should be one in Burgos, today's stop. That's also where we'll board a bus and skip ahead to the last hundred kilometers of the *camino*, that way we make it to Santiago in time for our flight home.

"Whoa, this place is a dump," Seth announces when we reach the city's outskirts.

I stop to tie my shoelaces in the sprawl of pavement and industrial fringe. "Yeah, after walking through the countryside, it does feels like we've entered the ninth circle of hell."

"Did you just make a reference to Dante's *Inferno*?" asks a female voice from behind me.

What can I say? Literature is my best subject.

"Because I said *the exact* same thing to my brother five minutes ago."

I turn around and see a guy and girl about my age—a rare sight, since most student pilgrims won't start walking to Santiago until the summer months. They're sitting on a bus stop bench covered in graffiti, eating homemade Nutella and banana sandwiches that smell delish.

I shrug. "A bleak abyss was the first thing that came to mind."

"*Genau*, I can't think of a worse place on the *camino* to send traitors for all eternity." The boy half of this pilgrim pair points to the white spires of a cathedral in the distance. "Good thing Paradise is on the horizon."

Okay, he's taking this Dante thing a little over my head, but at least this exchange gives me a chance to identify their accents. "Where are you guys from in Germany?"

"From the town of Otterbach. You've probably never heard of it," the guy replies with a smile that would make any girl stammer. "I'm Jens and this is Katja."

I'll be blunt. Jens (pronounced Yens) is kind of gorgeous. Both he and his twin sister wear their dirty blond hair in dreadlocks, only her strands are dyed hot pink. Jens pulls off the wandering vagabond look much better than she does, but guys are lucky like that. Somehow they look roguishly masculine in their dishevelment, whereas we just look filthy.

"Otterbach? As in the Otterbach north of K-town?"

"You mean Kaiserslautern," Seth corrects, since these siblings may not be familiar with American *Deutsch* slang. That's his only contribution to the conversation, which is fine by me because the twins are talkative and speak perfect English.

"Correction," I say with a smile. "I mean Kaiserslautern."

Katja laughs. "*Ja*, that's the only Otterbach I'm aware of. Do you know it?"

"I live nearby. On the U.S. Army garrison."

"I figured. We have a few American friends who live there, too." Jens tosses a subtle nod in Seth's direction before whispering, "Plus, Katja has a thing for men in uniform."

Katja jabs her brother in the ribs, telling him off in German. Their sarcastic quips remind me of the way Lucas and I communicate, which makes me want to latch on to them like an emaciated leech. As we head into Burgos, we discover all kinds of things we have in common, from our deep love of the Bavarian pretzel, to our World Cup fanaticism.

"So you play *fussball* then?" Katja asks when the subject of soccer comes up. "Why don't you join the Otterbach women's team this summer? We've had a few American girls play with us over the years."

"Sounds fun," I reply. And I mean it. "What are the odds of us living down the road from each other, but meeting all the way out here on the *camino*? Talk about a coincidence."

Jens gives me a wink that makes my stomach flop. "Ah, but there are no coincidences on the *camino*. There are only circles of destiny that occasionally overlap."

Seth rolls his eyes, though thankfully he doesn't say anything rude. I'm not sure if I agree with Jens's thoughts on destiny, but I like these twins a lot. Once we reach the city center, we exchange phone numbers so we can meet up back in Germany. Jens and Katja will stay in Burgos an extra day so they can experience the nightlife, which was nonexistent across this recent stretch of cow towns.

"*Buen camino*," the twins call out as we go our separate ways. It dawns on me that they're the first people I've made social plans with since I moved overseas. A strange *camino* side effect, I guess. Though according to Jens, *not* a coincidence.

"Now what?" Seth asks, glancing around the square.

Unlike Burgos's urban outskirts, the city center is a beautiful collection of narrow streets packed with *tapas* bars, plazas lined with ornate balconies, and walking paths along lush river banks. I stare up at the clean white façade of the Burgos Cathedral and shield my eyes from the glare.

"Want to go in?" Whenever I run into a church to light a candle, Seth waits outside, but the Burgos Cathedral isn't some country bumpkin house of worship. It's a UNESCO World Heritage site and one of the finest examples of High Medieval Gothic architecture outside of France. Again, according to Rick Steves.

"No thanks." Seth points across the square to a café of wicker tables and red umbrellas. "I'll be sitting over there in the shade, enjoying the view with a nice cold *cerveza*."

I point to a six-pointed star in the cathedral's rose window. "But look, a Star of David."

Seth snickers. "And that just makes up for centuries of persecution, now doesn't it?"

"Fine. I'll be quick. Be a pal and order me a few *tapas* while you wait."

Too bad my visit requires way more than a minute. There are *a ton* of tourists waiting to take pictures with a statue of this Spanish knight named El Cid, so I stop by to see what all the fuss is about. While waiting for my G.I. Lucas photo op, I study the iridescent colors cast across the stone floor by the rose window. I'm zoning out, soaring through a realm of Pink Floyd records and dancing rainbows, until someone taps me on the shoulder.

"Yes?" There's no one there, until I lower my eyes and see a woman so tiny, she could probably fit inside my pack. I'm guessing she's Mexican because she wears a T-shirt with Our Lady of Guadalupe proudly stamped on the front. Her huge smile eclipses her small stature.

"*Hola guapa*. You take my photo *y* I take yours?"

"*Sí, por supuesto*," I reply, though what I really want is G.I. Lucas in the shot, not me. When it's my turn, I set the action figure on the back of El Cid's horse and say *queso*.

After that box is checked, I try to visit all the little side chapels along the nave. Each has its own altar, and my plan is to light a candle for Lucas on every one. Unfortunately, the chapels are also packed with people who are convinced their photo albums will not be complete unless they include *every single* stained-glass window and statue on the *camino*.

"Uh, excuse me. Trying to say an actual prayer here," I grumble, annoyed that there isn't a drop of transcendence to be found in this entire sanctuary. Politeness is futile, so I speed up the process by jogging from chapel to chapel, dodging pilgrims and pillars with the spiraling moves of an all-star running back. Each time I manage to light a candle, it feels like I'm one leg further in some bizarre Catholic relay race.

"How was it?" Seth asks when I return to the plaza. "Filled with gaudy, morbid art like every other cathedral dominating the skyline of Europe?"

"This one was really beautiful. No, *majestic*. That's the word. Sadly, there were so many people treating it like a roadside tourist trap that it kind of diminished its power."

"Majestic, huh?" Seth leans back in his chair, soaking up the sun. "Well, so is this gorgeous day and that's the only temple of worship I require. Now have a seat before I eat all of this delectable blood sausage by myself."

I scowl at the chunks of purple pork lining his plate. "*No, gracias*. But speaking of blood, who's this El Cid character? It sounds like he killed a lot of people."

Seth pops the last few bites of sausage into his mouth, opens the guidebook, and clears his throat. He imitates a highbrow British accent, like he's on a BBC documentary. "El Cid was a legendary nobleman and warrior, considered the national hero of Spain. He was born in 1043 near the Castilian capital of Burgos and led many campaigns against the Moors, which brought him much fame due to his military prowess."

"Moors?" I ask while making a vain attempt to wave our waitress over.

"The Moors were the Muslims who controlled southern Spain for seven hundred years. Every part of the Iberian Peninsula, except for this narrow strip in the north, was under Islamic rule for centuries, and Christian knights like El Cid spent their free time trying to regain the lost territory."

I rest my feet on an empty chair, glad to be off of them after hours of walking on joint-crushing concrete. "I really don't get this age-old conflict between the West and the Middle East. It seems so endless. Not to mention pointless."

"That's because you're thinking about it from a twenty-first-century Western perspective," Seth replies. "What we have are two completely different ways of viewing the world, and any time that happens, there's bound to be conflict."

"But why? How hard is it to live and let live?"

"Really hard, actually. Maybe even impossible. Beliefs matter more to humans than almost anything else, no matter how we try to suffocate them." Seth passes the olive bowl. "Think about it. No one is willing to die for a bigger house or better 401(k), but people *are* willing to sacrifice themselves for the things they believe at the deepest possible levels."

"So what you're telling me is the only way to achieve world peace is for people to stop caring about anything that actually matters?" I pick at a plate of stuffed peppers, smothered with enough garlic to wipe out a vampire coven. "That's pathetic. If we can only play nice with each other when we're too comfortable, or distracted, or apathetic to fight, then I don't have much hope for our species."

"What other truce can there be besides a world united beneath the flag of superb HBO programming and funny cats on YouTube?" Seth shrugs, as if this topic doesn't concern him, even though he's spent half a year living its consequences. "We see them as patriarchal religious fundamentalists content to live in the Stone Age, and they see us as decadent, materialistic scumbags with no moral values. No real room for compromise."

Speaking of cultural stereotypes, I've failed miserably at securing our Spanish waitress's attention, though in the process of craning my neck in every possible direction, I saw a neon sign across the square that looked like an Internet café. "Sorry Seth, I'd love to continue this enlightening discussion on the clash of civilizations, but I've got a boyfriend to talk to."

"Run along then." Seth downs the last half of his beer. "I'll be waiting."

From: calipunk4ever@hotmail.com
To: gabigirl7@gmail.com
Gabi,

I hate to do this over e-mail, but you haven't called in a while and I really need to tell you this so . . . it looks like I'm about to become "that guy."

We need to end it, Gabi. We should have done it a long time ago. I know it and you know it, but neither of us likes change. The acceptance letter I got in the mail last week confirms that it's time to go our own ways. And no, it wasn't from UT-Austin (that letter came a month ago. I just didn't have the heart to tell you it's no longer my first choice). I got into UC-Fresno, so I'm moving out to California right after graduation. I know this wasn't part of our plan, but how can I pass up this opportunity just to stay in Texas for the rest of my life? SoCal, Gabi! The music scene. It's my chance to finally make it big!

I know this is really bad timing, what with your brother being injured and all. But that guy you're walking with in Spain, Lucas's buddy, he really helped me put everything into perspective. He made me see that I was holding you back, that being with me was causing you to put your entire life on hold. And because I'm being totally honest here, I'd rather tell you about the other girls I've hooked up with than have Seth tell you. (He threatened me with a complimentary waterboarding demonstration if I didn't. Be careful around that guy, Gabi.)

I know this sucks and I'm sorry. I hope helping you get to Spain counts for something and that you don't completely hate my guts. I also hope Lucas gets better soon.

Good luck in life,

Brent


*Good luck in life?* Are you kidding me? It's so lame I almost burst out laughing, but that's only because I'm on the verge of bawling my eyes out. I don't know who I despise more—Brent for being a sniveling coward who cheats and dumps girls over e-mail, Seth for being the whirlwind disaster who somehow caused all this, or Lucas for not being here when I really need him. That last petty thought makes me hate *myself* most of all.

I read through the message one more time, then log off the computer so I don't bash in the monitor, even though I have eight paid minutes left. Brent's pathetic message isn't worthy of a response. And no, the fact that he's been meaning to dump me for weeks and decided to soften the blow with a plane ticket doesn't make him any less of a two-timing turncoat.

I speed walk across the plaza, envisioning the scene I'm about to make—me picking up Seth's umpteenth glass of beer and throwing it in his face in trashy American girl fashion. I can't believe he had the nerve to go behind my back and tell Brent whatever he told him. I can't believe I was actually starting to trust him.

Seth is no longer seated in the café. Our stuff is still there, but he's gone.

"Your army friend had to use the loo," a familiar voice announces. "Spanish beer goes right through you, see. I told him I'd watch your bags."

I turn around. Yep, good old Bob is back. The sleep apnea didn't kill him, and neither did a lynch mob of REM cycle-deprived pilgrims, which was my forecast for the poor old guy if he kept up his snoring.

"Thanks, Bob," I mutter, searching for a pen so I can write on the back of Seth's bill. My hand shakes. I can feel my skin breaking out in red, blotchy hives, which only happens when I'm especially pissed off. As soon as I finish my infuriated scribbling, I grab my backpack and the guidebook, then leave the café without once looking back.

*Walking on my own now, traitor! Buen frickin' camino!*

# CHAPTER 13

Burgos is a big city, so it's the perfect place to go missing. Unfortunately, there's only one bus station with a single bus per hour headed in the direction of Santiago, so I've got to plan ahead in order to ditch a trained tracker like Seth. I don't care what motivated him to tell Brent we should break up. Seth isn't my father and he's definitely not my big brother. Now he's not even my friend. From this point on, I'm walking alone.

But first, I'm going to splurge.

"*Un habitación, por favor.*" I slap my passport down on the front desk. "Preferably a room with a view."

The concierge at the Meson del Cid hotel is a severe woman with penciled-on eyebrows who wears a red scarf around her neck like she's about to go run with the bulls. She studies the crushed leaves in my hair, trying to determine if I'm serious. I open my passport, pull out my last one-hundred euro bill, and slide it across the counter.

Funny. After that, the woman doesn't utter a peep.

"*Gracias.*" I take my change and the room key, then search for the elevator in a lobby with one too many fake potted plants.

I figure a hotel stay is the best way to throw Seth off my scent. Literally, since the first thing I intend to do when I enter my budget yet blissfully private room is take the longest, hottest shower of my entire life. The bathroom is huge for a European hotel, and once it's nice and steamy, I jump in and do nothing but watch water swirl down the drain for the next thirty minutes, wishing I could clean up my life with so little effort.

All my blisters have hardened into calluses—little islands of rhinoceros flesh no longer susceptible to pain. If that's what it takes to make it on the *camino*, then maybe that's what it takes to make it in life. An armor of thick skin.

I rinse the hotel's coconut-lime shampoo out of my hair and wrap myself in a fluffy white towel. The feather duvet on the double bed feels like a homecoming, so I lie there in silence, staring at the flamenco dancer paintings decorating the room's crimson walls.

*What now?*

Why go back to Texas at all? Sure, I had friends there, but we were a cohesive group of couples. Couples who are still together minus the pairing I happened to be a part of. UT-Austin was supposed to be *our* school, and it was the only college I applied to. The worst part is that Brent couldn't tell me the truth face to face. Instead, he chose to dump me in an e-mail so devoid of emotion, it sounded like a request to disconnect his cable.

I do not cry. I *will not* cry. Brent isn't worthy of my tears, though the wasted months of waiting and saving every penny to see him again *are* worth weeping over. But I can't do it. There's this dead, hollow space inside me instead, like I have nothing left in me worth loving. Like I am now—cue the *Les Mis* soundtrack—on my own. Lucas, my parents, Brent. None of them are here, and none of them can tell me what to do after I hand over my military ID card and become a stranger to the only life I've ever known.

Okay, this pity party has got to stop. I sit up and rifle through my pack for the *Odyssey*.

*For a friend with an understanding heart is worth no less than a brother,* reads the first highlighted quote I find. Kill me now. Seth may have had his moments of understanding, but he will never be like a brother.

*A brother.* Do I even still have one?

I flip through a few more pages. *Out of sight, out of mind.*

Now that's more like it, Homer. Lucas isn't here. Brent isn't here. And now, thankfully, Seth isn't here. It's time to stop giving this troublesome trio real estate in my brain.

I turn on the TV and flip through the channels. Apparently European TV is the same as American TV: lots of infomercials, spandex-clad girls gyrating to musical lyrics that could have been written by a three-year-old, and a Spanish version of *The Jerry Springer Show*. Great, now I'm even more depressed.

*Get over yourself, Gabi.* My conscience, inner voice, whatever you want to call it, is right. It's stupid to worry about the future, especially when my main concern should be finishing this pilgrimage. That's one good thing about the *camino*. The main objective is simple: Get to the next dot on the map. Everything else comes day by day, kilometer by kilometer.

• • •

I must have fallen asleep because the next thing I know, the sharp clang of church bells has me shooting up in bed with a start.

*Lucas.*

My first morbid thought? I'm late for a funeral.

*No. Not yet.*

My body trembles, which probably has something to do with the fact that I'm wearing nothing but a damp towel. I walk over to the window, pull back the curtains, and get a glimpse of the view that cost me an extra fifteen euros.

It was worth it. The Burgos Cathedral is right on the other side of my balcony, and its bright white stones glow an eerie green in the fading twilight. The melancholy view makes the depressed just-got-dumped part of me want to dive back into the crisp sheets of a bed that is thankfully not my sweatbox sleeping bag, and play sappy break-up music on repeat.

Forget *that*. I'm in *Spain*.

And I'm not wasting a single moment because of one stupid boy.

I open the door to my balcony and let in the sounds of the street. The breeze that tags along assures me it's balmy out, almost summer-like. That means I can finally wear the one outfit I packed that's suitable for a night on the town—a black tank top and a ruffled red skirt that reminds me of the Spanish dancers I've been staring at for the past hour.

I dig through my backpack for the travel tube of mascara I've never used. After braiding my damp hair and twisting it into a low bun, I secure my favorite pair of silver hoop earrings, and *voilà,* my gypsy flamenco look is complete.

A few dabs of roll-on perfume and I'm out of here, even though I have no idea where I'm headed. I certainly didn't get all dolled up to go to church, but the illuminated cathedral beckons me back into the main square, buzzing with chatter from all the outdoor cafés. Buzzing is the perfect word to describe what's happening to me, too. There's this strange energy building up inside me, waiting to burst through. I feel brand new, like anything could happen. Like tonight I could become anyone I choose.

Boys lie and television is crap, but the cathedral before me is *real* and it has stood here for centuries, created by people who didn't have a forklift, let alone a phone app. Yet somehow they believed they could build something beautiful. Something people would walk hundreds of miles just to see in the flesh.

That's it. That's the question I need to ask the *camino.*

*What am I going to build that will leave a mark? That will last?*

I'm feeling all profound and deep, until my stomach growls out a less sophisticated question: *When are we going to eat?* My nose selects one of the many tantalizing aromas floating around the square, and I spy a café serving up seafood paella.

Whirling around in that direction, my bare shoulder collides with something solid.

"*Scheize!*"

"Sorry!"

The stranger's eyes widen as he catches me in the midst of my stumble. "Oh. Hey, Gabi. We meet again."

That "something solid" is Jens. Have I mentioned that Jens is gorgeous?

"Gabi! How are you?" Katja is close behind, as excited to see me as her brother. "You look fantastic! It'd take me ten hostel showers to look that pristine."

I'm not a big hugger of trees or of strangers, but I can't help throwing myself into Katja's homemade sweater–wearing arms. "I'm so happy to see you guys!"

*Now* I want to cry, though I'm guessing that would freak out my new friends. At least their sudden appearance means I won't wallow around in self-pity all night.

"What happened to your soldier?" Katja asks.

*I will never have a soldier.*

"Let's just say we decided to go our separate ways."

Jens's already big smile widens even further. "In that case, follow me, ladies. I have a suspicion Gabi needs to celebrate her newfound freedom."

We hit up a few *tapas* bars for some pre-party fuel, then head off in search of nightclubs that allow minors in until 1 A.M. It's almost eleven—right about the time Spain starts to come alive—so the streets are crowded. Every other face we pass belongs to someone our age, which is an unusual sight. I had an 11:30 P.M. curfew back in the States, and a "big evening out" typically meant going to a late movie, but here young people own the night.

"How about this place?" Katja points to a sign above an inconspicuous alley doorway. It reads *Buenas Noches.*

"Sure," Jens and I reply in unison. Our eyes meet, the small flame flickers, and we both look away to avoid getting singed. Jens and I have either blurted out the same thing or finished each other's sentences multiple times. And we don't even share the same first language.

Inside the club, the music and strobe lights are so overwhelming, I feel like I'm going to have a seizure. With its sticky floors and dark corners, the place is kind of a dive, but people seem to be having fun.

"Want to dance?" Jens shouts over the roar.

"Um, yeah, okay," I stutter. Truth be told, I haven't danced with anyone besides Brent since my sophomore Homecoming dance. And that was with a fumbling football player who stepped on my feet and treated every track like a slow song that gave him permission to hold my hips.

Jens, on the other hand, is an amazing dancer. I've only seen Germans dancing on top of tables to polka music at a *bierfest*, and believe me, it wasn't pretty. But this kid has moves and he knows how to use them—house, swing, hip hop, salsa, you name it, we dance it. The pulsing beat of the music and the heat radiating off of every body in the room create a warm fuzzy feeling that's intoxicating.

"I need a drink," Jens gasps after a popular song that has the whole club cheering and singing along. "How about a sangria?"

"Sure. I could use a break." I step away from the neon lights and scan the crowd for Katja. Ah, there she is—glistening with sweat as she dances with a smoldering Spaniard who looks like a cross between a young Johnny Depp and an even younger Antonio Banderas.

Jens returns with our drinks, his smirk sharpening into a scowl. Katja and her new friend aren't leaving much room for the Holy Spirit. "Be right back."

My jaw drops as Jens walks over and *actually* separates them, like a fearless nun armed with a ruler. I smile because Lucas would do the same thing, only in this instance, Jens would be the one getting told he needs to take a step back. As I sip my grown-up fruit punch, the deafening music fades to white noise. All I can hear is the voice of my father invading my head.

*Gabriela, you are not a person who can be trusted.*

*This is Spain, Dad, where the drinking age is sixteen and parents aren't so spastic,* I silently snap back. By the third sip the voice fades and by the fourth I couldn't tell you a thing about Sergeant Major Francisco Santiago, other than he's a major pain in my ass.

Jens returns, clutching Katja's arm. "I think it's time to go."

"Yeah! Let's go back to the cathedral," Katja squeals in a pitch that tells me she's had *waaay* more sangria than I have.

Once we're outside the club and far from the seductions of Don Juan, Jens loosens up. He keeps smiling at me in a specific way. A smitten way. I'm surprised he hasn't made a move yet, but then again, I can't imagine kissing someone with my sibling around. And these two are attached at the hip.

Katja walks ahead of us, swirling through the streets in a dance all her own, high on the hundred percent natural drug of being young and alive. "Your sister is adorable."

"*Ja*, Katja is . . . what's the phrase in English? A free spirit?"

"You mean you have those in Germany?" I joke.

Jens smiles and drapes his lanky arm over my shoulder. "Ha. Ha. Yes, despite the stereotypes, not *all* of us are Type A, rule-abiding robots."

Then Jens starts philosophizing, as the wasted are wont to do. As I half-listen to him babble on about how Ikea is destroying Europe the same way Walmart is destroying America, I keep my eye on Katja. She's stopped in front of the cathedral to talk to a dark-haired girl about our age. The brunette hands her something small and walks away.

Great. I tried not to judge these two by their hipster-hobo, riding-the-trains look, but I *really* hope Katja and Jens aren't into drugs because I don't need that kind of trouble on top of everything else. Between my overbearing father and those terrifyingly effective anti-meth ads, I'm already scared straight. Not to mention that trouble with the law could end Dad's career and result in federal government agents on my family's collective behind.

A mistake I've already made once.

We catch up to Katja, who looks sleepy and all danced out. She hands each of us a tealight. "That friendly girl said we were welcome to light a candle in the cathedral. It sounds like there's some sort of music event going on inside."

"Let's go," I reply, relieved. Not only because Katja gave me a little candle instead of a little baggie of mysterious white powder, but because I suddenly have an intense desire to feel closer to Lucas through the simple act of lighting one.

*Stars. Sleeping bags. Sanctuaries.*

Thinking about my *camino* ritual brings to mind Seth's face, washed in the moonlight of Eunate. I squash the association like a roach beneath my shoe.

*Traitor.*

"Earth to Gabi. Come in, Gabi."

I look up from the candle in my palm. Jens is waiting by the cathedral entrance. His slightly plastered grin is lopsided and goofy, but in the most adorable, genuine way possible.

"I must have heard that NASA line in American movies a hundred times, but I've never had the chance to use it," Jens says, holding out his arm for me to take.

We follow the soft acoustic strumming of "Stairway to Heaven," and enter a space unlike anything I've ever seen. There are candles *everywhere*—hundreds, maybe even thousands, of tiny, flickering tealights. The soaring ceiling pulls our eyes skyward. My chest tightens as the empty space above us swallows up my breath. During the day, this cathedral was dominated by camera-flashing tourists, but by night it radiates a beauty that almost hurts. A beauty that can't be fully absorbed, only admired at a distance.

A few kids sit in pews by the altar, where the guitarist strums his gypsy-inspired melodies. Others sit on the ground, talking quietly in clusters. This cathedral could easily be the lawn of any university campus, only with giant stone pillars instead of trees. There's even a group of kids playing Hacky Sack in a far corner.

It's almost two in the morning.

"What *is* this place?" I whisper. Whatever it is, it's warm and inviting and I love it.

"The girl who gave me the candle said this is part of a movement that started back in Germany," Katja explains with pride. "Young people in the city were bothered that their cathedrals, once the centers of urban life, had become little more than tourist attractions. A group of university students in Cologne decided their cathedral should be a house of refuge once again, especially at night when young people need a place to talk about important things that are hard to discuss in a noisy bar. The bishops agreed to open up cathedrals across Europe a few evenings each month—not for an official service or anything, but just for a contemplative space. For a reminder that sacred places still exist."

The sea of serene faces before me, representing almost every nationality under the sun, convinces me this space is most definitely that. "So what's with all the candles?"

"That's how they get the word out. Once you've lit one—for yourself, for someone you love, or to remember someone who has died—you're supposed to take the peace that comes from that small act and pass it on to someone in the street."

I love everything about it. I love that this wonder of the world isn't sitting empty all night, but is still used as a communal meeting place. I love that there are hundreds of twinkling tealights, each one representing the soul of another human being. "And the clergy don't mind?"

"Guess not." Katja nods towards a row of confessionals. The intimidating, old-fashioned kind made of shiny wood. A bearded priest sits out front, talking to a group of kids our age. Most have black stamps on the back of their hands from nightclubs, just like us. I watch as a kid with a green Mohawk and full arm-sleeve tattoos approaches the priest. The cleric nods along as the guy talks with animated gestures, almost like he's angry. Without saying a word, the priest places his hand on the young man's forehead, as if imparting a blessing.

I turn to see Jens's reaction, but he's wandered off. I spot him lying in the middle of the transept with outstretched arms, looking straight up at the vaulted ceiling.

"That must be quite a trip," I whisper to Katja. "If I lie down, I'll get the spins for sure."

"My brother says there's a reason German monks brewed beer. Hops have a natural calming effect that puts your mind in the right mood for contemplation." Katja grins and gestures to a stone bench in a shadowy corner. We brighten the space by setting our candles on the windowsill next to a statue of St. Francis, who's holding a bunch of baby animals as per usual. The quivering flames make the darkened colors of the stained glass flicker across Katja's cheeks. She seems completely sober now.

"So what's your brother's deal?" There's something about Jens I can't put my finger on. I've wanted to ask Katja about it all night, so I'm glad I finally have her alone.

She flashes me another serene smile. "Jens is different. Special."

I knew it. I could have sworn I felt a spark between us, but I also got the sense that maybe I wasn't his type. "Special how?"

"Those monks I mentioned? Jens is thinking about becoming one." Katja states this fact like it's the most normal thing in the world. "That's why we're here. We're walking the *camino* to find out if he has a vocation."

I almost choke. "Come again?"

This is *so not* the explanation I expected.

To start, I didn't think guys in this day and age even considered such a thing. And while Jens may be deep, he doesn't seem especially devout. Although this does explain why he only let his flirtation go so far.

I release a defeated sigh. "Well, I can tell you one thing. Those dreads will have to go. If my grandmother was here, she'd grab scissors and do the honors herself."

Katja laughs. "He hasn't decided yet, but there's been a monk or priest in our family for every generation going back a hundred years, so Jens is trying to figure out if the next one might be him." A peaceful expression—the expression of someone who knows exactly who she is and what she stands for—settles on Katja's face. She passes her hand over our candles, like she longs to feel the heat.

"So is your pilgrimage similar to how the Amish send their kids out to party for a year before they decide if they really want to be Amish?" I ask, hoping my question isn't offensive.

"Kind of. We needed to get out on our own. See the world for what it is. Figure out who we are and who we're meant to be. Learn to love people who are difficult to love, which tends to be the people closest to us. People like brothers."

Her eyes shining with a hope I've witnessed in very few people, Katja leans back against a wall built hundreds of years before we were born. A wall that will likely be here hundreds of years after we're both dead. "In the end, isn't that why we're all here?"

# CHAPTER 14

"*Café con leche*," I groan to the barista behind the counter. He responds to my demand for this last of the legal stimulants with a cocked eyebrow and a knowing smirk. I'm not hung over, but I didn't get much sleep, which means I feel (and look) like Death.

Katja throws back her espresso. "What time are you hitting the road?"

"I need to take the first bus out or I'll lose an entire day of walking," I say, stirring three packets of raw sugar into my coffee. I can already tell it's going to be a three-packet kind of day.

Pilgrim purists that they are, my friends will continue on foot, which means we won't cross paths again until Germany. After we finish our coffees, we say our *auf wiedersehen*s. Jens turns about six shades of pink when I wish him good luck figuring out if he has "the call," before casually suggesting that he give me a ring if he ends up choosing girls over God.

Apparently Death-Warmed-Over Gabi is also Extra-Bold, No-Filter Gabi.

Speaking of higher authorities, when I board the bus, my father calls. I hesitate to answer. He hasn't called me once, but I can't imagine Dad would want to chat unless it was about something serious. That leaves two options: really good news or really bad news. I'd rather choose Door Number Three: not knowing either way. The other paths are too final.

As the phone vibrates in my hand, a lump forms in my throat. My eyes fix on the blur of the passing scenery, which is orange, dusty, and flat.

The dreaded *meseta*.

I answer on the final ring. "Hi, Dad. What's up? Has Lucas improved?"

My chipper words pour out like a tidal wave of optimism I have yet to feel.

"*Nada*, Gabi. No changes."

Dad's frigid words harden into an uncomfortable silence. The acidic coffee sloshing around my empty stomach starts to eat it. That lump is now stuck, as though I inhaled a handful of the copper dirt lining the *camino*. It feels like every swallow for the rest of my life will be like forcing down a mouthful of saltine crackers without any water.

"Dad, I never meant to—"

"I don't want to talk about that right now, Gabriela. *You* are not my main concern. Not when we have more important matters to discuss."

"What happened?" My question comes out as a croak. If Dad isn't calling to chew me out for disobeying direct orders yet again, that means a major decision is about to be made, and Mom is too torn up to dial the phone.

I didn't want to know the outcome, but I already do. The words slam against me like a blow to the head: *life support*. "How much longer . . . ."

"His condition is worsening. The doctors think Lucas may be slipping into a vegetative state." My father's voice cracks. I can practically hear the tears sliding down his face. "Once that happens, there's only a slight chance he'll come out of it. And if I have to deploy suddenly, I can't leave your mother to deal with this alone."

"What are you saying? You'd actually consider taking him off life support?" I don't hide my disbelief. Dad has always made it clear that he's firmly against anything that threatens the sanctity of life. "Can you even *do* that?"

"Allowing nature to take its course isn't the same thing as assisted suicide, *mija*." Dad sighs deeply into the phone. "We're not at that point yet, but if nothing changes and the doctors tell us Lucas is gone, brain dead . . . *no se*. How can we ever know for certain what it is that makes a person truly alive?"

I can see this is a moral gray area, but why in the world is my father sharing his dilemma with *me*?

"Lucas isn't gone yet. He's still here; I know he is!" I'm blubbering now, displaying the ugly cry for all the world to see. Other passengers on the bus stare, but I couldn't care less.

"Calm yourself, Gabi. We're not making any decisions yet. But I thought you should know, seeing how you're an adult who can handle the realities of life on her own." Dad's words drip with resignation and resentment, not with the unshakable faith I'm used to.

Why is he doing this? When I told Dad he should trust me more, I meant I should have a later curfew and be able to get my own car, not be involved in determining my brother's end-of-life status.

Fine. If my father wants me to cast my vote, here it is: "I swear, Dad. If you take Lucas off life support before I get home, I will never forgive you."

With that, I hang up the phone, but my hands won't stop shaking for the next five minutes. My father never mentioned Seth, which means the jerk hasn't tried calling my parents to let them know we got separated. That also means he's still trying to find me, though Seth should be kilometers ahead of me by now.

The bus drops me off in Astorga, a decent-sized city with a lot of concrete. I stop for my second coffee and a *mantecada* (this spongy, orange cake thing that looks like a flattened muffin), but I can hardly choke it down thanks to my resident throat lump. Once the city sprawl is behind me, I pass through a landscape of undulating hillsides, manicured Merlot vines, and wildflower carpets the *camino* cuts in half.

None of it matters. I might as well be walking through the movie set of an apocalyptic wasteland, through a painting drained of all pigment. All I see is ugliness and death. Not a natural world that is perfectly ordered, but a natural world that is chaotic and cruel.

An army of ants devouring a baby bird fallen from its nest.

A hawk dive-bombing a field in search of unsuspecting prey.

A trail of litter that proves we humans are nothing but highly evolved parasites.

Then there are the allegations, the constant reminders that I'm as much of a beast as the rest. Accusations about how I used to tease Lucas for his stutter, not to mention the countless promises I made to him that I promptly broke. We were solid until I joined Lucas in high school. Somehow I ended up in the semi-popular crowd, whereas Lucas remained on the fringe like usual. He could have moved up the food chain if he actually cared, but he didn't. What kills me is there were many times I *did* care.

Times I chose *them*—people whose faces I can hardly picture now—over him.

*What about the night before his deployment? Remember that?*

The reproachful question stops me dead in my tracks. What the hell *is* that? I hear a rattling in the bushes to my left, but I'm pretty sure rattlesnakes aren't native to Spain.

Do I remember the night before Lucas's deployment? Of course I do. It's easy to recall moments when you sucked at life on an epic scale. I'd been out with Brent and lost track of time, *again*, which meant I was an hour late for Lucas's farewell dinner. He shrugged it off like it was no big deal because that's how Lucas is—gracious, forgiving, generous—but for the next five miles, all I can think about is how I could have had *one more hour* with my brother.

Now I'd trade all my months with Brent for one more minute.

The road descends and my thoughts spiral down with it, until I'm in full on ranting and raving mode. "It isn't fair!" I scream across the valley.

My cry bounces off the rock walls and slams back into me, as hot and oppressive as the afternoon sun beating down on my bare shoulders.

*You're right. Life isn't fair. Get used to it.*

"But why Lucas? He was perfect! What's the point of trying to be good, of following rules, obeying orders? Things get screwed up regardless!"

Yes, I'm talking to myself like a crazy person, but it brings relief like nothing on this pilgrimage has so far. Not last night's binge session, not all the candles in all the pretty sanctuaries, not the array of nice people I've met with their "Kumbaya" outlooks on life.

A bend in the road leads to a pilgrim shrine made of stacked stones. Without a second thought, I smash it to pieces. Karate kick it, actually. With the foot I use for crossing soccer balls, which isn't the smartest move, since my big toe starts bleeding through my sock.

This journey is starting to involve a lot more pain than it's worth. How like life.

I pick up one of the toppled stones and carry it to a small grotto in the distance. The shallow cave is filled with colorful flowers planted in clay pots, along with a collection of random saint statues. I'm no good at softball, but I'm tempted to use the stone in my hand for pitching practice. Rage pumps through my arteries and Dad's nickname rings truer than ever: I am a bull who sees nothing but a world painted red.

*Do it. Do it!* screams the sinister voice that keeps following me.

*No, Gabriela,* says another.

While the angel and devil on my shoulders battle it out, something inside me stays my trembling hand. I drop the rock and pull out a candle, muttering as I light the match, "See? I'm playing the game. It's a really *stupid* game, but I'm doing it."

And I'll do whatever it takes to keep Lucas with us. I will pray, do penance, and petition whatever deity requires it. Jehovah, Allah, Thor the frickin' god of thunder—I don't know or much care who I'm talking to anymore.

I just want my brother back.

Reluctantly, I set Lucas's candle in front of some local saint I've never heard of. The guy probably doesn't get as many intercession requests as the A-list of saints, so I'm sure he needs something useful to do. Well, now he has a task.

*What do you say, Gabi?*

This voice belongs to my mother. Another memory flashes across my mind. When I was eight, right before I made my First Communion, I was anxious about memorizing all the right prayers. I'll never forget what my mom said as she secured the lace veil *abuela* sent from Mexico over my mass of unmanageable curls.

"Prayers are like good manners, Gabriela," Mom announced in her classic Army wife style. "There are really only two you need to remember: *please* and *thank you*."

"Please, please, *please*," I pray now with everything I've got.

• • •

My next stop is Rabanal del Camino. From there the dirt road takes an even steeper turn skywards, and a hand-painted road sign tells me I'm about to climb to the highest point of the entire pilgrimage trail. Awesome. If I'd known that, I'd have stayed on the bus a few more hours.

*Push through the pain, mija.*

That's Dad's favorite mantra. It used to serve as the film score for our trio treks, not to mention the ten-mile jogs we'd take when Lucas and I trained hard for soccer. It's legit advice, given the euphoria most athletes experience once they push past their breaking point. Too bad my limit should have shattered miles ago. Or kilometers. Whatever.

It smells like rain. Sure enough, it starts sprinkling as a massive cloud swallows up the road in front of me. I pull out my headlamp and put on my waterproof gear. There was only one poncho in stock at the BX and it was bright pink—my least favorite color—so I'm sure I look like a giant Easter egg.

The sky darkens. I can only see a few yards in front of me, and that's with the headlamp. One wrong step and I'm sliding down a precipice. One wrong turn and I might wander into the forest and lose the path entirely. No one would find me for days. If ever.

Then my parents would have two children to mourn.

*Aaaannd* now I'm hyperventilating. That sad image is enough of a reason to stay alive.

I reach for the tiny rosary around G.I. Lucas's neck. I don't pray it, but it's enough to feel the beads between my fingers as I steady my breathing. Soon I notice a trail of periwinkle flowers growing alongside the road. The five-pointed petals look like little stars, and this fills me with a strange reassurance. So long as I keep my eyes fixed to this purple path, I won't end up in a proverbial ditch somewhere. I'll be okay. I'll make it.

That reminds me. Hippie Harmony said some people believe the *camino* lies directly below the Milky Way, the "pathway to the gods" in multiple mythologies. She claimed the *camino* radiates a special energy due to the stars above it, which is why so many people are drawn to this path specifically. Now, Harmony also claimed she was an inhabitant of the lost city of Atlantis and a gazelle on the Serengeti in her former lives, but the trail of amethyst stars gives me a shred of hope that someone up there is watching out for me.

The dense fog dissipates, revealing another hiker in the distance. I should be relieved, but the heavy atmosphere surrounding this person fails to rise with the mist. At first the pilgrim looks like another Easter egg in a blue poncho, but as I get closer, I make out the distinct image of a woman on her knees. It's hard to tell how old she is because I can't see a single feature of her face, but her weeping sends a shiver through me.

This isn't just a good cry with a pint of ice cream. These are loud, uncontrolled sobs—the kind people only indulge in when they think they're alone.

The woman, her poncho flapping in the wind, bends over before what looks like a giant telephone pole sticking out of a mountain of stones. My plan is to pass by her quickly so she can mourn in peace, but then I notice that the rock pile is manmade.

This is the Cruz de Ferro, one of the most popular stops on the entire pilgrimage. Pilgrims leave their mark here in the form of a rock brought from wherever they started. That's why Lucas gave Seth the crazy blue stone from Afghanistan. That's where this journey truly began.

Seth told me lapis lazuli was a prized mineral during the Renaissance because artists used it to create a deep blue pigment that drew the eye to the most important person in the painting, most often the Virgin Mary.

If this pilgrimage is my masterpiece, then Lucas is the focal point.

I reach into my pocket, but a part of me doesn't want to let go of the stone. I've grown accustomed to its weight, to its rough edges and smooth center, to the sapphire swirls that make it feel like a souvenir from outer space. It's too beautiful to part with.

The sad woman sees me approaching, so she heads down the other side of the rock heap. Her weeping goes with her, leaving behind a harsh wind that harbors her pain and pierces my heart like a sword. I want to know what this woman left behind as her offering, so I climb to the top, to the very spot where she stood.

Photographs, handwritten notes, and torn pieces of clothing cover the thick pole, secured to the beam with tattered rope, fishing wire, and rusted staples (seriously, who carries a stapler on the *camino*?). The random mess makes it impossible to determine the source of the woman's grief, given that her problems blend in with everyone else's agony.

It makes me wonder if my family's situation is all that unfair or even excessive. Maybe it's just life. Normal. A painful part of the journey that must be pushed through.

I unclench my fist and drop the lapis lazuli onto the pile—a brilliant blue beacon in a world of granite. Thousands of stones sit beneath my feet and each one tells a different story. Each one proclaims the truth that there isn't a person on earth who has escaped suffering and loss, the mandatory prerequisites of love.

I descend to the base of the rock pile, and my eyes climb back to the top. Lucas's stone is still shining, and it's the brightest of them all.

# CHAPTER 15

The sun returns beyond the Cruz de Ferro, right when the road drops into a valley of snow-white broom and Spanish lavender. I don't see any other pilgrims until I reach an old Roman bridge at the entrance to the town of Molinaseca, where a woman rests in the middle of the stone arch. She stares into the glass mirror below like she's having a conversation with her own reflection, but lifts her chin when I approach. My eyes travel from her shiny black hair to her swollen belly.

Really now. Who walks the *camino* pregnant?

"What part of the pilgrimage was that for you?" the woman asks. She's wearing a cornflower-blue skirt, not an ugly poncho, so I can't tell if this is same woman I saw weeping. Something tells me it is, but right now her face is the kind of calm made for playing poker. The woman's accent and almond eyes make me think she's Middle Eastern, but her ageless expression gives nothing else away.

"I'm not sure I understand what you mean." I slip off my pack to give my aching shoulders a break.

"A friend once told me there are three stages to every pilgrimage. The first battle is purely physical, because all you can think about is the pain. Then comes the *meseta*—a period when our bodies grow stronger, but the flat landscape grows boring and our spirits are assaulted by regrets we didn't even know we had."

"Yeah, I skipped most of the actual *meseta*, but I've figuratively been there and done that." I take a few gulps from my water bottle. "What's the third stage?"

"The third stage is when our hard outer shell is shed and our true desires are revealed, something that can only happen when you begin to forget yourself entirely. Only then will you feel at home in your own skin. When you accept that this journey, with

157

all its ups and downs, is not an accident." Smiling, the woman rubs her belly bump. "Or so I hear."

"Are you really walking the *camino* like *that*? All alone?"

By which I mean, *Uh, do you really want to risk giving birth behind a bush?*

"Oh, I'm hardly walking alone." She pats her stomach again, her face glowing with a radiance I've never seen in anyone. "None of us are."

This woman reeks of tranquility. If that was really her weeping by the cross, how did her grief transform into such calm? I want to ask her so many things, but before I can say another word, she waves goodbye and crosses the bridge, disappearing below the dip on the other side.

I grab my stuff and start to follow, but by the time I get my pack back on, she's gone. The fastest waddling pregnant woman ever.

Something brushes against my feet. I look down at the piece of windblown paper sticking to my hiking boot. The neon green flier reads:

WANTED: INFORMATION ABOUT PILGRIM KILLED IN RECENT ACCIDENT

*Two days ago, the body of a camino trekker was found at the bottom of a ravine between Cruz de Ferro and Molinaseca. The pilgrim was a young male between the ages of 18–25, with dark brown hair and blue eyes. He carried no identification, so police are unsure of his nationality and do not know how to contact his family. If you know anything at all, please call....*

*Not possible.* I brace myself against the solid bridge. It can't be him. It *isn't* him. The description is too vague. This poor pilgrim could be anyone.

So why can't I stand up without the support of stone?

Guilt. That's why. It's one of the heaviest things on this planet and right now it's threatening to crush my bones to dust. The fog, the mist. It was stupid to walk through that alone. Maybe Seth walked through it, too. Maybe he fell off a cliff and bled out or died from exposure before anyone could do a thing about it.

All because of me. All because I left him.

"Don't be stupid." I force myself upright. Seth has military dog tags, so of course he's identifiable. Unless he took them off. No, stop being paranoid. It isn't him.

Regardless, I think I need a drink.

Molinaseca's town center is tiny, so I step into the first bar I come across. Sweat pours down the back of my neck, and my throat burns with thirst. I push through a wall of people, searching for an open seat at the bar. A surge of shouts tells me this afternoon crowd has nothing to do with the food and everything to do with the soccer game playing on the flat-screen TV.

I find a stool and order a soda, which comes with a complimentary *tapa*—a terra cotta bowl of green olives and potato chips. Good, I could use the extra salt. A few seats down, two guys are in the midst of a debate that's escalating into an argument. The stockier guy has a broad, pancake face and pale, bulging eyes. His companion's sharp features are striking against his olive skin, shaded by whiskers that suggest laziness, not a disheveled look he intended. Based on their accents, the first guy is English and the second is French. Or maybe Belgian. They're squabbling over which team is better: France's FC Lyon or England's Arsenal.

"Oh, who the hell cares?" I mutter, which is strange because when it comes to soccer, I'm usually as much of a freak as the rest of these people. Why am I suddenly so irritable? Why do I want to turn around and slap these diehard fans for failing to realize the world has bigger problems than what they're bickering about?

I unfold the neon flier and set it on the bar. *This* is my problem. This stupid piece of paper, which has the same power over my sweat glands as the *Odyssey* had moments before I learned Lucas was hanging onto life by a tattered thread. A thread those three hags from the underworld are threatening to cut at any moment.

The bartender points to the flier. "Quite a tragedy, eh? Losing someone so young. The kid probably made one mistake, but it cost him everything. It isn't fair when a person your age can't come back from a wrong turn. It isn't right."

One mistake. One wrong turn.

Is that all Seth made by talking to Brent? Was I too hard on him? What if he really is this hiker found at the bottom of the ravine, and I never even gave him the chance to tell his side of the story?

"You know, I think I might have seen him. The young man who was killed," the bartender continues, staring into space as he polishes silverware. "The weather was getting bad, but this guy seemed determined to keep going. Said he needed to reach Santiago by a certain date. Said he had a non-negotiable deadline."

My eyes snap up from the condensation rings on the bar. "What was he like, this guy? Did you catch his name?"

"No name, and an accent that was hard to place. But I remember his drink." The bartender almost smiles. "Red Bull and vodka. An unusual choice for a pilgrim walking the *camino* in the middle of the day."

Yes. It is. And it fills me with relief. There's only one thing Seth—no snob when it comes to a midday drink—despises more than Red Bulls and vodka, and that's "bros" who drink Red Bull and vodka.

Seth is alive. And it gives me wings.

Without warning, the stocky soccer fan next door turns my way. "How about you?"

"Huh?" I almost choke on my soda.

"Yeah, what's your team?" his French/Belgian buddy adds.

*No sudden movements.*

If I take my eyes off the TV and engage the enemy, it will only encourage them and I'll be stuck here all night. I keep my gaze fixed ahead and name the first team that comes to mind.

"Bayern Munich."

"You don't sound German," says the English guy.

"You don't look German either," his French (I'm pretty sure) friend observes.

"I'm not German, but I live in Germany."

"So you're American?"

"That's right. My father is a soldier stationed there."

Frenchie casts a not-so-subtle glance down my tank top. "Explain something to me. Why are there so many American G.I.s here in Europe? Do you really need bases all over the world to feel secure in your superpower status?"

I don't know what to say. Curious eyes from around the pub drift towards us, but I don't want to do this right now. I don't want to play the sole representative of the United States, as if I'm qualified to speak on behalf of my government. My father is still my father, and my country is still my country. Maybe our tribal loyalties are the reason we humans will always be at war, but I don't know how to love some vague notion of *all* humanity. We reserve the ferocity of love for the people and places we have ties to. To the things we know because we live and breathe in them and recognize their scent.

Take these two football fanatics. They're willing to go to blows because of the passion they feel for FC Lyon or Arsenal—*their* team—not for the sport of soccer in general. The line between love and hate may be fine, but I'd rather attempt the tightrope walk than not be able to feel either. It's a fine line between acceptance and apathy, too.

"Look guys, I didn't ask for my country to go to war, or for my family to move to Germany in a manner that you clearly regard as occupation," I finally reply. "As a matter of fact, most soldiers don't want those things either. So lay off, all right?"

"But that doesn't change the fact that your troops are still here. And there. And everywhere. Or that more innocent people are dying in these wars than the soldiers who wage them." My verbal assailant tosses back a shooter of schnapps before swiveling his stool in my direction. "You seem like a smart girl, so perhaps I'm missing something. If you're not a soldier yourself, then why do you defend them?"

Now there's a thought. Why *do* I defend them? Why do I care what the rest of the world thinks when I'm not part of the military—officially, that is—and never have to be?

Maybe it's because I have a strong suspicion this guy has never stuck his neck out for anything greater than a soccer team. Maybe it's because I'm part of a miniscule group of people *not* in uniform who actually know what it's like—the terror of loss lurking around every corner, the turmoil people like my dad and brother have to wade through as they navigate defending the nation they swore to protect, without losing their souls in the process.

I turn to the Brit, hoping to revive an old alliance. "Want to back me up here? It's not like we're fighting overseas alone."

The bloke studies the bottom of his beer glass, both elbows resting on the bar. "Sorry, luv, but no one in Parliament asked me what I thought before they launched the most pointless mission in recent memory."

Awesome. Guess I'm flying solo, then.

Team France scoots closer and his sleazy sneer comes with him. There's enough alcohol on his breath to assure me this situation could take a nosedive real quick. "So you have no justification? No argument? Or are American schools still failing to teach you kids how to think for yourselves?"

There's a line in the sand and this jerk is about to cross it. Living overseas, I've gotten used to bouts of good old American bashing, but this guy's arrogant I-Googled-some-statistics-once attitude makes me want to throw his beer in his face.

"I thought she told you to *lay off*."

This time, I do choke on my drink. That voice. I know that voice. It's a not-lying-at-the-bottom-of-a-ravine voice. I turn and see Seth behind me, his sunburned face unsmiling, his arm no longer encased by a sling. I'm what he's been searching for all this time, but his livid eyes stay glued to the two football fans, not me.

"Ah, now I see. Your boyfriend is a G.I." My bar mate gives me a smirk that suggests this puts me on par with a prostitute. Not to mention makes me a fascist. Then he turns to Seth, his bell glass of fancy beer twirling in his hand. "We were merely engaging the young lady in a friendly political debate that doesn't concern you. Then again, most of the conflicts you Yanks insert yourselves in don't concern you."

"Funny, you frogs didn't say that when the Nazis overran your ass and several thousand American soldiers dead on the beaches of Normandy helped put a stop to it."

That particular zinger makes me tingle all over, I'm not gonna lie. But it doesn't stop me from snapping my head in Seth's direction to hiss, "What are you *doing* here?"

Seth's eyes stick to his foe, but his anger transfers to me like a rerouted current. "What do you think I'm doing here? Once I figured out that you stayed in Burgos, I decided to wait it out. You're lucky I'm patient."

"Hey, you giving the little bird trouble?" the Englishman interjects. Because *now* is the perfect time to come to my aid. "Maybe she doesn't want you following her about."

"That's right," his occasional ally joins in. "Maybe she wants to stay here with civilized men who've progressed further up the evolutionary chain."

"Uh, thanks guys, but I can speak for myself."

No one hears me.

"By the way, I'm Belgian, not French," the scruffier guy continues. "Could you even find it on a map? I'm sure geography isn't one of your strengths."

Based on the toxic levels of testosterone in the air, that last jab is all it takes to light the dynamite. One second Seth and the Belgian guy are standing chest to chest like two enraged roosters, and an instant later a fist slams into Seth's jaw. The punch knocks him back onto a barstool and the pub goes silent. Seth just sits there, rubbing his cheek while the kindling ignites in his eyes. To everyone's surprise, he maintains his composure.

"Glad you got that out of your system, pal, but I'm not looking for a fight," Seth seethes through gritted teeth.

"Too bad." His assailant rolls up his sleeves. "Because I've been waiting for some imbecile with an attitude to walk through those doors all day. What are you doing on the *camino* anyway? Out here seeking forgiveness for your many sins?"

That does it. Game on.

My eyes stay glued to the pompous jerk with more unfounded opinions than a Facebook newsfeed, but I don't need to see Seth's face to hear him suck in his breath like it's the last one he'll ever take.

I jump out of the way seconds before Seth and the Belgian collide. Their bodies twist in a hostile bear hug as they topple pint glasses and send my olive bowl soaring.

"Do something!" I shout to the bartender. He just stands there drying dishes like this is no big deal. After a solid minute, he moves into his office and casually picks up the phone.

"Guys, stop!" I try to get between them, but Seth pushes me out of the way before giving his opponent a solid blow to the gut. "The bartender is calling the cops!"

They don't listen. Two guys in the heat of battle never hear anything but their own raucous grunts and the smack of flesh against bone. Seth didn't start this fight, but it's clear he'll finish it. He's not nearly as smashed as his adversary, plus he has the guy beat in size and formal training. The Belgian only has one thing going for him: Seth's sprained arm happens to be his good arm.

The entire bar gathers around to watch and cheer, including the Arsenal fan—a fair-weather friend in the end. To be honest, I'm surprised people don't start making bets. Our perverse love for the coliseum endures, no doubt about it.

"*Mira! Policía!*"

Three cops burst into the bar before this round of drunken UFC can conclude with a decisive victory. The officers pull the fighters apart, dragging them towards the nearest exit in handcuffs. As they push Seth out the door, he frantically scans the bar for me. Our eyes meet for the first time since Burgos. Blood trickles down his lip and one of his eyes is swelling shut, but the straightforward stare of its adjacent companion tells me all I need to know.

This wasn't just a bar fight. If assault charges are pressed, this is a potential discharge from the U.S. Army, and not an honorable one. Seth is in deep and can't speak more than two words of Spanish to tell his side of the story, which means I'm the only one who can haul him up the cliff he's thrown himself down.

The question is: do I want to?

• • •

It's as startling as it is in the movies—the harsh echo that ricochets along concrete when the lock is turned and the jail cell opens. Seth lifts his eyes from the assortment of stains on his cot. Despite the new facial welts he's added to an already impressive collection, he looks like a little boy. A boy in trouble for throwing rocks through his neighbor's window, though he doesn't have much of a defense because there are chunks of granite lining his pockets.

We don't talk until Seth signs the paperwork and we exit the small police station. Seth rubs his eyes as we step into the bright sunlight. "How'd you do it?"

I shrug. "I told them the truth. I said you weren't the one who started the fight, and that you defended yourself only after the second attack."

Seth's relief is surpassed only by his disbelief. "And that's it? They're not going to press charges?"

"Well, I also told them you were a soldier on R&R, walking the *camino* on behalf of my wounded brother. Officer Fuentes's sister went to university in Madrid and was injured in the terrorist train bombings back in 2004, so he seemed sympathetic to your situation."

Seth massages the red cuff marks around his wrists. "It's nice to know not all Europeans hate my Yankee guts."

My job is finished, so I turn in the direction of the nearest *albergue*. I'm glad Seth is okay. I wasn't about to let my brother's best friend rot in some foreign jail, but that doesn't mean we are any less *done*.

Seth puts a hand on my arm to stop me. "Gabi, wait. Thank you. You're still angry. Obviously. So why didn't you just leave me here?"

Seth doesn't look like a little boy anymore, but he isn't the invincible warrior he once was, either. He looks humbled, taken down a peg or two. It makes his scarred face slightly more inviting, which makes me want to run from it faster than ever. Against his bronzed skin, Seth's irises pop with a blue that contains the entire sky, but his newfound humility isn't enough to soften my resolve. He betrayed my trust. Defending my "honor" in some stupid bar fight doesn't change the fact that he went behind my back. That he still sees me as a kid who needs to be protected, not as a partner.

"A pilgrim died not far from here the other day," I say. "He was about our age."

Seth drops his head. "I heard. How tragic."

"So that's why. I did it for Lucas." I pull my arm away and walk. "I did it because he would have a hard time forgiving me if I hadn't."

# CHAPTER 16

Today is the hardest day of the entire *camino*—a straight uphill climb that lasts several hours and doesn't quit. The full-body assault feels even worse with Seth on my tail. At least the guy took the hint and keeps his distance, letting me walk up ahead alone.

Finishing this trek together doesn't mean we have to like each other. Seth doesn't try to explain why he encouraged Brent to dump me, and I don't care to ask. If I'm honest, I'm afraid to ask. Afraid to know the reason Brent and Seth both think going to college with me, planning a future with me, is an especially bad idea.

I look up and see wet-cement clouds rolling in, clouds that could crack open at any moment. The coverage is a good thing after climbing for two hours without shade. For the next few kilometers, the road levels out and the yellow *camino* arrows guide us through ghost towns of crumbling buildings tagged with slogans like *Una Galicia libre!* After living in Texas, I'm familiar with separatist sentiments, but I never knew there were multiple parts of Spain that want to break off from the rest of the country. All the visual reminders make me wonder what happens to a functioning union when it loses one of its most vital limbs.

To a family when it loses its Lucas.

"You out here all on your own, sugar?"

I've steadied my breathing by keeping my eyes fixed to the white line hugging the shoulder of the asphalt road, but this melodic voice calls me to attention. The distinct Texas drawl belongs to a woman sitting in a small shack that resembles the roadside fruit stands near my grandparents' farm in Michigan.

I almost walked by without noticing her, which is hard to believe since this woman is larger than life, like most things from her home state. She's fit, busty, and her orange skin suggests she's spent much of her life by pools or in tanning beds. The woman wears a bejeweled, cherry-red cowboy hat that's so stereotypically Texas, it's laughable. The hat clashes with the rest of her sporty hiker ensemble, making it clear she "ain't from around here."

"It's a joke," the woman says when she sees me staring at the ridiculous boat on top of her head. "A few pilgrims I met back in Pamplona got a kick out of my accent, so they bought me this tacky cowboy hat."

I laugh. "I've never seen one like it outside of a Miss Rodeo America pageant."

"Which is ironic, since I hate rodeos almost as much as I hate beauty pageants. But at least the wide brim makes for good shade," the woman chuckles. "You look about my daughter's age. What are you, eighteen?"

"Not quite." Come to think of it, what *is* today's date?

"Why don't you come in and take a load off. I won't bite."

I join the woman on a rickety bench beneath the shack's metal awning. Something stirs inside me. It's a feeling most would call homesickness, but is it even possible to feel homesick for multiple places? "I take it you're from the Lone Star State?"

"Now what on earth makes you think that?" The woman gives me a smile as generous as the rest of her demeanor. "The name's Nancy."

Nancy takes a gulp from her water bottle, then raises a hand to her mouth, struggling to hold the liquid in. "Wait a minute, that's *him*! Hell, I was hoping to run into y'all!"

I glance down the road, relieved to see she isn't gesturing at Seth. Nancy isn't pointing to a person at all; she's pointing to G.I. Lucas, back in his privileged position at the top of my pack.

I don't get her enthusiasm. "Uh, are you an admirer of circa 1990 collector toys?"

"Ha! No, though I think my son had that exact same doll." Nancy drops her thick accent and imitates the tone of a snooty art collector. "Pardon me, I mean *action figure*."

"Yeah, my brother gets mad when I call it a doll, too."

"Lucas, right? I gotta say, I really admire what you're doing for him, darling."

Now it's my turn to almost choke. "How do you know my brother's name?"

Nancy whips out her hot-pink phone. "Girl, don't you know? Your medieval pilgrimage has gone viral, twenty-first-century style."

She hands me the phone so I can see the blog page, one that's received thousands of hits, according to the stats bar. Now, either I'm super dehydrated, or someone is playing a sick joke on me. As I read the blog's title, I feel faint. And not from the altitude.

*In Honor of PV2 Lucas Santiago.*

The website documents G.I. Lucas's entire journey. The silly doll is everywhere, living it up like an actual pilgrim. G.I. Lucas standing in front of a yellow arrow marking the *camino*. G.I. Lucas crossing a medieval footbridge on the back of a *burro*. G.I. Lucas with red Irache wine all over his face. G.I. Lucas next to the hotel Hemingway stayed in when he wrote about the running of the bulls.

I read the short blurb describing my brother's condition and my blood bubbles over. Talk about an invasion of privacy. The blog is simple, but I have to keep scrolling because there are so many comments. Hundreds of comments, all posted by people I do not know. All well-wishes from total strangers.

*Wake up soon, Lucas. Come on back home.*

*Thank you for your sacrifice. I'm sorry it cost so much.*

*We're praying for you, Lucas. For you and your family.*

On and on the comments go, but I can't read too far before they blur together. The boil inside me reduces to a simmer as I lift my watering eyes. "Who did this?"

Nancy's smile fades. "You're tellin' me you don't know, hon?"

I shake my head, but of course I *do* know. There's only one answer to my question, it just happens to be the answer that makes me want to crawl inside myself and collapse like an imploding star. "I am such a jerk."

"Oh, I doubt that." Nancy points to a link in the blog corner that reads: SUPPORT LUCAS HERE. "You should probably find a way to check that PayPal account, though. I'm sure lots of folks are showing their sympathy in more material ways."

With that, Nancy wishes me luck and continues up the mountain. I'm too shaky to walk. Soon the rain mist becomes a monsoon, and I glimpse a lone figure ascending the hill—a walker wearing nothing to protect him from the elements but a soaked ARMY T-shirt that gives him away at once.

"Need a break?" The roadside hut provides some shelter, but by now the rain is blowing in sideways. "I'm willing to share this prime piece of real estate."

Beads of water drip down Seth's face. He studies me with suspicion, as if he's trying to figure out if I've set some kind of booby trap. It's a legitimate concern, considering the intensity of my silent treatment. With an exhausted groan, he removes his pack and starts digging through it for his rain jacket. "What made you wait for me?"

"Www.lucasonthecamino.com."

"Oh." He flops down beside me. "That."

"What do you mean, *oh that*? Why didn't you tell me sooner?"

"Well, first because you disappeared, and then because you wouldn't answer your phone, and then because I was in jail, and finally because you refused to speak to me."

"Okay, I suppose that made things difficult," I concede. "Sorry I split, I just . . . wait a minute. I still have a right to be pissed about Brent. What'd you say to make him kick me to the curb like a piece of frat house furniture?"

"Why does it matter? You don't seem too torn up about it."

On the surface, no. I'm probably more upset than even I realize, but now is not the time to enter a chasm of repressed emotions. Dad isn't the only Santiago with a strong sense of pride. Brent was the one who cheated, but being played like a fiddle still feels like a major character flaw. Like something I should be embarrassed about because it says something about *me*.

"I am torn up, but the situation with Lucas put things into perspective real quick." My voice cracks, so I keep going before it splinters. "Then there's Brent's big confession. Who knows how long *that's* been going on. Since the day I left, probably. Whatever, it's for the best. It's not like there'd be any less opportunity for him to cheat at a massive state school like UT."

"Which isn't where you belong anyway," Seth replies.

"What do you mean by that?" I assume he's slamming me, saying I'm not smart enough to do well there, or at any college for that matter.

"Just what I said. You don't belong at a school like that. It's too big, too impersonal, too much of a playground for stunted adolescents."

I release a clip of a laugh. "You talk like you know me."

Seth holds his water bottle to his lips and smirks. "I do know you."

Okay, so based on his last insightful comment he actually *might*, but that just freaks me out. There's nothing as disturbing as a person who can pinpoint personality traits you've failed to recognize yourself. It means there's nowhere to hide. "Back to Brent. I want to know what you said to him. Word for word."

"I'll show you the e-mail if you want, but all I really said was that I knew he was messing around on you. His social media updates made that clear. Nothing overt on his part, I could just tell. I told him I'd let you know if he didn't have the guts to do it himself. And then I'd hunt him down without mercy."

"How can you *just tell* something like that without any proof?"

Seth shrugs. "You girls have your ways of communicating things only other girls can read, and so do us guys. It also helped that he kept posting nonstop about 'Cali,' as he liked to call it in his more asinine 'I sooo wish I was the backup bassist to 311' moments. That's how I guessed he was leading you on about UT-Austin, so I contacted a few friends back in San Antonio and they confirmed that your beloved Brent is a bit of a sleazebag."

"Yeah, he can't be the brightest bulb in the store if he actually thought he could get away with cheating," I admit. "The Army takes 'it's a small world' to a whole new level."

Seth cracks his knuckles. "You sure know how to pick 'em."

I feel sick, but also relieved that I escaped Brent's lies before I gave the creep any more of me. "Look, I appreciate you looking out for me, but it's still annoying that you took it upon yourself to mediate the termination of my two-year relationship."

Seth pats me on the knee in a brotherly fashion, only Lucas's support taps never left me with goose bumps. "Pardon the Dr. Phil moment, but I'm pretty sure it isn't the length of the relationship that matters. It's the depth. And trust me, you'd never dive very far with a guy like that. He's shallower than my cousin's kiddie pool."

After all this, I don't plan on trusting anyone for a long time. Still, I can't help snickering at Seth's relationship advice. For as long as he's been friends with Lucas, he's never mentioned a single steady girlfriend. Not one. "And you're telling me you've had enough failed romances to know the different degrees of depth? Yeah, right, Romeo."

"You're right. I haven't." Seth's lips curl into a funny half-smile, but his eyes stay fixed on the rain river rushing down the mountainside. "Maybe I haven't found a girl brave enough to wade into the deep end yet. Maybe I never will, now that the chlorine has been replaced by toxic sludge."

"Uh, this pool analogy is getting out of hand. I don't follow."

Seth chuckles, but his fading smile tells me he's laughing away something that requires stronger ammunition. "Think about it, Gabi. I'm a soldier who's spent the past six months hanging out with a bunch of smelly dudes. No respectable girl will want to wade the depths of my perverted mind now."

No, that's not it. He's hiding something. Seth's mind may be plenty randy, but lust isn't the vice he's trying to conceal. His secret has something to do with Lucas.

"You've got to stop blaming yourself, Seth. What happened to Lucas was—"

"A *mistake*." Seth cuts me off, slipping back into shutdown mode. "Got that? What happened to Lucas *never* should have happened. Don't let anyone try to smooth things over and tell you otherwise. If they do, I don't care if it's a room full of five-star generals and congressmen in expensive suits, they're lying. And you can tell them Private Russo said so."

# CHAPTER 17

We hit the road as soon as there's a break in the rain, but walking together feels awkward. The comfortable silence we established weeks ago is strained.

"What made you start the blog?" I ask Seth.

He shrugs. "I had our G.I. Lucas photos stored on my phone, so I figured I'd upload them and see if I could rake in some donations while I was at it."

He makes himself sound so mercenary, but I know that isn't the case. A blog is *so* not Seth's style.

"Who knows how much physical therapy Lucas will need later on," he adds. "That stuff can get expensive."

Yeah, so can funerals. I don't say it out loud, but I can tell Seth is thinking it, too. The f-word hangs between us, putting a damper on a plenty-damp atmosphere. I don't want to think about the sand trickling down the hourglass. I can only keep moving if I know I'm walking for a *reason*. At least the generous response to Seth's blog gives me hope that what we're doing matters. Maybe it even has the kind of meaning that a miracle requires.

"So the website just blew up all on its own?" The fact that Seth exposed my brother to the world without my permission should make me furious, but deep down I know Lucas wouldn't mind. "You must have a lot of Facebook friends."

Seth laughs. "I have, like, thirty Facebook friends."

That's an understatement because I've seen his profile and he easily has a hundred, but I get what he means. Online as in life, Seth runs with a smaller, closer circle than most.

"Nothing really happened until I shared the link with one of those goofy websites—you know, the kind that post things like '10 Funniest Cats of the Week'? Anyway, they ended up featuring it, and from there the whole thing spread like a kindergarten cold virus."

"So what you're telling me is the best way to get people to care about our troops is to highlight their suffering alongside videos of Siamese sneak attacks?"

This comes out whinier than I intended. I appreciate that so many strangers shared their condolences on Seth's blog, but why does *reality* have to go viral and become a trend first? We've been at war for years. Guys like my brother are nothing new.

"Speaking as a soldier, I don't want anyone's pity," Seth replies. "I willingly signed up for this life, but yeah, it would be nice if more civilians noticed how much it costs. I haven't even been back to the States yet, but talking to old friends makes me feel like I've been living on another planet. It's like nothing ever changes. Like no one even realizes we're at war. Back home, life goes on like normal and the main topic of conversation is which character from a favorite TV series got the axe, even though there are *real* people dying overseas every day."

Wait, what home is he talking about? Texas? No, that's right—because Seth's parents are divorced, he's basically lived a double life. An Army brat upbringing with his dad, but with consistent summer vacations in the small New England town where his mom lives.

"I mean, I could have just killed someone, but when I call home all my mom can go on about is how so-and-so is dating/marrying/having a baby with so-and-so, and I can't even force myself to pretend I care." Seth sighs. "It'll be weird . . . going home."

*Has* Seth killed anyone? Before I can ask, a low rumble in the distance warns of an approaching thunderstorm. We're off the highway now, back on a forested dirt trail that's become increasingly rocky and narrow. If the rain comes now, it's going to get muddy.

"Gabi, get back!" Seth grabs me by the pack, slamming me against the embankment that rises up on both sides of the road. I turn to see what he's freaking out about.

It's a stampede.

The "thunder" comes from six gigantic cows, racing down the steep path in a single file. That's several tons of organic, grass-fed beef, just as deadly as the cows on steroids when there's nowhere to hide. The earthen walls on either side of us create a kind of tunnel, and there isn't enough time to scramble up the steep ridge.

"There's no way out!"

"Get back against the wall." Seth stretches his arm out across my chest, as if his bicep, impressive though it may be, can actually prevent me from being trampled to death. Blood races to my head; it's like someone is beatboxing inside my brain. I pinch my eyes shut, press myself into the wall of soil, and wait for the bone-crunching body slam.

A musty, barnyard smell blows past my cheeks. I hear the heifers' labored breathing as they race by. Heavy hooves pound the ground inches from our feet. Seth squeezes my hand, but the searing pain of broken toes never arrives. I open my eyes. They're gone.

The cow scent lingers, but manure has never smelled so sweet. The earthy aroma reeks of life—the kind of life that only becomes precious when it's *this close* to being snatched away.

"Holy crap," Seth exhales.

"No kidding." Right now cow dung really does feel sacred, just like everything else in the natural world that reminds us of mortality.

"What the—? Look!"

I follow Seth's index finger. A large black donkey rounds the bend, the caboose to this wagon train of destruction. On his back sits the madman responsible for our near-death experience. The *burro* blows past us at top speed (for a donkey), and the rancher raises his hat in a friendly salute, as if his wild beasts did *not* almost kill us.

*"Buen camino, peregrinos!"*

Seth and I look at each other, mouths hanging open. Then we burst out laughing.

My legs give way and I slide down the wall to the dirt floor, relishing the feel of mud between my fingers. "That was crazy! Not to mention close."

Before Seth responds, a loud *crack!* has me scrambling back to my feet. The weight of my pack shifts and I lose my balance, face planting right into a puddle.

Seth helps me up. He's laughing so hard he's almost crying. "That time it really was thunder. Poor Gabi. You're disgusting." He wipes a smudge of dirt from my nose.

My response to this semi-sweet gesture? Scooping up a handful of mud and slamming it down on Seth's head. Top that, bucko.

For a moment Seth looks pissed, but his eyes give him away. They're smiling and as far as I know, he isn't Irish. "That's how you want to play, Santiago?"

"Bring it on, Russo."

This is not a game. This is an all-out war. I may not have Seth's training, but Lucas and I used to dress up in Dad's old fatigues and played a more violent version of Capture the Flag that involved organic projectiles. In other words, I'm an expert at flinging mud balls.

*Bull's-eye!* I get a good hit in, but before I can strike again, Seth wraps his arms around my waist and tackles me to the ground. Shaking his head like a wet dog, he flings the lovely mud hat I made him back on my face.

"Truce! You're violating international law. Remember the Geneva Convention! The *Geneva Convention!*" I scream as Seth tickles me. I'm laughing so hard my insides hurt.

Seth's face is inches from mine. I can't tell if he wants to kiss me, or slam mud into my mouth. He's covered in so much sludge that he looks like Martin Sheen in *Apocalypse Now*, but instead of shouting, "The horror! The horror!" he flashes a white smile. "Come on, we should get cleaned up. I think I saw lightning."

We exit the cow alley of death only to find another dilapidated village at the top of the hill. The place is a total time warp. All the houses have the same tile roofs and sea-green shutters, but the only signs of life are the pigs in the front yards and the gardens filled with this huge leafy plant that looks like a cross between cabbage and kale. I try to wash up in the fountain at the center of this ghost town, but that only smears the mud and makes the mess worse.

"How about we hang out in there?" Seth suggests as a flash of white streaks across the dark sky like chalk on a blackboard. "Looks like a nice place to ride out a storm."

The sarcastic lilt in Seth's voice tells me the shelter he has in mind is far from ideal. Sure enough, I turn around and see an old, abandoned house with boarded-up windows, covered in out-of-control weeds. It's a total dump.

We take off our backpacks so we can squeeze through a gap between the boards nailed over the opening where the front door should be. Thankfully, the house is semi-dry, even if it's rotting from the inside out. Seth gathers scraps of wood left over from a staircase lying in shambles. He pulls out a piece of flint from his pack and starts making a fire in the hearth, its stone covered in a layer of lichen. I peer over his shoulder, impressed by yet another useful Boy Scout skill. Or maybe I'm just impressed by the way Seth's damp shirt clings to his lean back as he crouches in front of the fireplace.

Wait, *what*? Where did *that* come from?

"Gross. All that mold has got to be a serious health hazard," I blurt out, alarmed by the thought that just passed through my head.

"Hey, if my underwear is soaking wet, then so is yours. Who cares about a little mold at that point?" Seth stands and takes a step back to admire the emerging flames. "Look at you—you're shaking. Get closer to the fire, silly."

I take a seat on the hearth's stone bench, and Seth sits beside me. We don't talk, but we don't have to. What happened outside in the mud—the play, the laughter, the *sparks*—was weird. And unexpected. And kind of exciting.

And neither of us knows what to do about it.

I'm as warm as I'm going to get. Too warm, probably. "I think I'll explore a bit."

"All right." Seth doesn't look up. He keeps his eyes fixed on the flames, almost like he's more afraid of getting burned by me.

I move from the fireplace to the adjacent dining room. There's no furniture. A dusty antique light fixture hangs from the ceiling and yellowed paper peels off the walls in torn strips.

"I wonder who used lived here," I call out. "And why they left."

Seth's voice echoes back to me from the other room. "Earlier this morning, I talked with a Spanish pilgrim who told me that a lot of the farming communities in northern Spain are shrinking due to the country's negative birthrate. Almost all of the young people are moving to big cities like Barcelona or Madrid to look for work."

"But this house has been empty for a long time." I kneel in front of a built-in bookcase in the far corner of the dining room. On the lower shelf, behind a curtain of cobwebs, a picture frame lies face-down. I pick it up and meet the stare of a stoic man, his chest lined with medallions that proudly announce his profession. "Hey Seth, come look at this."

By the time I feel Seth's solid presence behind me, I've had a chance to get familiar with the other faces in the black-and-white photograph. Standing beside the imposing man is a short, pear-shaped woman and two young children, a boy and a girl. The same look of longing haunts each pair of dark eyes.

Seth studies the family portrait. "I bet they're Sephardic Jews."

He points to the large pendant hanging around the woman's neck—an open hand with a jeweled eye centered in the palm. "That's a *hamsa*, an amulet of protection popular in Sephardic Judaism. My grandma has them all over her house to ward off the evil eye."

"Sephardic?"

"Jews who lived in Spain until they were kicked out of the country in 1492."

"But this photograph was taken in the 1930s or 40s," I observe. "Why would a Jewish family still live in Spain if they were exiled centuries earlier?"

Seth shrugs. "Some converted to Christianity on paper, but still practiced their religion in secret. I heard a rumor that during World War II, Spain's leader, Francisco Franco, drafted a list of all the Jewish families still in Iberia and handed it over to Hitler. Spain was officially neutral during the war, but if the man in this photo was a soldier, maybe he caught wind of Franco's list and got his family the hell out of Dodge while they still had a chance."

"How do you know all this?"

"My grandma is Sephardic. Her family also left Spain right before the war," Seth explains. "She used to tell me all kinds of stories about growing up in Andalucía. 'In Granada there are pomegranates as big as your head,' Grammy always said."

How strange. Seth and I both have Spanish ancestors, but they emigrated for very different reasons. Mine left to seek a better life in a virginal land across the sea, and Seth's fled to seek any life at all. I think of his family scattered across the planet—first because of their ethnicity, then because of their military legacy. "Do you think it will always be like this?"

"Like what?" Seth asks.

I run through a mental list of all the places I've lived, including the pit stops along the way. "Do you think there will always be people destined to wander? People who never get to feel like they have an actual home?"

Seth brushes the dust from the photo's frame and sets it upright. "Yes."

That's all he says, but it's enough. The thought of other rootless pilgrims scattered throughout history is strangely comforting. It means having a home might just be the exception, not the rule.

It means we're not alone.

• • •

"What. The. Heck."

Back at the fireplace, a gray striped cat lounges on top of my bag. In G.I. Lucas's spot. The friendly feline gets up to rub against our ankles, but his angry, scrunched-up face and the chunk missing from his left ear tell me he's more of a fighter than a lover.

"Hey, little guy. Where'd you come from?" Seth crouches down to pet the purr machine, but I've got other concerns.

"Seth, what did you do with G.I. Lucas?"

"Don't look at me." Seth glances around the room. "Did you move him for a photo op?"

"No. He was on my pack when we entered the house." I study the cat, trying to determine if an animal his size is capable of dragging a doll to some hidden lair. Then I hear it. Laughter, followed by the hollow ricochet of a ball being kicked down the street.

Seth is out the door in two seconds flat. I've never seen him move so fast, even though the cat had him enthralled an instant earlier. I'm right on his heels, just in time to see Seth chasing two boys down the block. A semi-deflated soccer ball sits at my feet.

What just happened? Maybe the two kids followed us into the house—thinking they were about to spy on a stormy make-out session—and saw a tempting toy marketed to their age and gender instead. But even if they lifted G.I. Lucas while we were in the other room, that doesn't explain Seth's intense reaction.

Something is wrong.

The rain slows to a trickle and the thunder has moved on, so I jog after Seth until I reach the village church. He's pacing back and forth in front of the entrance, kicking rocks.

"Whoa, calm down, dude. It's just a doll."

"No. It's not. Wait until I get my hands on those little punks," Seth seethes through gritted teeth, his eyes ablaze. He points to the church. "They ran inside. What's the protocol here, Gabi? Cause if I go in there, I'm going to raise hell."

"I'll go," I reply, still bewildered. Why is Seth so upset? Sure, G.I. Lucas has sentimental value and it's messed up that the little brats stole him, but they're just kids. "Wait here. And take a few deep breaths while you're at it."

I pull open the heavy door and enter an empty sanctuary— small, cool, and dimly lit. Filled with perfect hiding places for two little boys. My footsteps trample the silence as I make my way down the aisle, peering beneath each pew, until I reach the altar where a large and intimidating crucifix hangs from the ceiling.

Not exactly the kind of refuge where you'd expect to find two thieves.

A door to the right of the altar opens and a robed priest steps out, dragging the two boys behind him. By the ears. He pauses to bow before the altar, pulling the boys' heads down with him in involuntary reverence, before approaching me.

"I believe these two took something that belongs to you," the priest grumbles. The boys remain silent, but they wriggle beneath the balding man's grasp, their big brown eyes locked on me. "*Elias, Javier. Dónde está?*"

Elias and Javier must be about ten or eleven. They start arguing, each blaming the other for what happened, until the irritated priest snaps, "*Alto! Mirad a la chica.*"

Both boys turn to me, surprised when I ask them in Spanish, "Can I please have the toy back? It's very special to me."

"You mean G.I. Joe?" one of the boys replies, his smug smirk giving him away as the instigator. He shrugs. "*Lo siento.* Haven't seen him."

"Javier!" The priest squeezes the haughty boy's ear and threatens to call their parents, which has his timid friend turning Judas in no time. The quieter boy points to one of the church's side chapels.

"Over there, *padre*!" Elias cries. "Javier hid it over there. We were going to give it back, *padre*. I promise."

"The only promise I want to hear after this blatant act of theft is that I'll be seeing you both in Confession this week." Without warning, the priest's tone turns gentle and he releases his grip. "Now. What do you say to the *pobre peregrina* you've tortured with your cruel tricks?"

"*Lo siento.* Sorry," the boys mutter in unison before racing down the aisle and out the door. All I can say is they better keep moving while Seth is down for the count.

"Little demons, the pair of them," the priest mutters, a playful glimmer in his eye. "But with grace and a lot of prayers, they'll turn out all right."

"Thanks for your help, father. Though I'm not sure you needed to be so hard on them."

"Unruly children *want* someone to be hard on them. There is freedom in self-discipline, for those ruled by their desires soon become slaves to them. Sometimes firmness is the only way boys like that know someone cares. Cares enough to hold them accountable for their actions. And boys like that soon become men." The priest smiles, which makes him seem less crotchety. "*Venga.* Let us go rescue our brave hostage."

I join him in the side chapel, where G.I. Lucas stands on the little altar before a row of vigil candles, smack dab in the middle of the Blessed Virgin and St. James. It's a slightly sacrilegious—not to mention slightly hilarious—sight.

"*Madre de Dios*." The priest snorts out a laugh. "*Que ridiculo*."

My buried chuckle never makes it out of me. That's because this mixture of camouflage and sanctity is a stark reminder of that September night when millions of Americans lit candles to remember those who met their end in smoke and tragedy.

Maybe that's what this tealight thing is all about. Maybe it isn't about bargaining with God or trying to buy an answer to a prayer. It's about remembering a person, a soul. The silent flicker of the flame embodies what it means to *wait*, to endure, to be a dogged ember in a pile of coal, refusing to crumble to ash.

"It is a bit of a contradiction," I finally say. "A soldier up there with the saints."

"We are all called to be saints," the priest replies, turning from the altar to a stained-glass window featuring the Spanish mystic, Teresa of Avila. "That sweet little boy, Elias. Once I asked him what made a person a saint, and he told me something very profound. He pointed to this window and said without hesitation, 'A saint is someone who lets the light shine through.'"

I think of Matteo's frequent pearls of wisdom and smile. "From the mouths of babes."

The priest smiles back. "You are a pilgrim, no? Then surely you've learned that your journey is nothing but one massive contradiction."

I pull out a candle and light it with one already on the altar. "What do you mean?"

"Many pilgrims walk the *camino* in search of solitude, but find themselves connecting with other people in deeper ways than they ever thought possible. Some walk it for recreation and are surprised to find religion, whereas others looking for a supernatural experience end up realizing how earthbound they are." The old man lifts his hand and makes the sign of the cross in the air. "*Sí*, it's all about the contradictions, the crossroads. That's where life's gritty, messy, wonderful truths are waiting to be found."

I survey the statue of St. James, dressed like a medieval pilgrim with his staff and scallop shell. For some reason, the face of Becky Anderson, a childhood friend from my years in the Bible Belt, comes to mind. One time, after seeing Grandma Guadalupe's impressive collection of saint figurines, a very concerned Becky informed me that my family was going to hell for idolatry. A few weeks later, we encountered my *abuela* on her knees in the middle of the living room, praying the rosary with a nun on TV. The final straw was the time we walked into the kitchen for an after-school snack and were greeted by an iconic image in loose, leathery skin. *Abuela* likes to iron Dad's uniforms wearing nothing but her bra and underwear, since the heat of the iron makes her "*tengo mucho calor, Gabrielita.*"

After that, traumatized Becky wasn't allowed to come over anymore. That's when I knew we Santiagos were different. That not all families asked St. Anthony to help them find their keys.

"So why pray to saints at all?" I ask the priest. "They're just people."

Yeah, *dead* people.

The priest's grin tells me this is one of his all-time favorite theological questions. "Tell me, *niña*, when faced with a serious problem, what do many people ask their friends to do for them? Send up a kind word to heaven on their behalf, no? It's the same with the saints. They *are* just people, but perhaps they have a better perspective than we have down here."

The priest points down the aisle to the open door the boys left ajar. A thick beam of sunlight cuts through the shadows at the back of the church, and specks of sparkling dust float in its wake. "The road out there is long and full of trials. It can't hurt to call on friends who have already walked the way."

"I guess that makes sense." I reach for G.I. Lucas and prepare to hit that road myself, only this talkative father isn't quite finished with his homily.

"Never forget, *niña*. The brightest lights are often so dazzling that it's hard to look at them for long. That's because the lights aren't meant to be adored; they're meant to illuminate. To point beyond themselves."

"Thanks, father." By this point, I have no idea what he's talking about.

"What's his name?" the esoteric cleric asks as I turn to leave.

I pause. "Who?"

He points to the toy in my hands. "The light that symbol represents. The bright boy who's had many people in his life who were hard on him because they cared."

I don't understand how this stranger can know all that just from looking at a crumpled photo taped to an action figure's face, but it assures me there are things in this world that cannot be rationally explained.

"*Lucas*," I reply. "*Su nombre es Lucas.*"

# CHAPTER 18

By the time our G.I. Lucas rescue mission is complete, it's raining again, but because it's so late in the afternoon, we have no choice but to put on our rain gear and continue walking.

"Do you think he'll follow us the rest of the way to Santiago?" I look down at the cat with the angry face and the relentless purr. He's been walking with us for a good mile. We reach a stone bridge and the feline jumps onto the ledge, arching his back and demanding to be petted. Aggressively.

"Hey, as traveling companions go, he's far easier to please than you." Seth winks, then stops to run his hand along the cat's damp back. The purring escalates.

I laugh. "Who knew a guy afraid of chickens would be so enamored with cats."

"Cats kill chickens, my friend. Which is why they're awesome."

This bridge must be the end of the kitty's turf, because he refuses to cross it. You'd have thought Seth was saying goodbye to his favorite childhood pet, based on the way he strokes the matted thing for a good five minutes before I drag him to the other side.

I can't help smiling at the pitiful expression on his face. "You are full of surprises, Russo. Is that an itty-bitty tear I see in the corner of your wittle eye?"

"You're pushing it, Santiago." Grinning, Seth gives me a gentle shove, right into a puddle. "Do I need to repeat the muddy lesson in respect I gave you a few hours ago?"

I hold up my hands in surrender. "I'm not stupid enough to challenge a proven war criminal twice."

I'm joking of course, but Seth flinches like I've slapped him across the face. Then it's radio silence for the next four miles.

Our destination is a mountaintop village that's supposed to have the most amazing views on the entire *camino*, but thanks to all the unexpected stops today, the sun is long gone by the time we get close. We pull out our headlamps and continue climbing into the darkness.

The mountain air smells of woodstove fires, fresh rain, and manure—a pungent mixture I'll forever associate with this place. As we enter the village, my headlamp light passes over a stone hut shaped like a beehive—our first clue that O Cebreiro is something special. The round cottage has a thatched roof and low doorway that gives it a distinct hobbit-hole vibe.

"Wait, I saw a picture of something like this in one of Lucas's history books." Seth stops to touch the wet straw. "Except that photo was of a medieval monastery in Ireland."

"Then we must have teleported through time and across the ocean, because that's exactly what this place feels like. And I'm not just talking about the abrupt weather change." I pause, straining to hear beyond the patter of rain. "Please tell me you hear the music too and I'm not losing my mind."

The haunting drone comes from the center of the village, which otherwise is as dead as the rest of the ghost towns we walked through today. Seth's gaping mouth confirms that I'm not the only one who hears the distinct sounds of bagpipes and a Celtic fiddle. The eerie duet dances through the darkness, growing louder with each step we take.

Honestly, I'm a little disappointed to discover that the wailing notes aren't emanating from a caravan of Irish tinkers or burly Scots seated around a campfire. The reality is far less romantic. A brightly-lit gift shop appears ahead of us, and we discover that the bagpipe music is blaring from loudspeakers in its open doorway.

"Uh, where *are* we?" Seth mutters.

"Spain the last time I checked, though I'm starting to wonder."

We duck inside the gift shop because: a) neither of us can stand to be in the rain for one more minute, and b) if the owner of the shop is trying *this hard* to attract customers, we've got to see what this place is all about. Most of the souvenirs are Celtic-inspired knickknacks—silver jewelry twisted into knotted designs, Irish penny whistles, and jars of Galician honey so thick and black it looks more like molasses. Also, a ton of Enya CDs.

We're the only people here. We warm ourselves in the store's heat for about twenty minutes, so I feel obligated to buy something. And what else does one buy in such a store but a sheep refrigerator magnet (made with local wool) that proclaims "I [Heart] Ewe"?

A studious-looking man sits behind the cash register, absorbed in an Umberto Eco novel. The flecks of gray in his goatee suggest he's in his forties, but when he raises his eyes and sees that he has a customer, the enthusiasm engulfing his face makes him seem younger than me.

"Will that be all?" he asks in a dialect that barely sounds like Spanish.

"Yes. Thank you." If I can get the guy to talk again, maybe I'll be able to figure out what's up with his bizarre accent. "You own a very unique shop. This village reminds me of Ireland. Not that I've ever been there."

The shopkeeper laughs, his brogue softening a bit. "That's because we Galicians are descendants of the ancient Celts. In fact, of the seven Celtic kingdoms, Galicia is by far the oldest, which makes us more Gaelic than the Irish *and* Scottish. Though don't try to tell them that!" The animated man produces a large instrument from behind the counter. "*Mira.* This, *señorita*, is a *gaita*. Made from a goat's stomach. Similar to the bagpipe, see?"

"Ah. Interesting." I smile and nod, but what I'm really wondering is how people came up with the disgusting idea to make musical instruments out of animal organs in the first place. I don't want to be rude, but with Seth's famished eyes boring into my back, I'm hoping I haven't just invited this shopkeeper to launch into a lengthy diatribe on the seven Celtic kingdoms and why Galicia is *numero uno*. He's super friendly, but the intense glimmer in his gaze also makes me question his sanity. "We had a long walk today, *señor*. Would you mind pointing us in the direction of the pilgrim *albergue*?"

The shopkeeper's eyes bulge behind his thick glasses. "No one told you, *peregrina*? All this rain has resulted in flooding on the lower level of the *albergue*, so an entire section of the hostel is temporarily closed off. I'm afraid the beds they do have were taken hours ago."

"What's he saying?" Seth asks beside me, picking up on the sudden change in the shopkeeper's tone. When I explain the situation, Seth's face reddens. He gets that look guys tend to get when they're about to punch a wall or do something equally impractical. "Awesome. This entire day is a disaster. Your turn, Gabi. What are we supposed to do now?"

"Uh, we're supposed to practice good OPSEC and not cause an international incident," I say through gritted teeth. Forcing a smile, I turn back to the shopkeeper and ask about hotels in the area. Staying in one would mean breaking Dad's supreme commandment yet again, but I'm sure even my prudish father would prefer that I not contract pneumonia from sleeping outside in the rain. Maybe.

"The village does have one private inn. *Un momento*, I'll give them a call."

This phone conversation takes a lot more than a minute, since it also involves an update on village news for the entire week. Seth and I are fidgeting by the time the shopkeeper hangs up. "*Lo siento*. I regret to inform you that the inn is also full."

I translate the verdict. Seth whirls around in frustration, nearly taking out a display of kitschy St. James statues with his pack in the process.

The shopkeeper holds up both hands. "Wait! No problem! You may stay here. Tell your bad-tempered friend, *peregrina*, before he destroys my shop. My wife and I have room. You may stay with us."

I'm not sure how to respond. Stay overnight with total strangers? Not to mention a stranger who seemed odd to begin with and *must* be a little off if he's willing to put us up after Seth's latest display of *camino* rage. Yet the more I think about it, the more I realize my kneejerk reaction to this man's exuberance is pretty sad. Since when did I start translating "nice and slightly eccentric stranger" into "potential serial killer"?

"Hospitality has a long tradition on the *camino*," the man explains, picking up on my anxiety. "In the medieval monasteries built along the Way of St. James, the monks used to open their home to any traveler who landed on their doorstep, whether rich or poor. Now we have the *albergues* to house pilgrims, but many of us locals who live along the route feel blessed when we are able to offer the same services our ancestors did so long ago. 'Do not neglect to show hospitality to strangers, for by this some have entertained angels without knowing it.'" The shopkeeper smiles in a way that's moderately creepy, but one hundred percent genuine. "Most of us have been, or will one day be, strangers in a foreign land, no?"

"I can't say we're angels, but that's very kind of you." Because I'm the one who speaks Spanish, I get to make the call. I accept the shopkeeper's offer before Seth even hears what it is. "Thank you. We'd love to stay."

Fact: there are a lot of messed-up people in this world, but there are some generous souls, too. And the more I hear about this man's love for the *camino* and its traditions, the more I trust that he's one of the good guys. Besides, at this point, any dry place will do the job.

Our host, Rodrigo, closes up shop and guides us to the small apartment above his store. There, his equally gracious wife, Pilar, pours us bowl after bowl of steaming hot *caldo Gallego*. It's the most delicious soup I've ever tasted, made with chorizo, potatoes, and the green leafy vegetable that seems to grow all over this province like an invasive weed. Seth has three helpings and I have two, but Pilar keeps rummaging around her kitchen like she's got more magic in store. The petite powerhouse reminds me of my dad's sister, Isabel, another woman who's never satisfied until her guests have eaten their body weight in whatever she's serving.

"And now *un postre!*" Pilar sets two thick slices of cake dusted in powdered sugar before us. "This is the *tarta de Santiago*—a special dessert for pilgrims on the Way of St. James."

"I assure you, *amigos*, Pilar's is the best *tarta* you'll try on the entire *camino*," Rodrigo insists. "It's a secret family recipe, passed down for many generations."

*From the ancient Celts, no doubt.* I smile, amused by Rodrigo's assertions that everything from Galicia is "the best." It's hard to argue with him, based on my experience so far. I'm stuffed from the soup, but every bite of this flaky almond cake makes me want another. The dessert is simple and rustic—the same characteristics of our hosts, the local cuisine, and this region in general. Simple, rustic, and *good*.

Dad used to tell us that the neighbors he grew up with in the humid hills of Oaxaca were the most benevolent, salt-of-the-earth people he'd ever known. The kind of people who looked out for one another and fed whatever kid happened to be hanging around, no matter who that kid actually belonged to. Sometimes life on a military base can feel like that, though I can't say I've ever met a couple as bighearted as Rodrigo and Pilar.

Even the skeptical Seth seems touched. "*Muchas gracias*," he repeats multiple times whenever Pilar sets down a new plate or takes one away. He's quiet during the meal since that's about the extent of his Spanish, but I can tell from the content look on his face that he feels safe here with these strangers. And the soldier part of him doesn't quite know what to make of that.

"Are you all right?" I ask later on when I'm stretched out across the sofa. Seth is tossing and turning on his air mattress on the other side of the living room.

He stops flailing. Rain patters softly on the roof. "I'd forgotten."

"Forgotten what?"

"That there are decent human beings out there."

I smile defiantly into the darkness. Seth is right. Turn off the news and avoid the mall during the holidays and people might surprise you. His words have me smiling myself to sleep. For the first time in weeks, I don't wake up in the middle of the night. Not once.

• • •

"Bloody hell!" Seth shoots up from his mattress like a busted spring.

Apparently in Galicia they don't believe in alarm clocks. They believe in *gaitas*.

The bagpipe music assails us from Rodrigo's study down the hall, where the light of dawn drifts in from outside in muted grays that signify another rainy day. Galicia's wet climate doesn't exactly encourage us to hop out of bed, but once I smell espresso, I throw on a sweater and stumble towards the kitchen. Seth just groans loudly and attempts to smother himself with his pillow.

"*Buenas dias,*" I mumble to Pilar. She's standing at the counter juicing half a bag of oranges, her foot tapping along with the *gaita* music while the percolator boils on the stove. Yes, morning people are annoying, but I will not bite the hand that brews my coffee.

Pilar returns my greeting by handing me a glass of fresh squeezed OJ, which kicks the crap out of the canned-from-concentrate stuff from back home. "You never told me, *peregrina*. What are your reasons for walking to Santiago?"

I ponder this question while sipping my deliciously pulpy juice. Maybe it's because Pilar reminds me of my Aunt Isabel, or maybe I'm still half-asleep, but I feel like I can talk to her about almost anything.

"I'm walking for my brother, Lucas. He was badly injured a few weeks ago." For some reason, saying the actual words stings like citrus in an open wound. "I also had a big fight with my father a while back and things haven't been the same between us since. He's relying on me to finish this pilgrimage for Lucas, and I'm hoping that once I do, things will return to normal."

Pilar smiles. "I'm afraid things never go back to normal after the *camino*. Look at me, eh? I walked to Santiago when I finished university, married a loveable lunatic I met along the way, and never left."

"You met Rodrigo as a pilgrim?" Somehow this doesn't surprise me. "Let me guess. He serenaded you with his early morning *gaita* tunes?"

"Actually, being a *señorita* from southern Spain, I serenaded *him* with my flamenco guitar." Pilar gives me a mischievous wink. "Your reasons for walking to Santiago are very noble. I wish more pilgrims walked on behalf of loved ones, instead of for the touristic reasons more seem to cite every year."

"That bothers you?" My mouth starts watering as Pilar presents a plate of toast topped with blood-red tomatoes and sea salt. Seriously, the woman never quits.

"I can't really say it bothers me, especially when the pilgrims motivated by tourism are more likely to purchase something from Rodrigo's shop," Pilar replies with a wry grin. "But it makes me sad when the *camino* isn't seen for what it truly is. It isn't a hike.

It's something sacred. It's a way to connect. Or maybe a way to *re*connect. The Way isn't about reaching a destination just to check it off the list and buy a postcard. It means so much more than that."

"I know, I know, and I need to find *my own* reason for walking it," I reply. "I get that, but I can't come up with one."

"Your own reason?" Pilar frowns. "Who told you such a silly thing?"

I shrug. "A lot of pilgrims seem to be looking for some big existential meaning behind their journey, but I'm not on a quest of self-discovery or anything like that. I'm doing this for my brother and for my dad. That's it."

"And what could be more meaningful than that?" Pilar laughs and pats my hand like she's scolding me for stealing from the cookie jar. "Do you think pilgrims in ages past had the luxury of walking across Europe to 'find themselves'? Of course not. They walked out of devotion to their faith and for the sake of those they loved. Your reasons for this journey are perfectly valid, *peregrina*. Don't listen to anyone who tries to tell you otherwise."

Pilar adds a dash of pepper to the tomatoes and breakfast is served. "You know what? I always said I wanted to make the journey to Santiago on foot one more time. I almost did it a few years back, when Rodrigo and I were trying to have a child."

The sudden sorrow in Pilar's eyes tells me they were not successful.

"What I'm trying to say is that true spirituality is rarely about warm feelings of fulfillment. It's often about duty and obedience and sacrifice. A pilgrimage *must* be difficult and it must involve suffering, otherwise it has no lessons to teach. Based on what I've witnessed all these years living along the *camino*, the best way this journey helps people find themselves is by teaching them to forget themselves. This is often done by learning to love your fellow travelers. After all, we're all on the same road, *mija*. All walking the same way home."

My ears perk up at the familiar Spanish shorthand for *my daughter*. The rest of Pilar's words settle down deep. I've never stopped to consider why anyone else might be walking this route, and that makes me feel ashamed. Maybe I've encountered someone recently diagnosed with cancer, or a couple having fertility problems, or a pilgrim who also has a loved one laid up in the hospital. Who knows what battle each and every person walking this route came out here to fight? I never bothered asking.

"That's wise advice, *Señora* Valente. Thank you."

Smiling, Pilar retrieves the coffeepot from the stove. "I'm no sage, *peregrina*, but in order to live with an insatiably curious man like my Rodrigo, it's vital that I come up with a halfway decent thought from time to time."

As Pilar pours me a cup of coffee, the bagpipe music falls silent. Rodrigo bursts into the kitchen humming the same upbeat tune, a local newspaper, the *Meditations* of Marcus Aurelius, and a nature book on hedgehogs in his hands. Pilar nods in her oblivious husband's direction as he sits down for his eclectic morning reading. "See what I mean? *Esta loco*."

I slurp my *café con leche* and smile. "Aren't we all?"

# CHAPTER 19

The sun comes out. Maybe it's going to be a beautiful day after all. After Pilar's delicious breakfast, it's time for Seth and I to say goodbye to our amazing hosts.

Rodrigo walks us back to the *camino*, lifting both hands to the increasingly clear sky. "See, *peregrinos*? You are very fortunate. It's rare to see sunshine in O Cebreiro in the spring. As they say on the Emerald Isle (though I believe the Irish stole it from us Galicians): May the road rise up to meet you. May the wind be always at your back. May the sun shine warm upon your face . . . ."

Seth extends his hand to Rodrigo. "Thank you for everything, *señor*."

The rain has stopped, but Rodrigo's farewell blessing makes me want to turn on the waterworks, so I quickly say goodbye before things get overly emotional. The further we walk, the more the morning fog lifts, showcasing views too gorgeous to leave behind right away.

"Do you mind if we stop here for a few minutes?" I ask Seth, gesturing to a low stone wall at the edge of town. The vista overlooks clover-green mountains sprinkled with yellow wildflowers. It's the perfect spot to lay out our wet clothes from the previous day. "I'm not ready to leave this place just yet."

"Yeah, me neither." Seth puts on his sunglasses, takes off his backpack, and pulls out the *Iliad*, stretching along the wall like a lizard. "Listen to this: 'Everything is more beautiful because we're doomed. You will never be lovelier than you are now. We will never be here again.'"

Pinpricks dance along my skin as I join Seth on the wall. These lines really do encapsulate this entire morning. Every time I visit someplace special, someplace like O Cebreiro, I think I'll come back one day and recreate the same sensations. But it will probably never happen, and even if it does, a moment like this isn't an essence that can be captured in a bottle and saved for later. If our lives are our own story, the fact that we're doomed—that the plot keeps pushing forward until we reach "The End"—makes every chapter that much more significant.

*You will never be lovelier than you are now.*

I don't feel lovely; I feel like I need to burn all of my clothes and start from scratch. Still, the thought that seventeen could be my prime—as it surely was in ancient Greece—doesn't leave me feeling depressed. It warms me from the inside, just like the sun's rays warm me from the outside. Seth could have skipped this line to avoid giving me the wrong idea.

But he didn't.

"You know what I realized this morning while trying to block out Rodrigo's bagpipes?" Seth asks.

"What's that?"

"We haven't had a round of questions for quite some time."

That's probably because they've felt forced and pointless ever since Burgos. Seth may never tell me what happened to him and Lucas. Not until he's ready, so why try to sneak in the same question a hundred different ways? Besides, we're getting along better than ever. I'm not about to risk our truce by rocking the volatile vessel that is Seth. He's too guarded and he likes it that way.

"What else do you want to know?"

Seth points to the unspoiled scenery before us. "Do you really think you'll be able to return to normal life after *this*?"

"Define normal," I reply, sitting up to wring out my damp socks. "Oh, wait. You're telling me this trek isn't what life in the Army is actually like? That's too bad. I thought the blisters and lack of laundry facilities were giving me some decent marching training."

Seth smirks. "You've actually considered joining?"

"No. I was kidding. You need to work on your sarcasm radar."

"Nah, I bet you marry a soldier one day. It takes a special woman to keep that little platoon in working order. You've already got the skill set. And the guts."

I don't know if I should be flattered or outraged. Seth meant his statement as a compliment, but right now my life goals consist of reaching Santiago ASAP, seeing my brother go on to lead a normal life, and graduating high school so I can get as far from the Army as possible. My mom rocks the military spouse role and I'm sure I could do the same if I wanted to, but the fact that Seth would even *think* to acknowledge this freaks me out.

So I set up a roadblock. "What about you? Think you'll re-enlist?"

"I don't know." Seth sighs. "Maybe. My dad was pretty ticked that I enlisted before going to college first, since that makes getting into Officer Candidate School a lot harder."

I'd almost forgotten that Seth is an officer's kid. His father is a colonel, so yeah, I can imagine his decorated dad was pissed when he learned his only son wouldn't follow in his footsteps by attending an elite military academy, but signed up to be a grunt instead.

"Why didn't you try for OCS?" I'd always assumed Seth was the one who came up with the idea that he and Lucas enlist together. "Or why didn't you guys go to college and do the ROTC route? It probably would have been safer that way."

For some reason, all my anger about this situation is gone, ground into the dust of a road I've already walked. I ask out of curiosity and nothing more.

Seth swings one leg over the wall, straddling it like a horse. "In that case, we would have joined Special Forces or done something equally dangerous." He removes his sunglasses and stares right at me. Right through me. "Lucas didn't want to spend his life behind a desk, Gabi. It was his idea, you know? Signing up right after graduation. I think he saw it as a sort of rite of passage. A surefire way to become a man, instead of spending his twenties playing video games in his parents' basement like most of our friends. He was enlisting with or without me. I figured *with* might give him better odds, that way I'd be around to watch his back."

But he was wrong. Even Seth couldn't watch it close enough.

I can tell that's exactly what he's thinking. And it makes me feel sick. I'd convinced myself that Seth pressured Lucas to enlist, but I know my brother and now that I know Seth, Lucas is definitely the more spontaneous of the two. I guess it was easier to blame someone else than to admit that Lucas knew what he was getting into when he signed that dotted line.

"So the only reason you didn't go to OCS was because you didn't want Lucas to enlist alone?"

Seth nods and it all makes sense. He was balancing my brother out, trying to be the stark realism to his romantic idealism. Seth's failure to protect Lucas is furrowed in the lines of a face way too young to even have such scars. Knowing that for every visible wound I can trace, there are dozens more beneath the surface makes me want to weep.

*You're a big girl now, mija. Too big to cry.*

That's what Dad told me the first time he deployed. I was barely seven. But I'd held back my tears like a true Santiago, saving them for my pillow that night.

"Come here, Gabi." Seth drapes his arm around my shoulder. "Go ahead. Cry. Curse. Get angry. You need to. But afterwards, after you get it all out, you go back to being strong for him, all right? Once Lucas wakes up, you be the tough little sister I already know you are."

"*If* he wakes up." The words come out as a sob, not statement. I press my face against Seth's chest as the lid containing my grief bursts open. The tears finally come. Hot, angry tears. Liquid rage at the thought of Lucas's boyhood getting blown to bits. And for what? What did his sacrifice even mean?

Seth holds me tight, solid as a citadel, a stable mast in the midst of a storm. He doesn't say he's sorry or give me any reassurance. We're way past the power of positive thinking by now, past empty promises that everything will work out for the best. All we can cling to is the fraying thread of hope that unites us, even if the unraveling strand is what strangles us both in the end.

"Gabi, look at me." Seth lifts my chin and stares into my tear-stained face. "No matter what happens, no matter where he is or where he's going, Lucas would be proud of you for doing this. And grateful. I know I am. This walk, this time to process everything—it was exactly what I needed. And I needed to walk it with *you*."

Suddenly, I am intensely aware that Seth's rough hand cradles my chin. He wipes the tears from my cheeks, but as he pulls his hand away, I lift mine to stop him.

The look on his face assures me we're in for it now. It's an irrevocable look, a no-going-back look. Seth cups my face with both hands and presses his lips to mine. I taste tears, and rage, and secrets, all mixed with a hope that binds us more than one kiss ever could. It's over in an instant, but things will never be the same. And we both know it.

"I'm sorry, Gabi. This isn't a good idea. You just make me feel so damn weak—"

Seth pulls away, but I pull him back into heaven. "We've got six more minutes."

The second kiss is more urgent and less sweet, but everything spins all the same. Seth wraps his arms around my waist and draws me closer, like I'm a lifesaver he'll drown without.

"*Ándale, ándale! Arriba!*"

We wrench ourselves apart at a loud wolf whistle and the laughter of passing pilgrims. I whirl around to glare at these gawking intruders, knocking my water bottle off the wall in the process. It rolls down the hill, getting caught on a thorny bush before a significant drop off. I want to cry out after it, but my tingling lips have yet to regain the power of speech.

"No worries. I'll get it." Seth jumps down from the wall. He seems relieved to have a reason to avoid the fact that he made a move on his best friend's sister and she made one back. I'm not fourteen anymore, so it kind of irks me, but I also get that there's an elaborate BFF rulebook and Seth has broken a major commandment.

"It's not worth it," I call after him. "I'll buy another bottle in the next big town."

"The next big town is two days away, and hydration is the key to hiking success." A shy grin on his face, Seth slides cautiously down the steep hillside. "Sit tight. I'll get it."

With this new mission before him, Seth slips back into soldier mode. There will be no stopping him, so I focus on *not* having a nervous breakdown as he climbs down the rocky embankment, inching closer to the ridge. It's a messed-up thought, but I can't help thinking that if Seth slips and goes over the edge, I may never be kissed like that again. Brent certainly never kissed me like that.

Seth kissed me like I mattered, like I gave him somewhere firm to stand.

It's only when he reaches the shrub and gropes for the runaway bottle that I realize I'm holding my breath. Why is it that the second I open myself up to caring for someone, he's immediately hung out over a ledge? Literally.

My champion raises his stainless steel trophy, a proud smile stretching across his sun-kissed cheeks. After securing the bottle's cap between his teeth, Seth scrambles back towards the wall, using exposed roots to pull himself up the hillside. He's almost to the top.

*Snap.*

The sound is worse than the crack of a shattered femur. One of the roots breaks. Seth loses his footing. And he's gone.

My stomach lurches up my throat as Seth slides down the steep incline, his shocked eyes locking onto mine before he vanishes from sight. He doesn't cry out. He just disappears.

"Seth!" I jump down from the wall and peer over the edge, my heart invoking every memorized petition I know in a single moment. "Please, please, *please.*"

Thank God. I see Seth lying face down on his stomach, both hands clinging to rocks and loose dirt. As I press my boots into the soft soil and creep down the slope, he releases a combination of curse words I've never heard before. The crude soldier language is music to my ears. It means Seth is still conscious. Seth is still Seth. What I would give to hear Lucas, who rarely swore before basic training, drop a string of serious f-bombs.

I inch closer and Seth pushes himself upright. Thankfully, there's no sign of blood, minus what's boiling in his eyes. "Are you okay?"

"If a busted ankle counts as okay," Seth growls, reaching for my extended hand.

His anger is a mask for his humiliation. I feel worse about *that* than I do about his injury. I'm sure the poor guy never imagined he'd survive firefights with the Taliban just to be taken out by a damn tree root. It's so tragic it's almost funny, but I'm too concerned about the pain warping Seth's face to so much as crack a smile.

"Walk it off, soldier," I say as I pull him up the hillside. Coddling is the last thing Seth's bruised ego needs right now. Only he can't walk it off. When we reach the wall and I remove his boot, it becomes apparent that Seth won't be walking for weeks.

His ankle is double its normal size.

"Serves me right." Seth shakes his head. He's frustrated about falling below his own ridiculously high standards on two accounts, but I see the hint of a smirk forming in the corners of his mouth. "Kissing you is dangerous business."

...

"It can't happen again. You know that, right?" Seth winces as I lay a bag of frozen peas across his ankle. We're back at Rodrigo and Pilar's apartment, back on the couch where I slept last night. Back, in many ways, to square one.

"You're assuming I *want* it to happen again." I expel the words like acid, that way Seth won't see how much his rejection hurts. There's no way I'm letting another guy kiss me and dismiss me without getting scathed in the process.

"Fine, but just know that it was a mistake. And I'm sorry." Seth bites his lip, which seems to have more to do with his sprained ankle than it does with the agony of wanting something he can't have. "You're amazing, Gabi, but your dad, your brother. They're both trusting me not to be that shady soldier who takes advantage of younger girls."

"And you think *that* was 'taking advantage'?" I get that Seth's fall probably felt like a divine lightning bolt, but this condescension is too much. "Maybe you've already forgotten, but *I* kissed *you* back."

"Dammit, Gabi. What do you want from me? I have no way of knowing how Lucas would feel about it, and I've got enough on my conscience as it is." Seth scowls like he's going over a very long list. "Besides, where would it go from here? You're heading back to Texas once you graduate, and who knows where the Army will send me next."

I transfer Seth's bum ankle from my lap to a pillow. "Relax. It was a kiss, not a proposal. Ever heard of a summer fling?"

Seth frowns. "You're worth way more than that, Gabi. And I'm pretty sure summer flings don't apply to your best friend's little sister."

If that's true, then why don't I feel worth anything? Why do I feel slighted yet again?

"Fine. It—whatever 'it' is—ends in Santiago."

Seth's cold silence tells me it's ended already.

Pilar enters the room carrying a tray of hot tea. "*Pobre peregrino*," she purrs, setting the tray down so she can feel Seth's forehead, as if sprained ankles somehow caused fevers. "After we ice it, we need to get that leg wrapped to help with the swelling. But first, a dose of the world's best medicine."

I'm thinking Pilar has brewed some kind of gross medicinal tea, but then she walks over to her husband's reading chair and picks up an acoustic guitar from the stand behind it. After cracking her knuckles, she starts playing some of the most gorgeous melodies I've ever heard. Seth lies back on the couch with his eyes closed, soaking it all in like the Spanish sun.

Pilar doesn't exactly sing, but every now and then she croons the guttural moans and gypsy yelps that give flamenco its flavor. "That song was by Paco de Lucia, *el rey de flamenco*," she says with a shy smile after Seth and I break into enthusiastic applause.

"May I?" Seth reaches for the guitar and Pilar obliges.

"I didn't know you played." Seth has never struck me as being creatively inclined, so it's hard to hide my astonishment.

"The number of things you don't know about me may surprise you," Seth says as he tunes the strings. "I do have other hobbies besides blowing things up, you know?"

On the surface he's teasing me, but Seth's tone has an edge to it that I don't know how to take. Then again, I'm too stunned by what happens next to care. Seth's guitar skills can't touch Pilar's stylized strumming, but his *voice* cuts me to the quick. Lush and a little somber, he sings the story of wandering vagabonds, abandoned churchyards, and a million stars in an empty universe.

In other words, he sings our story. Our song.

"Sorry, I'm a little rusty," Seth says when he's finished, bashful like a kid after his first talent show. "I haven't tried putting that one to music before."

Pilar's face glows like she's just had a religious experience, which is entirely plausible since Seth's lyrics remind me of a psalm. Tortured yet timeless, they evoke a melancholy nostalgia that never goes out of style. Listening to Seth sing is like looking at a world photographed in sepia tones.

"*Un momento,* I must tell Rodrigo. He would love to hear you play!"

After Pilar leaves us, I turn to Seth, straining to form a coherent sentence. "When, exactly, did you write that?"

"After Eunate," he says, like it's a confession he's been holding in for years.

He doesn't look at me, but he doesn't have to. The name Eunate tells me everything I need to know. Every confused emotion I feel for Seth started that cloudless night. The night I caught him wishing on a shooting star for a person both our universes would be emptier without. The night I was consumed by something big. Something as vast and mysterious as that illustrious night sky.

Apparently I wasn't the only one.

"Brent played music too, right?"

I know Seth is really asking: *How do I compare? How do I measure up?*

"If you call whining other people's lyrics into a microphone music."

Seth grins like he's won the lottery and will never have to work another day in his life. "Kid has no guts. See, I knew those tight pants didn't reveal much."

I laugh. "I'll give you that. You saw what I couldn't see."

"What about your dad?"

"What about him?" I ask.

"You said things haven't been great between you two, and I get the sense Brent has something to do with that."

Am I that transparent, or is Seth just especially good at reading me?

"So what happened?" he continues.

"I've never talked about it."

And why would I now? Seth kissed me, but he stopped himself because he didn't want to disrespect my family, which means he didn't want to disrespect me. What will he think when he knows my reputation is already tarnished?

"Okay, so tell me."

I breathe in Pilar's special tea and exhale my shame. "Brent and I were headed to a party at Kristina Newman's house—"

"Wait," Seth interrupts, "you mean *General* Newman's house?"

"Yep. He was out of town. Still stupid, but we're talking about Kristina here."

Seth nods. "Yeah, her dad may wear a lot of brass, but I'm pretty sure the last gold star that girl saw on schoolwork was way back in kindergarten."

"Don't be so mean," I say. "But yes, Kristina wasn't the sharpest crayon in the box and yes, she hosted a huge party at her high-ranking officer father's house."

"In his general's mansion? On post?" Seth shakes his head at such a folly.

"On post," I confirm.

"And you guys actually went?"

"Well, we would have. If we hadn't been arrested first."

Seth nearly jumps from his seat, then remembers that he's in extreme pain and eases himself back on to the couch. "*You?* Arrested? For what?"

"Brent was in charge of picking up booze since one of his bandmates is twenty-one, and being the connoisseur that he is, he decided to bring a case of Boone's Farm Strawberry Hill."

Seth smirks and shakes his head. "Such a rookie move."

"Yeah, if you're going to get busted for underage alcohol possession on federal government property, might as well get caught with something a tad more sophisticated than a malt beverage that tastes like Welch's strawberry soda and air freshener."

Seth adjusts his frozen bag of peas. "So how'd you get caught?"

"On our way to the party, we stopped in the PX parking lot for a make-out session in Brent's car. Brent opened one of the bottles of 'wine' for us to drink—I guess he was trying to be romantic or something. The next thing I know, a military police officer is tapping on the foggy window above my head. He asks us to step out of the car, finds the Boone's Farm, and two minutes later we're in the back of the police cruiser in handcuffs. My dad was called to the MP station to pick us up, and that's when he pretty much stopped talking to me. For a year."

Seth studies me closely, like he's envisioning me in the back of Brent's car and doesn't know what to think. He doesn't seem upset or disappointed, just confused.

"We never had sex, if that's what you're wondering." I pour Seth another cup of tea. "There were a few close calls, but I never went through with it."

"Why not?" Still no judgment in his voice, just relief.

"I don't know," I reply. "Deep down, I figured there was something more. That I'd be making a vow I couldn't keep. That Brent wasn't worthy."

"Gabi. Look at me." Seth's eyes are resolute. "He wasn't."

• • •

"This is it, *peregrinos*! The solution to all your problems."

Somehow I doubt that, but Rodrigo's gusto will not be diminished by the skeptical glance Seth and I share. In one swoop,

Rodrigo pulls off the dusty horse blanket like he's unveiling an artifact at a world-class museum. The item beneath the blanket *is* ancient, I'll give him that.

"No way." Seth shakes his head like his hair is on fire. "*Gracias,* but no way."

We're in Rodrigo's garage behind his shop, which houses so much Celtic overstock it looks like we're bidding on a storage unit that once belonged to a leprechaun. But it also contains an alternative mode of transportation for my injured *compañero.*

An old wheelchair that belonged to Rodrigo's mother, may God rest her soul.

"Come on, Seth. What other option do we have besides taking a bus the rest of the way, which means no *Compostela* certificate for Lucas? This is the only way we can finish the last hundred kilometers on foot. Well, sort of."

"You think you can actually push me in that thing?" Seth's Adam's apple flinches as he tries to swallow his pride.

"I can push you." I ignore the fact that this wheelchair is in worse shape than he is.

"There's no time. We need to reach Santiago in a few days and I'll only slow you down."

"I can push you," I repeat, my voice firm.

The rare reception in Seth's eyes tells me I've almost convinced him, which is proof he really will do anything for Lucas. At least I think it's for Lucas, though the goofy way Pilar looks at us makes me wonder. Regardless, dodging bullets and building fundraising blogs are cakewalks compared to Seth putting his weakness on display for the entire world to see.

I grab his hand. "I'm not finishing this without you."

Seth's fingers tighten around mine. He sighs and says some of the hardest words he's likely ever spoken. "Okay, Gabi. You win."

# CHAPTER 20

Every muscle in my body screams like a boiling lobster, but my calves hurt most of all. Rock-hard calves are what you get when you spend multiple days pushing a 175-pound man in a wheelchair across varied terrain. I don't do it alone, thanks to the other pilgrims walking this last leg of the *camino* who offer to help out when we reach a steep/muddy/crappy section of road. The most arduous parts of the trek are behind us, but it isn't all downhill yet.

Seth handles his humbling circumstances like a champ. He's visibly grateful for the assistance from strangers, even when he has to explain *ad nauseam* that no, despite his dog tags and cropped hair, he didn't injure his ankle in combat—unless a heroic campaign to reduce littering on the *camino* counts.

Neither of us brings up our kiss again, which is probably for the best. Still, I can't stop thinking about it, and I kind of hate myself for thinking about it. Why should I let myself get all gaga over a guy when this journey is about something bigger than both of us?

That's just it. I can't. And I won't. Our pilgrimage is almost over and I need to focus all my thoughts on the reason we're walking it in the first place: Lucas.

I lift the phone to my ear and wait for the repetitive ring. The signal should be stronger now that we're back near civilization, but my parents haven't been answering their phones. That means something has happened. Some sort of *change* has taken place.

And if it was good news, they'd have called me already.

What if Mom and Dad are waiting until I get home to tell me that Lucas is dead? The thought makes me so ill I can't even entertain it, not when I'm this close to the finish line. This walk is the only motivation I've had to get up in the morning. It's the only thing keeping me from spending hours in bed, tallying up a long list of *what ifs?*

*What if* Lucas doesn't get better?

*What if* I walk 500 miles for him and he never gets to hear about it?

*What if*, after everything we've been through, Seth and I never speak again because the one bond holding us together doesn't wake up in time to save us both?

*What if* repentance and atonement don't mean a thing because nothing we do ultimately matters, which means ultimately there's nothing to forgive?

*What if* cells in various stages of decomposition are the only thing that's real?

*What if* there's no point to *any of it*? To life, to death, to war, to *love*?

I dig through my pockets. If a passerby studied my jerky movements, he'd assume I'm an addict searching for her next hit. Oddly enough, that's what this ritual has become: a respite, a moment of relief. The feel of wax between my fingers is like a surge of serotonin. A promise that not all lights—not the brightest ones—have to go out.

Up ahead, Seth talks rugby with a young South African who volunteered to take over the reins of his rusty chariot. I take this opportunity to light a candle for Lucas, given that I've been slacking ever since my new wheelchair workout routine. I set the tealight below a plain wooden cross on the side of the road, decorated with worn-out boots hung by their laces, along with other random items pilgrims realized they could do without. The assortment of offerings includes a cherry-red cowboy hat, which brings a smile to my lips.

"Is there something you must let go of to lighten your load?"

The unexpected voice startles me. As I whirl around to face it, I accidentally knock Nancy's hat off of the shrine. A man with a full head of white hair and skin the color of cardamom sits in the grass behind me. He wears an embroidered shirt made of linen that matches his mane, and kneels on a small carpet, facing east.

"I don't know if my load needs to be lightened," I reply as the man rolls up his mat. "I, uh. I'm sorry if I interrupted your prayers."

"I doubt the Almighty minds." The man smiles and joins me on the road. He gestures to the stack of random junk. "May I ask for whom you are lighting that candle?"

"For my brother. He's injured. Pretty bad." It feels strange to be telling *this* man, of all people, about my brother. "Are you, uh . . . where are you from?"

"Iraq originally, but I live in London now."

Talk about awkward. At least Lucas never deployed to Iraq.

"And why, if you don't mind me asking, are you walking the *camino*?"

The man doesn't flinch. "What am I doing here as a Muslim, you mean?"

I nod. There's no point trying to be PC when that's *exactly* what I mean.

"I came to Spain to visit relatives in Barcelona. They told me about this ancient pilgrimage route and I wanted to see it for myself." He shrugs. "Simple as that."

"Muslims have to make a pilgrimage too, right? To Mecca?"

The serene man nods, still smiling. "You might say this is my warm-up."

I smile back. "And it's been *okay* so far?"

"It has, in fact," the man replies, sensing what I'm getting at. "Most pilgrims have been very welcoming, though they are curious about my intentions, just like you. Now, if you don't mind *me* asking, why are you walking the *camino*, my young pilgrim friend?"

This question is getting as old as "So, where are you from?" Yet the way this stranger asks it somehow feels fresh. For once, I come up with a halfway thoughtful answer, even if I'm not quite sure what it means. "I'm walking to heal what's broken."

"Ah, I see. Then you picked a good route, for this land is a symbol of what's been broken in our world for centuries. Yet it also shows us ways the wounds might be mended."

He must be referring to Spain's long history of religious conflict, seeing how this peninsula was once home to Jews, Christians, and Muslims alike. We pilgrims may seem like a peace-loving bunch, but there are lots of statues along the *camino* that depict St. James on horseback, slaying Moors with his sword. "I imagine seeing all those images of *Santiago Matamoros* is a little insulting."

The stranger shrugs. "Not really. *Santiago Matamoros* does not offend me, for he tells a story we would do well to remember. Besides, many of the people I've met along the Way practice what Muslims must also accomplish: welcoming the stranger, giving alms to the poor, and sharing with others everything one has."

The man studies the busted hiking boots dangling from the cross. "Perhaps now is the time for me to lighten my own load."

He doesn't even have a hiking pack, just his prayer mat and the clothes on his back. The man digs through his pockets until he finds a small item, holding it out for me to take. When I open my hand, another hand stares back at me. It's a red *hamsa* pendant with a turquoise stone in the center of the open palm—the same symbol worn by the Jewish woman in the family portrait I found inside that abandoned house.

The charm leaves me speechless. I'm probably overthinking it, but the tingling in my toes makes me wonder if this man and I were destined to meet from the moment I stepped on the road.

"This is my gift to you, fellow pilgrim," the stranger announces, his face aglow. "May your brother be healed, *Insha'Allah*, and visited only by good, not evil."

• • •

218

We reach Arca, the last overnight stop before Santiago. The weather is warm and the road is crowded. So are the pilgrim hostels, but there's an electricity of anticipation in the air that makes it impossible to be *too* cranky about the increased lack of personal space. We're almost there. We've almost made it.

Now I'm the one who waves the flashlight in Seth's face. "Rise and shine, gorgeous."

Seth groans, rolling over to face the wall. "This little light of mine is busted."

Most of the days in the wheelchair he's been fine, upbeat even, but this is our last morning on the *camino* and I can tell Seth is disappointed that he won't be able to walk it. Honestly, he isn't missing much. We pass through a forest of amazing eucalyptus trees, but it's hard to appreciate their gigantic, peeling trunks when you're crammed onto the footpath with a hundred other pilgrims who are all ready to be *done*.

The forest is the last scrap of nature before we reach the urban outskirts of Santiago de Compostela. The sound of traffic grates on my nerves after weeks of listening to grass grow, and nearly getting hit by a deranged scooter as I push Seth across the street isn't exactly the warm welcome I anticipated.

Seth is as underwhelmed by this pilgrimage finale as I am. I can literally see the tension traveling up the back of his neck. It doesn't help that one of his chair's wheels has gone berserk, like a sticky grocery cart wheel that makes you run into all the stacked cereal displays.

"Stop. I can't do it anymore," Seth says when the wheel keeps squeaking. "I'm walking."

"Do you really want to backtrack on all the progress you've made?" The swelling in Seth's ankle has gone down a lot, and the nurse who examined it last night said it should heal soon, as long as he stays off it. Which means he needs to *stay off it*.

Seth hits the breaks by planting his good leg on the ground. "I tried, Gabi, I really did. I tried to think about Lucas lying in that bed so I'd be grateful for the mobility I do have. I tried to suck it up and deal with feeling weak and helpless. But this is the last day of the *camino,* and I want to walk it. I don't care how much it hurts."

Before I can protest, Seth stands and starts pushing his chair towards a highway overpass, where a small crowd has gathered. Three nuns in full-on habits stand behind a picnic table, handing out cold drinks to the pilgrims arriving to Santiago. The small, smiley ladies wear white saris with blue trim, which means they're members of Mother Teresa's order.

Vulgar swear words decorate the concrete walls behind them and litter covers the ground, making this spot a shoo-in for Ugliest Place on the *camino,* but the simple beauty of kindness in action overshadows all of it. One of the pilgrims waiting for a drink is the Muslim man I met yesterday. He bows in gratitude as he accepts his lemonade.

"Would one of you sisters like to rest?" Seth asks, wheeling over the chair he no longer thinks he needs.

"Thank you, young man," the most elderly of the nuns replies. She trades Seth's chair for a paper cup. He gulps down its contents in seconds. The sight of Seth's chugging skills reminds me that he hasn't been drinking much lately. Maybe he knows he shouldn't mix alcohol with pain medication, or maybe he's found other ways to deal with his inner ache.

"Have you been healed?" the Indian sister asks, lowering her old bones into the seat.

"Not quite. But I'm working on it," Seth replies.

The sister smiles, her brown face wrinkling like a peach left out in the summer sun. "Be faithful in the small things first."

Seth doesn't respond. Telling a competitive soldier to start small is like telling a bird not to fly. A quiet calm as light and fluffy as the clouds above us fills the Indian woman's eyes, but it's propped up by beams of steel. Just like my *abuela*, this is one little old lady I wouldn't mess with. It's like she's strong precisely because she knows where she is weak.

"Do you believe your friend will be healed? That all will be well?"

I turn to respond to this gentle inquiry and find myself facing the youngest sister in the group—a Filipino girl in her early twenties. At first I think she's talking about Lucas, but then I realize she's a nun, not a psychic, so that's impossible. She must be asking about Seth.

Or maybe, somehow, she's asking about both.

"I sure hope so."

The sister smiles, like she knows a secret I don't. She nods in Seth's direction. "I can see the pain you feel for him. Mother Teresa spoke of this pain, the knife of compassion, as one of life's greatest paradoxes. After working with the poor her entire life, she learned that if you love until it really hurts, eventually there can be no more hurt, only more love."

"Well, the hurt isn't going anywhere fast, so I hope she's right."

"Me, too. In fact, I've bet my entire life on it." The young woman's face radiates pure joy. "Life is a gift, but most of its pleasures are fleeting and grow stale as soon as the novelty wears off. Yet I've found that serving those in need never gets old. Only the deep well of love lasts forever, long after everything else goes cold."

How can person so young already be so wise?

The sister's words feel like an invitation to a vow. The promise is one I automatically accept, even though the words never leave my mouth. If my brother wakes up, forget college. I will spend an entire year giving back. I'm not trying to strike a bargain with heaven or anything; I just want whatever it is that makes this young woman glow.

But what if Lucas *doesn't* wake up? Then there will be no light left in me to give.

"Here, have some wisdom for the road." The sister hands me a little saint card with a charcoal sketch of Mother Teresa on one side, and a quotation on the other. "After all, this is only the beginning of your pilgrimage, not the end."

*Life is an opportunity, benefit from it. Life is beauty, admire it. Life is a dream, realize it. Life is a challenge, meet it. Life is a duty, complete it. Life is a game, play it. Life is a promise, fulfill it. Life is sorrow, overcome it. Life is a song, sing it. Life is a struggle, accept it. Life is a tragedy, confront it. Life is an adventure, dare it. Life is luck, make it. Life is too precious, do not destroy it. Life is life, fight for it.*

*Fight for it.* That's it. That's why I'm walking the *Camino de Santiago*. My pilgrimage is my own small protest against meaninglessness and annihilation and despair. It's my war on nothingness, my own small way of fighting for light and for love.

For Lucas's life. For Seth's life. For all our lives.

I thank the sister for her gift. On the other side of the underpass, Seth is having an intense conversation of his own.

With the Muslim man.

Panic shoots down my spine as the man shakes his fist, then grabs Seth's arm.

*No, Seth. Please.*

We are steps away from being done with this pilgrimage. Please don't get into another ugly confrontation now.

As I get closer, I see the tears in the older man's eyes. He's clutching Seth's shoulder, but his face twists in pain, not anger. I can't see Seth's reaction because his back is to me, but as I approach, the weeping man turns and walks away.

"What was that about?"

Seth swallows hard. "He was telling me to call my father. He said not all children, his own son being one of them, make it home from war."

Seth has mentioned that he and his dad aren't as close as they used to be, especially after he snubbed the colonel's offer to get him into West Point. That's the main reason Seth isn't in a hurry to return to the States, though he of all people should know that holding grudges is a luxury soldiers can't afford.

"He's right, Seth. Call your dad. Tell him you're on your way home."

# CHAPTER 21

Santiago. We're here. The cathedral's baroque bell towers beckon us closer, standing tall and proud like a pair of watchmen guarding their post. Seth hones in on them like they're brothers in arms. With every step, the thin red line of his grimaced mouth tightens.

"Do you know how the *Iliad* ends?" Seth asks out of the blue.

He must be striking up a conversation to distract himself from the pain. "Tragically, if I remember right. The most honorable warrior in the entire poem gets cut down."

"And the only way his father, the king of Troy, can get his son's body back is by paying a visit to his mortal enemy, Achilles, and groveling at his feet."

"Does he do it?" I ask, wondering if my dad would ever swallow his massive ego for Lucas. For Matteo. For me.

"He does," Seth says.

Yeah, my dad would, too.

"It wasn't the way I expected the war epic to end," he adds.

I look around and realize this isn't how I expected my senior year to end either. We've fallen behind the rest of the group that departed our hostel early this morning. Seth leans on a wooden Gandalf staff, while I push his backpack in the wheelchair. Our pace is super slow, but step by painful step, he'll reach the cathedral on foot.

I offer my shoulder as additional support. "You gonna make it?"

Grimacing, Seth nods.

His visible pain makes my stomach ache. I don't know what I expected our arrival in Santiago to be like, but so far I don't feel any sense of accomplishment. We fulfilled Lucas's wish, but so what? Was it even worth the time it cost me by his bedside?

I press my phone to my ear and replay the voicemail Mom left earlier today when we passed through a dead zone with no coverage. Her voice is dead, too.

*Hi Gabi. Just wanted to let you know that we got your messages. Things are pretty crazy here right now, but we'll be in touch soon.*

*Crazy?* What does that even mean? Why is it so hard to answer the stupid phone?

"Stop obsessing, Gabi," Seth says as I put the useless device away. "They're there and we're here. There's nothing we can do."

"Since when are you one to give in to Fate?" I snap back.

Seth's grip on his staff tightens as he studies his ankle. "Since I got a taste of what it's like to not be in control of it."

Checkmate.

We fall silent as we follow a trail of pilgrims in brightly colored windbreakers through the winding streets of Santiago's old town. The buildings are the color of old coffee stains and the wet cobblestones gleam beneath our feet. After a lot of twists and turns, we reach a staircase that leads us to the Praza do Obradoiro, the main cathedral square. As we pass through the arched doorway, we're greeted by two bearded musicians wailing on a ukulele and a bongo. Inside the plaza, statues of St. James and his cockleshell stare down on us from every building.

Holy humanity—there are people everywhere. Some are tourists, but most are pilgrims, and highly emotional pilgrims at that. A few race towards each other, embracing like long-separated lovers, while others sit on the ground weeping tears of elation mixed with tears of exhaustion.

What's wrong with me? I should be overcome by *something*, but I'm not. After dozens of days and hundreds of miles, the pain has faded and I finally feel numb. And I don't like it.

A man with two blue icepacks taped to his knees limps in our direction. He's a living reminder that the strain of this journey can break a person down in more than one way. Our bodies seemed invincible on Day One, but none of us were built to last forever.

Walking, like life, takes its toll. And the fare is usually steep.

Seth's eyes flit from the people standing in clusters, to the garbage cans on the perimeter of the square. He hasn't been in a public space this crowded since he got back from Afghanistan, and I can tell it's making him a little anxious.

"Relax. I doubt anyone here is an enemy." I could be wrong about that, but if the goal of terrorism is to cripple us with fear, the most defiant weapon we have is refusing to bow the knee. Seth's face softens when I grab his hand. A slow and steady warmth spreads through me. His touch makes me feel less anesthetized.

We stand in silence, staring at the detailed carvings of the cathedral façade, at the trail of white algae that twists and turns across stone faces that have endured centuries of harsh weather. Seth's hand is like a jumper cable to my battery. All of a sudden, so many emotions are racing through me that no single feeling stands out. The volume of the square is turned all the way up, like we're at a massive reunion of old friends, even though I haven't seen a single person I recognize yet.

But apparently someone recognizes me.

"Gabi! Hey Gabi, over here!"

Jens and Katja sprint towards us. They engulf me in an embrace that reeks of sweat and patchouli, but hippie B.O. is the last thing on my mind.

"What are you guys doing here?" I exclaim. "How did you make it so fast?"

The delight fades from Jens's face. "A few days after Burgos, *Mutti* called to let us know that her sister, our favorite aunt, got in a bad car accident."

"We needed to get home, but we wanted to walk the last hundred kilometers first. For her." Katja's voice drops like she's about to confess a mortal sin. "So we took a bus."

"I'm so sorry about your aunt." I know from experience that my response is inadequate, but really, what else do you say?

"We've told just about every person we met along the way, so now there are hundreds of pilgrims praying for her." Jens smiles weakly. "We haven't given up hope yet."

Is that what it takes? Hundreds of whispered hopes, a swirling mass of pleading voices about as easy to ignore as a tornado? Is that the best recipe for a miracle? I know it's what my *abuela* believes, what my dad believes, what Jens and Katja seem to believe, what the thousands of medieval pilgrims who walked this road before us believed.

The doubt on Seth's face tells me it isn't what he believes, and I'm still not sure if it's what I believe. But I do feel better knowing our silly blog led to total strangers passing the name *Lucas* across their lips, adding a kind word to the storm cloud of resistance. It also helps to know that in between this sacred spot and the Pyrenees mountains, there are dozens of candles dedicated to my brother; a brigade of little lights standing guard against the despairing darkness. No matter what happens, it means I walked to Santiago for something.

It means I had a reason all along.

· · ·

Over the next hour there are more reunions with more pilgrims—including Bob from Australia (yet again), Harmony and her entourage, and the young Sudanese man with the smile of contagious joy. For lunch, we grab *doner kebabs* with Jean Paul and eat them on the steps across from the cathedral. As I take my first bite of garlicky goodness, I look up and see Rodrigo and Pilar crossing the square. They approach us slowly, tears filling their eyes like we're their own children. Rodrigo places a scallop shell on a red cord around Seth's neck, and Pilar drapes an identical one around mine.

"Our twenty-fifth wedding anniversary is this week, so we decided to walk the road where we first met," Rodrigo explains, beaming at his wife like it all happened yesterday. "We hoped we might surprise you, too."

"Your brother has been in our hearts the entire way," Pilar adds, squeezing my hand.

"Thank you. So much." That's all I can say without blubbering, but I hug Pilar tighter than I've hugged anyone in a long time. I can tell by the way she embraces me back that no other words are needed.

We finish our lunch while Rodrigo describes their walking adventure with his usual animation. And embellishments. The man could seriously make gardening in the backyard sound like a life-or-death rainforest expedition.

Finally, Pilar cuts him off. "Are you *peregrinos* ready to go inside?"

I take a deep breath as we approach the cathedral entrance. Seth stops at the doorway.

"Seriously, Seth? We walked all the way here and you're going to wait outside?" I can't believe he's going to be such a grump again. This is a pilgrim ritual *everyone* participates in, no matter their beliefs or lack thereof. "Loosen up. I doubt you're going to burst into flames just from crossing the threshold. Though I recommend staying clear of the holy water."

"Go ahead and go in. I'll be right there." Seth's flat tone means he doesn't pick up on my teasing. I follow his gaze over to the real reason he's stopped.

We've seen plenty of beggars throughout the trek, but there's something about this man that draws Seth in. The ancient, shriveled shell of a person has a patch over his right eye, and he holds a cardboard sign with words written in three languages:

*I'm a German veteran of the Second World War. Many years ago, I walked to Santiago to repent for the evils I took part in, but I never made it home. Lord, have mercy on me, a sinner.*

Seth drops a few coins into the man's basket, but he doesn't look particularly happy while he does it. In fact, he kind of looks repulsed. Based on his family history, I can understand why. This small gesture makes me admire Seth more than I've ever admired him before. He's showing compassion, he's doing the right thing. In *spite* of what he feels, not because of it.

"All right. I'm ready."

We enter the cathedral. The Pórtico da Gloria is bathed in sunlight and shadows at the same time. A large statue of St. James, the apostle himself, looks down on us from an elaborately carved pillar known as the Tree of Jesse. I place my fingers in the pillar's five grooves as we walk by—five deep impressions formed by the millions of pilgrims who have passed through these same doors.

The glitz and gold inside the church is a little much for my taste, but the forest of stone trunks are like magnets pulling us down the central aisle with an irrefutable force. Hundreds of pilgrims have gathered for the Pilgrim's Mass, which is celebrated daily. Same time, same place. Some attend because they're truly pious, others because it's a cultural tradition associated with the pilgrimage, and still others because they're curious to see what all the fuss is about.

"Did we lose Rodrigo and Pilar?" I ask Seth, scanning the crowd.

"Yeah, but we better find seats anyway. It looks like the service is about to start."

The Mass is predictable at first—stand, kneel, sit, and all that—but then a group of eight men in maroon robes gather around a large silver object up by the altar that looks like a giant teapot, tied to a pulley on a thick rope hanging down from the cathedral's dome. It makes me wonder what kind of circus tricks the latest Pope has added since I've been away.

Seth cocks his eyebrow and whispers, "And I thought Jews had weird rituals. Is this where the piñata originates?"

I stifle a laugh and poke him in the ribs. He grabs my elbow in the process, sliding his hand down my arm to lace his fingers with mine. It feels way more risqué, given the context, than it is. If my *abuela* ever saw me holding a boy's hand in church she'd have an absolute fit.

"That's a *botafumeiro*. The ritual dates back to the twelfth century," the man beside me explains when he overhears Seth's comment. He looks Spanish or Greek or Italian. Something Mediterranean. "It's normally saved for the evening Pilgrim's Mass, but today is a special feast day. Hard to believe the Church is still using such a thing, eh?"

"Hey, someone's got to keep the Middle Ages alive," I whisper back, smiling.

To be honest, I'm glad some things remain constant. Change is unavoidable, but it usually happens so fast that we don't even stop to consider if it's for the best. The view from our seats can't be much different from what pilgrims saw a thousand years ago, though thanks to the strong cologne worn by the gentleman beside me, it surely smells a million times better.

"What's that saying you Americans have?" the Mediterranean man asks. "If it isn't broke, do not proceed to fix it?"

I know he's making lighthearted small talk, but these words alter everything. What if things *are* broken, and they can't be fixed? Things like my brother?

A cloud passes by the window above my head, and the serenity of the space evaporates. Suddenly, I want nothing more than to chuck my hymnal at the choir's screeching cantor up front. How can all these people just sit here with placid looks on their faces, praying to a God who may or may not be listening, when millions of people are hurting and starving and dying beyond these doors every day?

*And what do you plan on doing about it?*

I don't know where this inner challenge comes from any more than I understand it. What am I *supposed* to do about it? This entire planet is groaning under the weight of pain. All I want is a sappy spiritual high like everyone else, where I get to cry and hug the stranger next to me before planting a big one on Seth like we're witnessing the New Year's Eve ball drop. This world is messed up beyond my repair, and it's not my job to fix it.

*If not you, then who?*

I have no answer to this question, but thankfully the giant teapot diverts my attention. The men in maroon robes grab hold of the eight handles splitting off from the thick rope, causing the *botafumeiro* to rise high above the pews. They pull the rope in a unified rhythm, making the silver receptacle swing back and forth down the center aisle. Before long, the thing reaches high speeds I never expected. Smoke pours from its crevices, and all I can breathe is church incense—a very specific scent that unleashes a torrent of memories. My entire childhood in a single inhalation.

Dad pissed off because we're late for Mass *again* and Mom still insists on marching us up to the first row of pews. Grandma Guadalupe with one of those white doily things over her hair, shaking her head at the teenagers in tank tops, muttering to me that this is how good girls get in trouble. Lucas sporting a comb-over and a little suit, speed-walking towards his First Communion because he figured the other kids weren't enthusiastic enough about receiving the Body of Christ. I'll never forget how he tripped and did a ninja-style tumble down the aisle, pumping his fists to the sky in victory when he bounced back on both feet. He tore a huge hole in his brand new dress pants, but as soon as he reached the priest—who turned beet red from holding in his laughter—Lucas's cracker/grape juice training kicked into high gear and he executed his task like a perfect angel.

I am both smiling and blinking back tears as the incense floats my memories up to the dome where sunlight pours down on us. It's hard to explain, but here in this ancient sanctuary, in a country that is foreign but somehow familiar, I am with my family.

I am home.

Seth's fingers tighten around mine. I can tell by the softness in his eyes that he watched me react to the reel of home videos playing through my mind. Only his eyes are trying to tell me something else. I follow his nod in the direction of the pews across from us. They're packed with people, so it's difficult to tell which pilgrim friend he's trying to point out, especially through the haze of incense smoke. Once it dissipates, I see the person Seth wanted me to see. A person kneeling calmly in a pew, both of his hawk eyes on me.

It's my father.

# CHAPTER 22

"Dad?" Despite my best efforts to steady my voice, it trembles across the sanctuary. Mass has ended and we are trying to go in peace, but the rushing waves of humanity make it hard to move until the crowd clears.

Finally, I make it across the aisle, where my father gives me a firm hug before looking me over with glassy eyes. "Well done, *mija*. You made it."

"But what are *you* doing here?" Because he shouldn't be here. Dad should be with Mom and Matteo. He should be with Lucas. Unless . . . .

I whirl around to Seth. "Did you text him our arrival date?"

Seth's silence tells me all I need to know.

"Come with me, Gabriela. Let's find a quiet place to talk." Dad shakes Seth's hand. "You too, son."

*No, no, no.* I don't want to talk somewhere else. Why won't he spit it out? Why does this ominous moment feel like receiving Lucas's package in the mail all over again?

The streets outside erupt with excitement as more pilgrims pour into the city, reuniting with kindred spirits they never thought they'd see again. The noise lessens the power of the silence surrounding my father like an invisible force field. I prepare myself for the worst, which is probably what my pilgrimage has been about all along. But now my time in this land of rainbows and unicorns is over.

It's time to face the facts: Lucas is dead.

My body suddenly weighs a ton. It's only when Seth grabs my arm and pulls me forward that I realize how far behind I've fallen. Dad marches down the cobblestones with his usual sense of purpose, but even after several hundred kilometers, I don't think I can make these final steps. Everything spins and I'm about to call out for Dad to stop, but he slips into an unassuming doorway. We follow him into a rustic restaurant where cured ham legs hang from the ceiling and wheels of stinky cheese line the display counters. My father grabs a table in a dark, private corner, and asks the waiter if the restaurant has Wi-Fi before ordering a carafe of the house wine.

"What's going on?" Quick like a Band-Aid. That's all I ask.

"One moment, *mija*." Dad's face reveals about as much emotion as a slab of marble. I'm shocked when he pulls an iPad from his bag and drags his finger across it like a Millennial pro. My heart is pounding and the ripe smell of olive brine makes me nauseous. Beneath the table, Seth rests his clammy hand on my knee. It's shaking, which tells me he's as terrified as I am.

Whatever my dad has to tell us, he came all the way to Spain to do it.

I glance at the other pilgrims celebrating their journey's end. Anger erupts in my gut. Not here. This is not the place to learn about the end of my brother's short life. *No* place is right for that kind of news, but once Dad says the words hiding behind his taut lips, a moan like no other will escape me and every pair of eyes will be on us.

Why is he torturing me like this? Dad's pride and joy may be gone forever, but *I'm* still here. After an eternity, my father slides the tablet across the table. Thanks to the dim lighting and my whirling head, I have to blink a few times before the blurry image comes into focus.

Lucas's corpse.

I'm staring at my dead brother's face, and I want to puke and cry and scream before sliding to a crumpled heap on the floor. But then the corpse moves. I realize there's a lag due to a weak Internet signal.

Two hazel eyes, both blinking. One mouth partially open, still breathing. Everything is motionless, yet spiraling. How is this real? How can someone who left us be looking right at me? Be looking right *through* me, since my heart has fallen from my chest and melted into a puddle beneath our seats.

"Hey, guys. How's it going?"

That voice. I don't recognize it. It isn't just groggy. Its defeated tone is foreign. If not for the moving picture in the center of the screen, I wouldn't believe what I'm looking at.

"Lucas!"

Tears pour down my cheeks with no restraint as I lift my eyes to my father, who is smiling a smile I've never seen before. A smile fashioned just for this moment. I look at Seth. He's stunned speechless, like he's about to pass out.

"Hey, Gabs. Mom tells me you were PMSing so bad, you needed to take a really long walk." My brother's voice is low and gravelly, but his soft smirk assures me it's really him.

Lucas is awake. He's alive! That he's already giving me crap is an extra-good sign.

"How are you feeling, man?" Seth's voice cracks.

"Oh, you know. Kind of like I've been in a coma for a month."

We both laugh—tense chuckles of relief and confusion and joy all at once. Lucas's face looks puffy on the screen and I can see a new sadness in his eyes that wasn't there before, but otherwise, he's the same guy. The same easy-to-love Lucas.

I hear my mother's voice in the background. "All right, sweetie. Time to say goodbye. You need your nap." Honestly, I'd think she was talking to Matteo if Lucas didn't roll his eyes.

"I've been sleeping for several weeks, Ma. Don't you think that's enough?"

Now all of us are grinning, but as self-effacing as Lucas can be, the exhaustion on his face confirms that even our short conversation has been a strain.

"Better listen to Mom," I say, trying to keep things light. "Otherwise they'll send you on a six-week walk of penance for failing to honor your father and mother."

The remaining color drains from Lucas's lips. Out of the corner of my eye, I see Dad shaking his head, as if to say, *Don't go there, Gabi.* I have no idea what I just said, but it makes Lucas go mute for half a minute. He looks away.

"I won't be going anywhere, Gabs, but thanks. Both of you. I'm glad you guys got to see the *camino*, though I'm shocked you walked it without killing each other in the process. You must have fallen head over boots in love or something."

Seth and I laugh nervously, as if the sheer thought is *sooo* ridiculous.

Lucas yawns. "Mom's right. This morphine is a trip. I better go."

"Bye, man," Seth says. "Rest up and we'll see you soon."

"Love you, Lucas."

The image flickers and he's gone. Seth and I keep staring at the little black screen, a miracle in its own right. We're elated, but apprehensive. I look up at Dad. His face confirms that even though it's beyond amazing that Lucas is awake, all is not well in the world.

Something is still wrong.

"He's alive. I can't believe it. He's awake," Seth keeps repeating, like he's in shock and doesn't know what else to say.

The waiter sets a carafe on the table and Dad pours out three small servings. He raises his glass. "A toast to Lucas, and to you both."

We clink our glasses. Dad drains his, then pours himself another. Okay, something is *really* wrong. My father has a drink maybe a few times a year. There's something else he hasn't told us yet.

"What is it?" I ask.

Dad sips his wine slowly, working up the right words. "I have no doubt that your brother's recovery is a miracle, but even miracles aren't always everything we want them to be."

Seth and I wait as dread builds a wall around us, brick by brick until we can no longer move, until we can hardly breathe. It feels like the only way I'll be able to wake up from this nightmare is if I scream. So I do. "Why all the unnecessary suspense? What the hell is wrong with him? Tell us, already!"

"Control yourself, Gabriela." Dad swirls his glass, then looks at me with renewed grief. "The doctors say your brother will never walk again."

*Never walk again.* Never. Again.

"How do they know for sure?" Seth croaks before he drains his drink.

"There was a severe injury to his spine," Dad explains. "The surgeon couldn't be certain of the lasting effects until Lucas came out of the coma, but he's been awake for several days now and hasn't regained any movement below the belt."

"Maybe it'll just take time." I'm crying all over again, but for very different reasons. Lucas unable to walk? The most active person I've ever known, incapable of moving one foot forward by himself? Everything hurts. It's an ache of utter helplessness. My brother is alive, but for a split second I almost wonder if his diagnosis is a fate worse than death.

It's only when Seth wraps his arm around my shoulder that I realize I'm trembling. His embrace—extra bold in front of my father—reminds me to breathe. It also reminds me of a truth as constant as cathedral stones and incense smoke. A truth that does not change no matter the circumstances.

Where there is love, life is worth it.

Lucas is still here and we all still love him, and that's what matters. We'll figure everything else out as we go, just like we figured out this pilgrimage.

Day by day, step by step.

"He'll be okay, Gabriela." Dad reaches across the table for my hand. I grab his like my life depends on it. "Your brother is still with us and I truly believe you helped bring him back."

I don't know if I'd go that far, but I'm glad my pilgrimage has given my father a reason to trust me again. "I'm so sorry, Dad."

There's no need to explain what I'm apologizing for. My father's brutally honest expression tells me he knows. "You are forgiven, *mija*. You already were. I just didn't know how to show it. *Venga*, I think I do now."

• • •

After dinner, Dad treats us to a fancy dessert at the Parador, a five-star historic hotel that was once a medieval pilgrim hospital. The hostess seats us at a small table with red velvet chairs, positioned below rounded arches made of pearly white stone. Little iron lanterns hang from the vaulted ceiling, like we're in an old wine cellar. Dad orders three *flans* and a glass of champagne for himself.

"What the heck—?"

My mouth is full of *flan*, but the tuxedo-wearing waiter hovering over me elicits this response. He's holding out a bottle of Boone's Farm Strawberry Hill, complete with a fancy ice bucket. "Uh, I *suppose* that was a good year."

My dad is beaming. Forget his career accomplishments or the fact that he came to the U.S. without a dime to his name. This parlor trick might be the greatest thing he's ever done. "I had it bubble-wrapped at the Kaiserslautern Shopette so I could bring it here for your birthday toast. I know how you like the expensive stuff."

Huh. Apparently I'm eighteen. The day came and went and I honestly had no idea, which goes to show how time passes differently on the *camino*, where calendars are not necessary.

Seth laughs. "Did you seriously forget your own birthday?"

"I don't even know what month it is!"

We laugh so hard that Dad can hardly make his second toast of the evening. I take my first sip of the fine rosé vintage and nearly gag. "Wow, this stuff is like cough syrup."

Seth grins. "I'm guessing your taste has matured recently."

Boone's Farm was Brent's illicit drink of choice, so I suspect it has. Six months ago, I would have said a car was what I wanted most when I turned eighteen, but this entire day has been the best gift I could ever ask for. Lucas is alive, and my dad still has a sense of humor.

The chasm between us is officially breached.

• • •

I can't sleep. It's way too quiet.

Dad got each of us single rooms so we could finally have a night in our own space, but the silence makes my thoughts deafening. Every time I close my eyes, I picture Lucas at a dozen different ages. There is one common theme: *movement*. Lucas riding his bike at age five. Lucas jumping off the pool's high dive at age eight. Lucas competing in a karate tournament when he was twelve. Lucas racing down the soccer field at sixteen. Lucas running 10K races in preparation for basic training just a few months back.

It's as if someone broke into the hard drive of my brother's soul and deleted all the images, erased his former life completely. Nothing will be the same. He's starting a brand new journey and there are places he'll be going that none of us can go with him.

*Bam, bam, bam!*

At the sudden sound, I jump out of bed and run over to the window. Our hotel isn't far from a modern section of the city that has a lot of *pintxo* bars, but this isn't drunken revelry. This sounds like someone getting beaten with a tire iron. The shadows in the street below refuse to give up any faces, but the attacker's white T-shirt glows in the moonlight.

Metal. Dog tags. Seth.

Seth beating someone's brains in.

*Sing, O muse, of the rage of Achilles.*

I try singing a scream of my own, but no sound comes out. My room is at the back of the hotel. By the time I race to the end of the hallway, down the stairs, and out through the lobby, it'll be too late. The guy lying on the ground out there could be dead. I'm not certain the assailant is Seth, but my heart tells me it is.

It also tells me I can't sit by and let him commit murder.

I open the window and rattle the fire escape. It doesn't seem super stable, but my room is only on the second floor, so the fall wouldn't be life-threatening. Seth's enraged grunts grow louder. The metal hits against something hard, something like bone.

I'll risk it. After throwing on shorts, I climb out the window and shimmy down the fire escape, forgetting to breathe until my flip-flops touch the damp sidewalk.

The prey of Seth's dormant war trauma—or whatever you want to call this darkness unleashed inside him—is bent over in the dark alleyway. Seth lifts a metal pipe over his head and slams it down. Again. And again. And again.

My birthday *flan* makes its way back up my throat. I open my mouth to hurl it all over the sidewalk, but instead, I scream.

"Seth! Stop!"

He whirls around to face me, sweat pouring down his face. The arm clutching the pipe falls limp at his side. His weapon clatters to the ground. "Gabi. I, I . . . ."

I inch closer, bracing myself for the hideous spectacle of some poor sap who said the wrong thing and is now a bloody pulp. At the sight of Seth's victim, I nearly collapse.

The wheelchair.

Seth has taken the wheelchair out back and given it such an alley ass-whooping, it's hard to tell what the twisted pile of scrap metal is anymore. The storm cloud lifts from Seth's face. He breaks my gaze. "I . . . I had to let it out somehow."

"Well," I sigh. "We all know that wheelchair had it coming."

Seth doesn't respond. The reason he chose this scapegoat is obvious. I walk over and grab his arm, leading him away from the crime scene. We sit down on the curb below the fire escape, our knees touching. I don't say anything. I don't have to remind him or even ask.

*Remember what you promised to tell me once we reached Santiago?*

The words pour out all on their own.

"In Afghanistan, our unit was assigned to a region known to have a large number of Taliban sympathizers. Lucas and I were on patrol in the village one afternoon. Nothing unusual about it, I just had this sense that something was different. Off." Seth licks his lips, like he's back in that harsh landscape. "There was this kid in the village who hung around the soldiers a lot, asking for gum or candy. Young kid, not much older than Matteo. Your brother, the big softie, took to him. He'd given the kid a soccer ball the day before. I told him it was a stupid thing to do, that he shouldn't be getting attached." Seth shakes his head. "But you know Lucas."

Yes, I do know Lucas. So well that I can almost see what's coming.

"Later when we're on patrol, we see that same kid squatting in the dirt, crying his eyes out, holding his flat soccer ball. Lucas goes over to see if he's okay and notices that the ball has been punctured. On purpose. He lets his guard down for *one second*, but that was all it took. The kid's older brother, a kid himself— fifteen, maybe sixteen—steps out from an abandoned building across the street holding an AK-47. He points it right at Lucas."

Seth gulps in a few breaths, giving me just enough time to wrap my mind around this impossible situation. "I raise my weapon and order the older kid to drop his, but he keeps screaming words I don't understand. Screaming like he's scared, like he doesn't *want* to be doing what he's doing, but someone's *making* him do it. Lucas doesn't even reach for his gun. He just stands there with his arms stretched out, talking to the kid, telling him not to shoot, trying to mediate like he thinks he's goddamn Gandhi. It's a stalemate. The kid pointing his gun at Lucas. Me pointing my gun at the kid. And Lucas standing there in the middle of it all, trying to keep the peace in a place that doesn't know what the word means. I inch closer to him, keeping the enemy in my scopes until my heart is racing so fast, I'm afraid it will give out before I can reach Lucas. The kid starts to lower his weapon. At least I think that's what he's doing. I exhale and loosen my grip on the trigger."

Seth clenches his jaw so tight, it sounds like he's grinding his teeth to gritty powder. "Once I realize the insurgent isn't dropping his weapon, just altering his aim, I hesitate. Why? Because he's a *kid* and I don't want to kill him. Lucas sees what's happening before I do. When the boy shoots the Coke can on the ground between us, the can filled with explosives, Lucas is already turning to throw his body against mine. He knocks both of us to the ground, taking the brunt of the shrapnel in his back."

Silent tears of rage and regret run down Seth's face, but he can't stop. He can't look me in the eye, but he can't stop. "Just before the IED in the can exploded, I'd panicked and shot off a round. The Afghani kid was dead. His blood was everywhere, Gabi. And Lucas was so messed up, I thought he must be dead, too." Seth trembles and meets my gaze. It isn't this cruel world he hates. It's himself. "I sprained an arm. That stupid kid is gone forever and your brother will never walk again. I had to wear a sling for a week, but that's it. I get off scot-free."

I pull Seth towards me, and he falls limp into my lap. "It's okay," I whisper, knowing things may never be okay again. But his grief *is* okay, and he needs to know that. "Odysseus wept. Even Achilles mourned."

Then I do the only thing I can think of: I stroke Seth's hair and kiss his cheeks until he has nothing left.

# CHAPTER 23

"Where do we go from here?" I ask Seth once he's sobered up. Neither of us will be able to sleep now, but at least this time Seth is drunk on tears instead of Tanqueray.

"We walk."

"You don't think we've walked enough already?"

Seth shrugs. "Sometimes it's the only thing left to do."

I get up from the curb. "Okay, let me grab a sweatshirt."

"Plan on going back the way you came, Catwoman?" Seth smiles weakly and glances up at the fire escape.

I give him a feeble grin back, knowing super-sensitive Seth could only stick around for a limited time. "Let's not tempt fate. I'll go through the lobby."

Seth has regained his composure by the time I return, almost like his late-night confession never happened. "Where should we walk to? Portugal might make for a nice evening stroll."

"I have a better idea," I reply. "Follow me, *por favor*."

It's after 2 A.M., but the night is still young. We soak in the pulsing sounds of life, grateful to be a part of the dance. Horns honk and people pour out of bars like a steady stream of bubbling champagne, filling this city with their celebratory songs. I can tell by the way his sweaty fingers clasp mine that Seth wants to go somewhere with less people, but there's still one Spanish tradition we haven't taken part in yet.

"What's this?" Seth asks when I stop in front of a modest building with a green and white awning. It doesn't look like anything special, but when we walked by earlier today, the chalkboard sign out front spoke to me in multiple languages.

"They claim to have the best churros and chocolate in town," I explain as the smell of fried bread and cocoa drifts out onto the sidewalk. "It would be a sin to leave Spain without trying this specialty midnight snack. Or three in the morning snack, rather."

Maybe it's a girl thing to crave chocolate after a good cry, but Seth humors me and steps inside. At least I'm not the only one with a sugar hankering. The tables are packed with groups of friends, couples, even families, all busy dipping the savory into the sweet. This confirms it. Spain is a culture for the nocturnal.

"*Hola guapa*," says an older man behind the counter, grinning as though this is the start of his midday shift. He wipes the powdered sugar dusting his hands onto his apron before pointing to the menu board. "*Que quieres, guapa?*"

"*Guapa*. I know that one," Seth whispers in my ear. "Looks like I have competition. This guy thinks you're hot."

"This guy could be my grandfather," I murmur back. "It's meant to be endearing. Every girl who walks through those doors is *guapa*, trust me."

"Maybe, but this time he means it," Seth replies. "Trust me."

My face feels flushed, so I turn back to the man behind the counter. "*Dos chocolates con churros, por favor.*"

"*Dos chocolates con churros!*" the man shouts to his partner at the other end of the blue-tiled bar. He, in turn, passes the message on to the cook inside the kitchen. None of the men working here look like they're under sixty. Their cocoa powder must have some amazing medicinal powers to keep them going so late into the night.

While we wait for our snack, I study the old photographs of bull-fighters on the walls, next to stuffed heads of all the *toros* who lost. It's like a Spanish version of the creepy taxidermy trophies you'd find in a Midwestern bar. Hanging on the wall beside us are additional photos of the three *compañeros* who own the joint, smiling with an assortment of celebrities.

"*De donde eres?*" the man who took our order asks when he sees me looking at a collection that would make *People* magazine jealous.

"*Los Estados Unidos*," I reply.

"America?" The man's face perks up as he steps out from the bar and grabs me by the arms. "*Mira!*" he says, dragging us to the wall of fame. "Look. Mel Gibson!"

Seth chuckles as the enthusiastic bartender shows off an autographed headshot of the actor, who must have been a patron here way back when he liked wearing blue face makeup.

"We *have* to get a picture of this for Lucas." I envision the *Braveheart* movie poster and its famous quotation, 'Every man dies, not every man really lives,' which hung over Lucas's bed when he was twelve. That should have been my first clue that my brother is more honor-driven than most.

"Did you bring the action figure?" Seth asks.

"Of course." I open my purse. "Never leave home without him."

As we position G.I. Lucas next to the headshot, capturing a celebrity image of our own, the churro man's eyes dance between us like *we're* the ones with some weird Hollywood fetish.

"*Amor. Nos vuelven locos.*" The man sighs and leaves us so he can assist the next customer.

Seth perks up. "What did he just say?"

"Didn't catch it," I fib. Because I'm a little freaked out. The bartender's comment—*Love. It drives us crazy*—means my chemistry with Seth must be visible to the outside world. I'm not prepared to call this chemistry *love*, since I think of love as a promise, not a transitory spark. But there's definitely something burning between us and it's bright enough to notice.

Our order is up, so we find a table by a window overlooking the street. The churros are piping hot, but I dig in despite my singed tongue. Eating distracts me from Seth's intense staring.

"Oh. My. Word," I say in between bites. "This is amazing."

Spanish hot chocolate is *not* of the instant-sawdust-with-cardboard-marshmallows variety. It's rich and dark and thick as soup, hence the churros, which serve as edible spoons.

"I'm not a big sweets guy, but this stuff is good," Seth says after a few bites. All of a sudden he laughs, which, given his status an hour ago, is music to my ears. "Napkin?"

I turn to look at my reflection in the darkened window. There's chocolate all over my face. "Guess I was hungrier than I thought."

Seth grins. "Sometimes we don't know what we really want until we taste it."

Why *hello*, double entendre. That comment has me blushing like crazy, so I stare into my cup, stirring my churro like a witch whipping up a cauldron spell.

Seth's confession has clearly established some sort of bond, but I don't know if I'm ready for that kind of responsibility. Not on top of Lucas. I care for Seth a lot, but in many ways he's hurt as badly as my brother, only his wounds are harder to see. If I fall for him now, what exactly will I be falling into? More than I can probably handle, that's for sure.

"When we get back home, what else should we do to help Lucas?" I ask, knowing this question will be a game changer. As intended, the sappy look in Seth's eyes solidifies at my reminder of the tragedy that brought us together in the first place.

"Get him a dog."

"Come again?" I assume he's messing around, but I don't get the joke.

"Get him a dog," Seth repeats. "There are a few charities that pair disabled veterans with retired MP and K-9 unit dogs. It won't fix everything, but I know of a few discharged vets who got pups and it made a huge difference. Sometimes it's nice to have a companion who doesn't offer up clichéd condolences when there's really nothing to be said."

Silence. Is that what Seth wants? Or does he want to acknowledge his wartime actions for what they were—an evil, perhaps a necessary and unavoidable evil, but an evil nonetheless? It isn't fair, but maybe that's how life works. Even when you *want* to walk the straight and narrow way, even when you're *trying* to stick to the honorable path, there are times where you're damned if you do, and damned if you don't. Like the sticky chocolate lining my cup, an unavoidable darkness lurks around every corner, coating every motive and tainting every move. None of us escape intact, even if we try to climb out of the muck by pointing fingers and passing the buck.

Seth was presented with an especially crappy choice, where even refusing to make it would have had disastrous consequences. I hate what happened, but I respect him for taking a side and accepting the blame, even if it costs him everything.

"So is that why you let me hang around?" I trace my fingernail along the tattoo inside his wrist, then press down hard. "Because I have the silent, steadfast loyalty of a dog?"

Seth grins. "You're a good listener, but I'm glad you talk back. Even if you do have a smart mouth. Besides, as you already know, I'm a cat person."

Seth leans forward and wipes a smudge from my nose. "Here, you missed a spot."

His expression of playful innocence makes me believe there are ways to get clean, no matter how big of a mess we make. Maybe that's what Lucas struggled with, why he poured himself into ancient warrior epics, in search of the secret for living with a fractured soul. Maybe that's why he wanted to walk the *camino*— to purge his spirit of all he'd done before returning home. Maybe *doing* something to show we're sorry when words don't cut it helps more than all the counseling programs and self-help books in the world.

If that's true, then Seth has a long road ahead of him, because I don't know how a person ever rights that kind of wrong. Maybe he can't right it on his own, but he can sure as hell repent of it. And for that, I'm glad. Monsters don't feel remorse, but men do.

"Can we talk about something besides Lucas?" Seth asks, suddenly looking sleepy. "I love your brother and all, but he's the only thing I've been thinking about for the past month."

"I get that. What do you want to talk about?"

A mischievous glimmer in his eye, Seth chomps down on his last churro. "Maybe I don't want to talk at all."

• • •

Unlike the newer parts of the city, the old town is quiet. Overflowing with dark corners made for kissing couples. Well, it's mostly quiet, until we pass through a courtyard where a public concert is taking place.

A small crowd gathers around an ornate stone fountain, where a group of men wear what must be traditional Galician garb: wool pants and white shirts with puffy sleeves, worn beneath gray vests. Each man dons a wide-brimmed hat that looks like it was stolen from a Mennonite. Each plays something musical, from the accordion, to the snare drum, to Rodrigo's beloved *gaita*. The few *hombres* not holding a physical instrument croon a controlled melody, clapping their hands in a consistent rhythm.

"Want to watch?" It isn't really a question. I'm already heading in that direction. The thought of being alone with Seth on an empty cobblestone street is both thrilling and terrifying at the same time. Better let the churros in my fluttering stomach settle first.

We work our way through the crowd, finding a seat on the edge of the fountain. I'm amazed by this musical spontaneity in the middle of the night, yet the people around us—locals and tourists alike—don't appear to find it strange at all.

At the start of a tune that sounds like a Scottish Highland ballad blended together with a finger-snapping song from southern Spain, a girl who looks about thirteen steps out from the crowd and begins to dance. She wears a full red skirt and a shawl that blends in with her long black hair. Soon she's joined by a few friends, all of them twirling in a circle around the fountain, their purple, yellow, and scarlet skirts billowing out like tulips. It isn't a sultry dance like flamenco; it's something sweeter and more traditional. Suddenly, in unison, each girl approaches a young man seated around the fountain and asks him to dance.

Naturally, Seth is one of those young men.

"No, no, no," he repeats to the smiling *señorita*, his panicked eyes pleading. "Tell her, Gabi. I don't dance. Seriously, tell her."

"*Le gusta bailar*," I say to the girl before turning to Seth. "Loosen up. It'll do you good."

"You'll pay for this, Santiago."

Seth is dragged from his seat with the other unsuspecting victims, all of them equally mortified. At least his ankle is feeling better and he doesn't have to do much. The young ladies are the ones who own this show. All the guys just stand there looking silly, while the girls swirl around them and everybody cheers.

Once the guys are sufficiently dizzy, the *chicas* return them to their seats before making one more rotation around the fountain. Each girl resumes her original position before her male counterpart. The music stops and the synchronized dancers lean forward, pushing their partners into the basin of water behind them. Seth seems to fall in slow motion, his shocked face sinking below the big splash he makes. The crowd releases a collective gasp and everyone cracks up, but all I can do is sit there with my hand over my mouth until Seth resurfaces.

He's going to be livid. A few of the other dunked tourists definitely look pissed. Seth emerges, but instead of cursing, he's laughing like a lunatic. He gets on his hands in the push-up plank position, then wades around the shallow fountain, spraying water on anyone near the edge like this is the splash section at SeaWorld. Amidst the screaming and the laughter, the music picks back up and the dancing resumes. Seth has an extra wet splash in store for me. I take it like a champ because I kind of deserve it, but I never imagined these tiny dancers could be so bold.

A huge grin on his face, Seth climbs out of the fountain, wrapping me in a soaking wet bear hug. "Well, that was refreshing. I feel like a new man."

"I had no idea it would end that way. I swear it," I mutter into Seth's soaked chest.

"Six months downrange only to be defeated by a little girl." Seth gives me that look again. The one that makes me shiver like *I* just climbed out of the dunk tank. "Let's get out of here. I think I've experienced enough Galician folk traditions for one night."

Dripping water the entire way, Seth leads me back to the main square of the cathedral. He's limping a bit, so we take it slow. The square is shielded by a silence that's almost unnatural, and the moon bathes the basilica in an ethereal light. Seth seems to absorb the solemnness of its afterglow.

He sits down on the steps, pulling me onto his lap. "Have any candles left?"

I try to get up. "Gross, you're still soaked!"

That only makes Seth wrap his arms around me even tighter.

I laugh and shrug him off, so I can dig through my purse for one last tealight. "I don't get it. Lucas is alive. What are we lighting this candle for?"

"For us."

Whatever Seth means by that, the way the hairs on my arm stand at attention tells me now is not the time to ask stupid questions. I hand him the lighter. He sets the glowing tealight down on the stone step.

The next thing I know, Seth is kissing me.

*Mist, coffee, shoelaces, dirt, hostels, rain, vino, pain, light.*

An entire *camino* in a single kiss.

For the record, I can honestly say that kissing a boy out in the open—beneath the holy glow of a cathedral and with all the wandering stars as witnesses—beats the back of a stuffy car any day. By the time we come up for air, all that's left of our candle is a puddle of wax and a thin trail of smoke reaching skyward.

# CHAPTER 24

"I don't understand." I pace in front of Seth while he shoves freshly laundered clothes into his backpack. "Why are you doing this?"

What I really mean is, why are you doing this *to me*? But saying that out loud would only solidify my selfishness and I don't want to give Seth the satisfaction.

"I'm doing this because I *need* to." Seth hands me the cardboard tube containing his *Compostela* certificate, sealed with the official stamp we received for finishing the *camino*. "Give this to Lucas, will you?"

He says it so nonchalantly, likes it's nothing, when it's everything. The simple gesture sums up everything I love about Seth, but right now I don't want to kiss him.

I want to kill him.

"Why don't you give Lucas the *Compostela* yourself?" I take the certificate anyway. "By visiting him in the hospital like the rest of us."

Seth stops packing. When he looks up at me, I see the fear in his eyes. Not the terror of someone who fears for his safety, but the look of one who is haunted. The dread of someone who fears for his soul. And then I know the truth. Send this boy back to Afghanistan, and he'd be fine. But make him visit my brother— half the man he was, at least physically—and the survivor's guilt would have Seth running from the room.

"I told you. You may have accomplished what you needed to by walking the *camino*, but I'm just getting started." Seth grabs my hands, interlacing his fingers through mine. "Something happened to me towards the end of the trek. I can't go home yet. I can't be in a place where everyone knows my name, but I feel anonymous. Not yet."

"I thought you were trying to get shipped back to Afghanistan as soon as possible."

Seth nods. "Before last night, all I wanted was to go back and get revenge for what was taken from your brother. But now I see why Lucas wanted to do this walk. I *want* to suffer, to feel pain and confusion and remorse, because that means I can still feel something besides rage."

"But where are you walking *to*?" I press. "Turning around and walking back the same way we came makes no sense."

"I'm not opposed to going backwards in order to go forward," Seth replies. "But there are a few old pilgrimage routes in England and Scotland, so maybe I'll hop on a ferry. Honestly, I don't really know where I'm going. I just need to keep walking."

"But you're not even religious!"

"I killed a kid, Gabi," Seth says softly. "I didn't want to, but I can't help thinking that if there *is* some sort of afterlife, that's one of the sins that counts."

*You're a kid yourself!* I want to scream. "What makes you think walking will change anything? How do you know it will bring you any peace when it hasn't so far?"

"Oh, it has. I feel much better walking than I do sitting still, but getting Zen isn't my goal. Peace may be a byproduct, but it's not the point." Seth turns to the crisp blue sky outside the hotel room window. "If there's anything up there besides stars and empty space, it's something that must be sought after, not summoned. I'm not interested in inner harmony or belief systems that soothe. I'm interested in ones that mobilize."

I have no ammo left, so it's time to play the girlfriend card (even though nothing is official) and start sulking. I cross my arms and take a step back. "What about your ankle?"

"It's getting better. Walking will hurt, but like I said, I'm okay with that."

No matter his reasons, I don't like the idea of Seth trotting the globe to atone for his mistakes, beating himself up for doing his duty, for trying to *save* my brother's life.

"What about you, kiddo? What are your plans now that the *camino* is over?"

His relapse to that nickname brings a half-smile to my lips, but it doesn't stop me from socking him in the shoulder—another attempt to hide that my heart is breaking a few hours after it finally felt whole. "I'm not sure. I'll have to make up schoolwork over the summer in order to graduate, but all I really want is to hang out with Lucas for a while. Who knows, maybe when he's well enough, we'll go on a long walk, too. At least I already have experience pushing a wheelchair over vast distances."

"I wouldn't count on that," Seth whispers. "Not yet."

Tears burn my eyes. Not yet. Not yet. The answer to everything I want is *not yet*.

Seth sighs. "I've got to go, Gabi."

And if I truly care about him, I'll let him. It may kill me, but I've been around the military long enough to know that if I don't let Seth heal in his own way, it may kill him instead.

"No matter what you do next year, you've got an incredible future ahead of you." Seth kisses my forehead gently, though his grip on my shoulders is anything but. "Don't let me or any other chump hold you back."

But what if I want to be held back? What if I want to stay here with him, free on the open road with nowhere to go and no one to answer to?

Seth reads my thoughts. "You know it would never last. Not like this."

"Yeah, I know."

There's a time for wandering, and a time for returning to your roots. A life severed from a mission is only liberating for so long. Pretty soon you're just another restless drifter with no ties and no loyalties; a slave on the lookout for the next high, the next escapade, never satisfied with the mundane tasks that are part of life's greatest adventure: love.

And now is the time for roots. My family tree needs me, one of its vital branches. If Seth is ever grafted onto us, it will have to be back in the real world, where soldiers harbor scars no one else can see, where miracles are harder to come by, and where people are a lot more lost.

I turn away and wipe my eyes. "You'll miss me, you know? Especially when you get thrown in a foreign jail or slide down a mountain and there's no one around to save your clumsy behind."

"You're right. I will miss you." Seth grabs my arm and pulls me in for a quick kiss. "But at least I'll have G.I. Lucas to keep me company."

"He may not be enough. Promise me you'll get real help if you need it."

"I promise." Seth says the words like he's making a sacred vow.

There's a knock on the door, already opened a crack. My father pokes his head inside. "There you are, Gabi."

Translation? *You should not be in a boy's hotel room alone, mija.*

Seth and I part like we've learned the other person has the plague. I swear I see a smile beneath Dad's fabricated scowl.

"Time to check out. You guys ready?"

I nod. Dad drops off our room keys at the front desk while I walk Seth out to the road. It doesn't take long to find the golden arrow guiding us back to the *camino*. I refuse to cry. It isn't like Seth is going off to war again. He's doing what he needs to do to get whole, to bring all the broken shards back together, even if the new stained-glass pattern ends up being a lot different from the one before. As long as a little light can shine through, Seth will be fine.

"Tell Lucas I love him." Seth squeezes my hand. I wonder if by not saying the actual words—which would make this a million times harder—he's telling me something similar. "Tell him I'll visit as soon as I can."

I focus my watering eyes on Seth's muddy boots, on the ACE bandage wrapped around his ankle. My entire life has consisted of one goodbye after another. I'm used to it, but this one cuts something out of me—something I may never get back. You don't take a journey like this without the person you walked it with taking a part of you, too.

"It isn't forever, Gabi. How can you not know that?" Seth lifts my chin. "Now go take care of my best friend. You might also let him know he has a competitor for the position and she's ruthless."

"But *when*? When will you be back?"

"I don't know." Seth smirks. "When will you be okay with surprises?"

One last kiss and I turn away, before I break down and start begging him not to go. I reach the hotel entrance, then glance back over my shoulder. All I can see is that ridiculous G.I. Joe doll riding on top of Seth's pack, until they both disappear over a rise in the road.

"*Buen camino!*" My strained voice bounces down the stones. Seth returns the pilgrim farewell, and I can hear his throaty laughter in it. Then, he's gone.

Gone in one way, but like Lucas, still with us. Still here.

• • •

"One last candle, *mija*. You never know. God answered our prayers the first time."

I want to believe this is true. I want to hope that Lucas will stand up one day. I want to trust that there are real, physical things we can do to help those we love—prayers we can utter and walks we can take—so I follow Dad into the cathedral, when a month ago I would have whined about all European churches looking the same inside.

The aisles are crowded with a whole new set of pilgrims. Dad seems to know exactly where he's headed. We pass a large statue of St. James the Moor Slayer, waving a sword high above his head, but this isn't where Sergeant Major Santiago stops.

He enters an empty side chapel at the back of the cathedral and kneels before a Pietà sculpture of the Virgin Mary, cradling the broken body of her son. I reach into my pocket for my lighter. The *hamsa* pendant comes with it. I did a bit of Internet research and discovered that the symbol is found in all three main monotheistic traditions, named for women important to each faith—the hand of Miriam, sister of Moses, in Judaism; the hand of Mary, mother of Jesus, in Christianity; and the hand of Fatima, daughter of Muhammad, in Islam.

As I gaze at this mother bent over the body of her dead child, I know each woman would react the same way. The way my mom reacted at Lucas's bedside. The way Seth's would react if his shame isn't defeated and, God forbid, he took his own life like so many of the soldiers who haven't found a way home. The way the mother of the Afghani teen no doubt reacted when she found her boy dead in the street. There's only one response to such a tragedy, and that's a woman's gut-wrenching wails—the high price of the pendulum that is the human heart, which can swing from wrath to love in the space of a few short breaths.

Dad lights his candle and says his prayer. ". . . blessed art thou among women . . . ."

I set the *hamsa* pendant beside the tealight, an extra offering for all the mothers made childless by war. There are widows and there are orphans, but for parents who outlive their children, there isn't even a name to designate the depth of the loss.

Then I join my father in reciting words I could utter in my sleep, even though I haven't said them in a long time. "Pray for us sinners, now and at the hour of our death."

And because I don't say the second part of Mom's go-to prayer often enough, I remember that Lucas is alive and whisper, "Thank you."

• • •

"You like him a lot, don't you?"

There is *no way* I'm having this conversation with my dad, especially not on the steps of the cathedral where I kissed Seth the night before. Boys aren't something I discuss with my father. In fact, pretending they do not exist tends to be the wisest move.

"Maybe. I don't know."

Dad smiles his knowing smile. "What about Brent? Won't he be jealous?"

"Wait. You *knew* I was still with Brent?"

"I wasn't born yesterday, Gabriela. Your mother and I figured that's why you weren't adjusting to Kaiserslautern very well, when normally you'd have new friends in a week."

"Don't worry. Brent and I are officially done."

"Good. That kid was a punk." Dad pats me on the leg. "Seth, on the other hand . . . ."

"I don't want to talk about him, Dad!"

"That's good, too. He's a loyal friend to your brother, but he's got a lot to deal with right now and you've got your own way to find. Maybe one day you'll meet somewhere in the middle. Until then, if you really want to spend the next year volunteering abroad, I can look into setting something up for you in Mexico. Your *Tia* Isabel would love to have you stay with her."

"You mean you'd actually allow it?" I stammer.

I'm waiting for Dad to launch into one of his "when I was your age, I had three jobs and couldn't dream of going to college" tirades, but instead he says, "Like I could stop you? Besides, it would do you good to learn more about your roots."

Dad breaks my gaze and clenches both fists. This tells me he's about to get sentimental, which makes me want to run back into the church screaming *sanctuary!*

"You're my only daughter, Gabi. I may have been harder on you, but that's only because raising a daughter in this world makes warfare seem easy. I never wanted to treat you like you were weaker than Lucas or less capable, so I'm sure I went overboard at times. The path I chose has given us many opportunities, but that doesn't mean it hasn't left me with scars of my own."

I chew my fingernails and avoid his eyes. "I never wanted to be treated like a princess. I just wanted to make you proud."

"You have, *mija*. You always have." Dad sighs. "One day you will stand by a good man, Gabriela. But first, I want you to stand on your own two feet."

Dad has given me a lot of lectures in his day and I've tuned out most of them, but these are words I will never, ever forget.

He squeezes my knee. "Come on, *mija*. Let's go home."

# CHAPTER 25

"ID cards, please." The uniformed guard utters these words without a trace of a smile.

Dad rolls down his window as I pass my ID card forward. I've been back in Germany for about three weeks, but after walking through a borderless world, these security stations still feel strange. Yet today, everything goes back to normal, even if it's a brand new normal.

Today, we bring Lucas home.

As soon as we reach his hospital room, my eyes hone in on the person playing cards by his bedside. The broad shoulders and dark fuzz on the back of the guy's head make my heart leap. The soldier gets up to leave, and I recognize him as one of Lucas's battalion buddies.

My brother looks great. He's clean-shaven and dressed in regular clothes. He may never live the life we all expected him to, and that makes me sadder than I can describe, but I won't show it. Despair is our worst enemy, so I'll be strong for him, just like Seth told me to be.

"Thought your long-lost love had returned from his vision quest, didn't you, sis?" Smirking, Lucas leans back in his wheelchair for a stretch. "Yeah, your smitten status is all over your face. Cut it out, okay? I know Russo way too well and the guy isn't worthy of your time."

"Oh, but he's worthy of yours?" Seth hasn't contacted me once since Santiago, so I'm not getting my hopes up, but that doesn't stop my cheeks from igniting. "Nice try, Lucas, but if there's an imminent wedding to plan, it's yours. Let me guess. Nurse Walker has already stopped by at least three times this morning?"

Lucas's face turns the same shade as mine. "Whatever."

It's true. All the nurses adore him, even if Lucas thinks he has a better chance of walking again than of getting a girlfriend while he's in a wheelchair. I disagree.

Exhibit A: The napkin with a telephone number peeking out from under his Jell-O.

My parents step out into the hallway to talk to Lucas's doctor while one of the nurses—Nurse Walker, I presume—takes Matteo down to the cafeteria for an ice cream. I haven't really been alone with Lucas since he woke up, so I'm not sure what to say. Usually we revert to sarcastic sibling bantering, but I can't stifle the question I've been dancing around for weeks.

"Lucas, can I ask you something?" I fidget with a teddy bear dressed in camouflage—a get-well gift from a visitor who, like the rest of us, has no idea what to give a wounded soldier. "Are you angry?"

Because he should be, but Lucas hasn't really shown it. And that means he's buried his anger way down deep, which is much scarier than if he wore his wrath on his sleeve.

Lucas goes quiet for a moment. "What, like am I angry at my CO for sending us on that patrol? Or at the government for keeping this war going? Or at God for giving humans the freedom to be complete morons?"

"That pretty much covers it," I reply.

"Yeah. I'm angry. Any time I'm in here alone, which thankfully isn't often, I just lie here simmering. But whenever you guys come to visit, I'm reminded that I have no right to be."

"Please. If anyone has a right to feel resentful, it's you."

"Oh, I feel plenty resentful. But why do I have the right?" Lucas picks at the uneaten mashed potatoes on his lunch tray with a fork. "Take a good look at the history of humanity, Gabs. Suffering must make up a good ninety-five percent of it. What makes me so special that I should expect to be exempt? If war has taught me anything, it's that we've been riding this wave of comfort and prosperity for so long that we've stopped seeing what life is like for the rest of the world."

"Then do you think there's a reason this happened to you?"
I regret the question as soon as I speak it.

"Ha." Lucas snickers and shakes his head. "What I wish I could say to people who utter that 'everything happens for a reason' crap. No. I don't think this BS with my legs is part of some grand Master Plan. Maybe it's the fire I have to pass through in order to become a halfway decent person, but no God worthy of the name would ordain something like this."

And by "this," my brother means something much bigger than his own plight.

"*We're* the ones who can't seem to get enough of war." He stares down at his atrophied legs and shakes his head. "But I still don't have the luxury of self-pity. At least, not for too long. Not when I'm one of the lucky ones. Supposedly."

"What do you mean?" I ask.

"Russo told you what happened, right? What went down in Afghanistan?"

"How do you know that? Has he called? Do you know where he is?"

"I didn't know for certain. Until now." Lucas chuckles. "Dang Gabi, you're in trouble. Seth is a vault. If he shared everything with you . . . well, I better start shopping for my best man tux now."

"Oh, shut up." I pinch Lucas's arm. Then I remember what we're talking about and my voice stiffens. "Seth told me how you got hurt, but he didn't go into details. Or talk much about the aftermath."

Lucas stares into his lap, as if willing his leg muscles to twitch. Any trace of humor evaporates from his tone. "Granger, the soldier just in here playing cards, was one of the first to arrive on the scene, along with the medic who kept me from bleeding out. They found Seth standing over me, refusing to budge despite the mob moving towards us. A mob made up of the Afghani kid's uncles and cousins."

Lucas's voice falls from a cliff of regrets, like he's already forgotten this kid is only dead because he put him in a wheelchair for the rest of his life. "Seth was on the verge of going berserk, but he wouldn't leave me, even though he thought I was already dead."

"Did Granger tell you this?" Seth's courage isn't surprising, but the thought of him refusing to abandon my brother's body pushes my heart to the edge. "Then what happened?"

"The medic who saved my life was shot and killed while getting me into the helicopter. Her name was Kendra Richards. She was twenty years old and from Jackson, Mississippi. She joined the Army as a medic because she wanted to be a doctor one day. A surgeon." Lucas lifts his eyes to mine, and his underlying fury evaporates. All that's left is a rock-solid determination. "Richards is dead and I will not, I refuse, to dishonor her by sitting here feeling sorry for myself when she gave her life for me, and Seth practically gave his soul."

A tense silence stretches between us, until my brother cracks a bitter smile. "Well, maybe I'll *sit* here, but that's beside the point."

"Ready to go, honey?" Mom steps into the room, her face as enthusiastic as a pep rally.

Ready or not, Lucas's belongings are packed. Dad walks over and grabs the handles of his wheelchair. Matteo races in behind him, a stream of green mint chocolate-chip ice cream running down his arm. "I want to ride with Lucas!"

"No, sweetie. It's not a toy. We have to be careful with—"

"It's all right, Mom," Lucas says as Matteo leaps onto his lap. "The kid could stab my thigh with a fork and I wouldn't feel a thing. I promise."

"Lucas!" Mom shrieks in horror. She doesn't get that his dark sense of humor is the only defense he has left.

Dad pushes my brothers down the hall. A few soldiers in hospital gowns come out to say goodbye, dragging their IV stands behind them. Each soldier knows he's fortunate, even if he doesn't always feel it. The glances that pass between them are a silent tribute to all the men and women who will never leave this hospital or the battlefield. Another generation gone.

Matteo, who can always be counted upon to lighten the mood, waves to every person we pass like he's riding a float in a Fourth of July parade. Two nurses give Lucas pecks on the cheek, reinforcing my theory about all of them wanting his bod.

This level of attention Lucas can handle, but I'm worried that when we get back to Kaiserslautern, it might be too much for him. I glimpse the crowd waiting outside our house long before we pull into the parking lot. At least fifty people are standing in front of our apartment building with welcome-home posters, colorful balloons, and mini American flags.

I see neighbors, soldiers from Lucas's unit, the little old German ladies who run the bakery across the street, my parents' friends, *my* friends (if you count the perky blond up front, waving her poster like a Dallas Cowboys cheerleader). Lucas smiles, shakes hands, and accepts hugs like a good sport, but he eyes our front door like it's the entrance to a holy haven.

As I help Matteo out of his car seat, Chloe runs over to me. "Hey, Gabi! Isn't this a great turnout?"

"It is, but how did so many people know Lucas was coming home?"

"Um, I kind of told them." Chloe stares at the electric purple toenails sticking out from her sandals. "I've been following your G.I. Lucas blog. It really inspired me, so I organized this committee at school and we put on a Wash It for Our Wounded Warriors carwash in front of the Exchange." Chloe hands me a check with a substantial number of digits. "I know money can't fix everything, but we hope this will help your family with the extra expenses."

This check, coupled with the donations from Seth's website, will help *a lot*. A few days ago, I logged into the PayPal account and was shocked to see a $5,000.00 donation I *never* anticipated. The note accompanying it was even more incredible.

Dear Gabi,

It was nice meeting you on the *camino*. We heard about your brother and this website from another pilgrim, a real nice lady from Texas. It's so easy for people like us to forget how much these wars cost those who wage them, so thanks for the reminder. We hope this gift will serve as a small indication of our gratitude.

Dennis & Natalie from Eunate

And that is how I know, without a doubt, that the *camino* can change us all.

I'm not sure who makes up this collective "we" Chloe speaks on behalf of, but they're making my heart burst. I throw my arms around this friend I never even knew I had. "Thank you, Chloe. You're amazing."

"No, your brother is amazing. So are you for walking all that way."

I should tell her it wasn't my idea, but I'm already scanning the crowd for the real *camino* mastermind. I sent Seth an e-mail with the date of Lucas's homecoming, hoping he'd see the message and drop in. There are lots of soldiers milling around our apartment's communal courtyard, but so far no Seth.

Once we thank everyone for coming and get Lucas inside, Mom prepares a huge dinner. It's a random assortment of my brother's favorites, and it reflects our mishmashed family culture: blueberry pancakes, chicken *tamales*, and German potato salad. While my parents get everything ready, Lucas wheels himself over to the sliding glass door in the dining room, where he watches hummingbirds flit around the feeder hanging from the balcony.

I walk over to him, shocked to see tears streaming down his crimson cheeks. These aren't tears of sadness, they're tears of frustration. Like when a wailing baby shakes with rage because he doesn't have the ability to ask for what he wants.

"I know people are being kind," Lucas says, keeping his eyes glued to the red glass feeder. "But I hated every second of that. I hate feeling so damn helpless."

I don't know what to say. I'd hate it, too. Any Santiago would.

Not knowing what else to do, I place a hand on Lucas's shoulder. Then I remember the other surprise we have in store— one I suspect will be more to my brother's liking.

I grab the handles of his chair. "Wait until you see what we've done to your room."

"What the—" Lucas gasps when he glimpses the full-grown German shepherd lying on his bed. The dog is mostly black, minus the little patches of tan near his eyes and on his paws. As soon as he sees my brother, the K-9's ears perk up and his tongue flops out in a way that makes him look like he's smiling. "Gabi. What's going on?"

We've never had a pet. Ever. From goldfish all the way up the food chain, my parents said we moved around too much. It never really bothered me, but Lucas always wanted a dog.

"His name is Homer." I am dead serious. The retired Army service dog came with that name, which was why I insisted he was the dog for us, though I'm pretty sure his former handler was just a huge fan of *The Simpsons*. "He's all yours."

Lucas doesn't speak, but I haven't seen his eyes light up like this in weeks. I help him move from his chair to the bed, where the big dog instantly lays his head on Lucas's lap. The comfortable silence that follows tells me this pair will be fast friends.

I unzip Lucas's suitcase. The first thing I see is the copy of the *Iliad* that Seth sent back with me. I run my hand over its cover, lingering on a stain that resembles Rioja wine. I open to a page bookmarked with a pressed almond blossom from the *camino*.

Like the generations of leaves, the lives of mortal men. Now the wind scatters the old leaves across the earth, now the living timber bursts with the new buds and spring comes round again. And so with men: as one generation comes to life, another dies away.

Life *is* short, and war can make it even shorter. But Lucas, Seth, and I—we're the new buds. We're still coming to life. We still have so much to experience and learn and love.

"Lucas, why did you give us these books?"

My brother, enamored by his new buddy, shrugs. "I reread them during the deployment, and I wanted to share the lines that meant something to me with the two people I thought would appreciate them most."

"So it wasn't some sort of message?"

Lucas and his dog stare at me blankly. "Uh, no. What kind of weird message would that be?"

Indeed. "Never mind."

Sometimes I get the feeling that life, like the *camino*, is more mysterious than we're willing to admit.

Once Lucas is settled in with Homer, I head to the kitchen to see if Mom needs me to set the table, but I end up getting distracted by the stack of mail on the counter instead.

At the top of the pile there's a letter for me. Postmarked in Scotland.

I rip open the envelope and pull out a glossy photograph of G.I. Lucas seated on a mossy gravestone. There's a crumbling cathedral in the backdrop, set against a lavender sky and a slate-gray sea. The structure is nothing like Santiago. It may have been opulent once upon a time, but now the cathedral is reduced to rubble.

Instead of Lucas's face on the action figure's head, I see mine. The image of my cheesy smile on a muscled, camouflaged body is so ridiculous that I laugh out loud, even though I want to cry when I flip the photograph over and read the words Seth scribbled on the back.

*You're still with me. The universe isn't empty.*

This photo isn't a promise, but it's close.

"Let's go, *mija*. We're waiting on you to say grace," Dad calls from the other room, interrupting an incredibly romantic moment like usual.

Smiling through my tears, I enter the dining room and see my brother seated at his designated spot, Homer resting by his side. There will be days—a lot of them—when Lucas is outflanked by anger and depression, but the rage of Achilles is something soldiers have fought since the dawn of time, and I have faith my brother will ultimately win the war.

Right now you wouldn't even know Lucas had a disability. He looks content, like he knows this is where he belongs. Yes, Lucas is still living up to his name.

Lucas is letting the light shine through.

I pause in the doorway and say a silent prayer for the mutual friend who also cares for Lucas like a brother, a friend who's walking across this hemisphere to prove it. That's when I realize there are three things I *love* about being a military brat.

Number 1: Being called a military brat. I am part of an invisible tribe I never asked to join, but, like Chloe and her rally of supporters have shown, it's one that will never forsake me.

Number 2: That perpetual question, "So, where are you from?" I am a pilgrim on an endless expedition, a link in a very long chain, a citizen of all lands.

Number 3: Surprises. Not all surprises are good, but some of them are, like the surprise of an unexpected journey, the surprise of a stranger's generosity, and the surprise of an answered prayer. Or even the surprise of the photograph in my hand, sent by a person I couldn't stand walking with a month ago. Now I can't stand the thought of walking without him.

People may be the only home the Army issues, but they're the only home that matters.

**Want to find out what happens to Seth in Scotland?**
*Learn more at www.ashleecowles.com/seth-in-scotland/*